INDISCRIMINATE

Howard Olsen

Beverley —
Get well soon.
This will help you
pass the time

Howie Olsen
12/9/15

This book is a work of fiction. People, places, events, and situations are the product of the author's imagination. Any resemblance to actual persons, living or dead, or historical events, is purely coincidental.

Copyright © 2001, 2012 by Howard Olsen
All rights reserved.
No part of this book may be reproduced, restored in a retrieval system, or transmitted by means, electronic, mechanical, photocopying, recording, or otherwise, without written consent from the author.

ISBN: 978-0-7596-2082-7 (sc)
ISBN: 978-0-7596-2083-4 (hc)
ISBN: 978-0-7596-2081-0 (e)

This book is printed on acid free paper.

1stBooks - rev. 6/27/2012

Acknowledgements

I would like to thank the chief of staff of the Massachusetts medical examiner's office, Doctor Stanton C. Kessler, for his generous contribution and expertise in helping with the research of this book. Few professionals would have set aside their well deserved and personal time to help someone they didn't know.

As always, I would like to thank my editor, mentor and friend, Bev Walton-Porter, for the professional and unselfish pursuit of quality she instills in everyone around her.

About the Book

Jake thought he'd left the stress of the Salem police department far behind when he left the force and opened up his own literary haven, a small bookstore named "Books." But when a series of brutal and vicious killings grips the city by the throat, Jake's called back to duty and into a tangled web of murder, mystique and witchy mayhem. Faced with a diabolical killer with a marred past and bent on a twisted revenge, Jake's wits and wisdom are pushed to the limit. Can he stop the sadistic killings before they destroy the town and Jake himself? Dive into the suspense and intrigue of **Indiscriminate,** the third book by Salem-based author Howard Olsen -- but only if you thrive on the thrill of a cunning mystery.

This book is dedicated to the 156 people who had legal action brought against them for witchcraft in the late 1600's. Twenty people in Massachusetts were executed for being a witch:

Hanged on June 10, 1692
Bridget Bishop, Salem.

Hanged on July 19, 1692
Sarah Good, Salem Village – Rebecca Nurse, Salem Village – Susannah Martin, Amesbury – Elizabeth How, Ipswich – Sarah Wilds, Topsfield.

Hanged on August 19, 1692
George Burroughs, Wells, Maine – John Proctor, Salem Village – John Willard, Salem Village – George Jacobs, Salem Town – Martha Carrier, Andover.

September 19, 1692
Giles Corey, Salem Farms – pressed to death.

Hanged on September 22, 1692
Martha Corey, Salem Farms – Mary Eastey, Topsfield – Alice Parker, Salem Town – Ann Pudeater, Salem Town – Margaret Scott, Rowley – Wilmott Reed, Marblehead – Samuel Wardwell, Andover and Mary Parker, Andover.

Other accused witches who were not hanged, but died in prison awaiting trial for witchcraft: Sarah Osborne, Salem Village – Roger Toothaker, Billerica – Lyndia Dustin, Reading and Ann Foster, Andover.

Thirteen others may have also died in prison, but sources conflict on the exact number. No one really knows if any or all of the people who were executed were actually witches.

You do not know my heart. I am as
clear as the child unborn.
Rebecca Nurse, Salem Village, March 24, 1692

I thank God I am free.
Sarah Wilds, Topsfield, April 21, 1692

ONE

Salem, Massachusetts is one of the most festive cities in the world during the Fourth of July holiday. With almost forty thousand residents, fireworks, parties and family gatherings are at the top of most people's holiday agendas. On Friday, July 2, Jake Burnett was like everyone else, looking forward to the holiday festivities.

Jake owned and operated a small bookstore called Books, located on Essex Street in the heart of Salem. At one time, Essex Street was paved with cobblestone and cars used its path to travel through town and shop in the many small stores that bordered both sides of the street.

The cobblestones have long been removed and the new age of brick has taken over. The entire street is covered with bright red brick. As the seasons came and went for many years, the weather has caused slight frost heaves in the brick giving it a rustic and beautiful appearance.

Although there are still many small businesses, there are

no cars driving through the center of Essex Street. Tourists by the thousands flock to Salem every year and are able to walk through the center of Salem without bumping into traffic. Salem's history of the witch trials has drawn an enormous tourist industry and most businesses have catered to their query. Every knickknack, hat and tee shirt reads "Witch City this," or "Witch City that." Salem even has its own *authentic* witch, Laurie Cabot, who also owns and operates a small business on Pickering Wharf called The Cat, the Crow and the Crown.

Three theaters that once attracted hundreds of local moviegoers have been torn down in favor of mini malls and modern office space. Jake Burnett was one of the locals, but he hardly remembered the movie theaters; they were torn down when he was very young. As an ex-Salem police detective, he recalled the old police station on Central Street and still harbored ill feelings of it being abandoned in favor of a larger, more modern facility on Margin Street.

Jake sat quietly in a fold-up chair in front of his store, watching and listening to the tourists as they walked past. Many of the women who passed by couldn't help but notice him. Standing at only five-feet-nine-inches tall, his 180-pound frame was muscular, toned and impressive. His wavy brown hair always gave him the look of needing a haircut. His teeth were straight and white when he smiled and this coupled with his tight frame always turned women's heads

He heard the accents of the people as they stopped and pointed to all the things that they'd read about and now were finally able to see in person.

German, French, English, Jake noted as he heard them

Indiscriminate

talk to one another. *They come from all over the world to take in the history that most Salem residents take for granted.*

Even at 5:00 in the afternoon the sun was hot and blistering, and with the humidity above ninety percent, shorts and tank tops was the dress code of the day.

Jake glanced at his watch and decided it was time to close shop. He folded his chair and put it away along with two racks of books he displayed in front of his store. Standing at the front door, getting ready to lock up for the night, he turned and glanced back. He couldn't help but notice how everything matched, the bookshelves, tables, desk and even the old wooden floors. Not only did everything appear to be made from the same type of wood, the color matched perfectly. He thought, *if I didn't know better I would think I was color coordinated.*

The only thing on his mind was a cool shower and a short walk to Pickering Wharf for a cold beer at the Chase House.

This local watering hole served most of the small shop owners in the area. The Chase House was famous for its food, and since it was located right on the water, its atmosphere was second to none.

After locking the store Jake walked down the alley where his 1965 Corvette Stingray was parked. He stopped, stared at his metallic blue Corvette and marveled at its sleek outline. He loved his car and took exceptional care of its maintenance. "Gotta get you an oil change, baby." He opened the door and slid behind the wheel. After starting the engine he backed out of his parking space and turned right onto Central Street and past the old police station. Glancing up at the old red brick building as he drove past, Jake made no attempt to squelch the feelings he held inside. He felt like he'd lost an old friend when the old, weather-beaten station was abandoned.

Turning left onto Lafayette Street, Jake headed for home. Approaching the intersection, the traffic light turned red. "Why is it I never make this light?" Jake said out loud. "I've had a red light at this intersection for as long as I can remember!" Turning up the volume on his Corvette's custom stereo, Jake tapped his hand on the steering wheel to the beat of "Ninety Miles An Hour" by John Berry.

He noticed two girls standing in front of the Engine House Restaurant. When he turned up the stereo they began dancing to the beat—it was obvious they wanted him to notice them. One girl hollered, "Can we come for a ride in your 'Vette?"

"Another time," Jake hollered back as the light turned green. He revved the engine and shot through the intersection. *Teenyboppers, they have no clue. I could be a serial killer.*

Jake lived on Lafayette Street only two blocks before the Salem State College. He pulled into his driveway and turned off the engine. Staring at his huge two-story home, he remembered when his mother and father had lived with him. He remembered how his mother would call him in the morning for breakfast, and how his father would always add, "She means now, Jake!"

A large grin spread across his face when he thought of his parents. His father retired from General Electric Corporation in Lynn, in 1995. Jake's mother, a registered nurse at Salem hospital, retired two months later. Jake bought the house he was born in on 242 Lafayette Street from his parents when they moved to a retirement community in Florida. "I gotta call them tonight," he reminded himself.

After showering and getting dressed, Jake called his parents in Florida. His mother overreacted as usual when he called. "What's wrong, Jason?" And, as usual, he assured her nothing was wrong and that he simply wanted to say hello.

They chatted awhile and then hung up. Jake was anxious to get to the Chase House early to find a table on the deck overlooking the water.

When he went to turn off the television a news bulletin pre-empted the regular programming.

The reporter for channel four repeated the broadcast, "The fully clothed body of twenty-two-year-old Sally Grogan was found on Gallows Hill in Salem, late this morning. An unverified source said she might have been strangled, but until the autopsy is performed, the cause of death remains unknown."

A surge of fear and uneasiness ran through Jake. His mind wandered back eight years to when a young girl was savagely beaten, raped and strangled. He had been assigned the case and it took an emotional toll on him. He couldn't sleep and worked on this case for eight months, never taking a day off. When he finally arrested the murderer, it was as though a huge weight was removed from his shoulders. He shook his head in an attempt to dislodge the vision.

The two young girls on the corner flashed through Jake's mind. *Why the hell don't these kids stop and think?* He wondered.

Jake turned off the television and walked outside. He decided to drive to the Chase House and hopped over the closed driver seat door and slid behind the wheel. Within five minutes he turned right onto Congress Street, then left into the parking lot where he could safely park his Stingray.

At 6:00 p.m. there were plenty of tables and booths available inside and, out on the deck. Jake peered through the plate glass window and noticed his friend, Dang Dung, sitting at a table on the deck. He was reading and sipping on some sort of fruit drink.

Dang was Vietnamese and was born in Salem. At twenty-eight years old and only 5'7" and 150 pounds, he wasn't the least bit threatening. He was a master of many forms of the martial arts, including Karate, Kung Fu and Aikido. His placid appearance, coupled with his mild manner often-enticed bullies to pick fights with him. Dang always backed away and tried to avoid an altercation, but when the fight seemed to be unavoidable he fought with fury.

Jake walked out on the deck and sat with his friend. Without looking up, Dang said, "Where the hell have you been? Being so hot today I thought you'd have closed the store and been here earlier."

"Some of us have to work, ya know." Jake waved for a waitress. "What are you reading now? Another child psychology book?"

"Yes," Dang replied without looking up, "there are new theories being developed every year and I have to be aware of new technology if I'm going to do my job properly."

"What are you drinking," Jake asked, "same juice-shit as usual?"

"Yes," Dang replied, "same juice-shit as usual."

"Let me buy you a beer," Jake offered.

Indiscriminate

Dang slowly lifted his head from the book. "You've been asking to buy me a beer for the past seven years. My answer hasn't changed, Jake. No thanks. You know I don't drink."

"Dang," Jake's voice changed to almost a whisper. "Did you hear about the kid that was murdered on Gallows Hill?"

Dang closed his book and nodded. "I have a hard time comprehending how anyone could do that? To snuff out a life in such a brutal way. They said she was strangled and left out in the open for someone to find."

"I'll have a Coors Lite," Jake said as the waitress walked past. Lowering his voice again, Jake added, "I don't know why, but I have a real bad feeling about this. I hope I'm wrong."

"What kind of feeling?"

"Don't know for sure, just a bad feeling. I think I'll ask around and see if I can come up with something."

"Jake," Dang said, "don't make this murder an instant replay of eight years ago. You were so possessed with finding the man who killed that girl that your personality changed. You turned violent and belligerent in a matter of days. You found nothing wrong with beating answers out of anyone. That's one of the reasons you're not a police officer anymore. You know Captain Reins doesn't look upon you as one of his own. In fact, he doesn't look upon you as being a member of the human race. He won't stand by and allow you to conduct your own investigation."

"Bull Reins is half-witted fucking idiot," Jake snapped. "He couldn't conduct an investigation in his own living room. He cares more about looking good in the media than he cares about digging out the truth."

Howard Olsen

Jake's mind raced back five years to when he resigned from the Salem police department. Or, more accurately, was forced to resign due to an out-of-proportion investigation spearheaded by Bull Reins. Captain Reins didn't like the methods Jake used to obtain information during an investigation.

Reins' reason for the attack on Jake's ability to perform police work was centered on the violent method he used. "Detective Jason Burnett is a disgrace to the department," began Reins' opening statement at the internal affairs hearing. He made reference to four different cases where Jake actually beat the answers from a suspect. He went after the detective with a vengeance, and he won. Jake resigned a week later.

Jake shook his head clearing the vision of Bull Reins from his mind. He looked up and noticed Cameron Baird standing in front of one of the little shops that bordered both sides of small, almost path-like, streets on Pickering Wharf.

Cam, as he was referred to on the street, was the lowest form of life on the planet, according to Jake. A drug dealer, whose customers were mostly children. He was thirty-years-old and had never held a job, other than destroying as many lives as possible. Most of his teeth were missing and the few he had left in his mouth were rotten and green. His greasy brown hair lay on his shoulders like matted animal fur after coming in from the rain. At 6'4" and only 130 pounds, his appearance was disgusting.

"I'll be back," Jake said. "Save my seat."

Dang watched as his friend got up and walked toward the street. He didn't know why he left until he saw Cameron

Baird. "Christ, Jake," he said out loud, "you're not on the police force anymore."

Without looking at Dang, Jake walked away saying, "Yeah, yeah, yeah."

Walking up behind Baird, Jake remained silent. He didn't want to have to chase the junkie through Pickering Wharf. He knew this low-life had nothing to do with the murder of the young girl, but knew Baird would have some information about it. Cameron Baird knew something about every illegal activity in and around Salem.

Baird turned and saw Jake walking toward him. His first instinct was to run until he heard Jake say, "Don't make me chase you, Cam. That will *really* piss me off."

Baird stood motionless and waited for Jake. "Ah, hey Jake," he said, "What up?"

Jake said nothing as he approached. He looked into Baird's eyes and saw how nervous he was. This observation solidified Jake's suspicion about something illegal going down. "Why don't you tell me, Cam? Why don't you tell me why you're hanging out in this neighborhood? You aren't here selling that shit again. Are ya, Cam?"

"No way, Jake." He shifted nervously. "I don't do that shit no more. Honest Jake, I'm clean."

Jake stood still as Baird took two steps backward and wiped the back of his hand across his nose. "You're fucking disgusting," Jake said. "You make my skin crawl. Why don't you clean yourself up?"

Before Baird could answer, Jake said, "I need some information."

"Ah…sure Jake," Baird's voice trembled, "what you wanna know?"

Jake looked away. "A girl was murdered at Gallows Hill." Without moving his head, Jake's eyes met Baird's revolting stare. "I need some information on how she died."

"I hear she was strangled," the junkie replied.

"You heard a lot more than that," Jake barked. "Don't fuck with me. You know every sleazy thing that happens in Essex County. I want to know *how* she was strangled."

Baird looked nervously over each shoulder and stepped to within six inches of Jake. He leaned down and softly said, "I have this friend on the newspaper, ya know, a reporter."

Jake moved his head back to avoid the stench of Baird's breath. "Don't you ever brush your fucking teeth?" Jake exhaled, hoping he could blow the bad breath away from his face.

Baird talked as if the insult held no merit. "He said there was a rope around the chick's neck, tied in a hangman's noose. Said there was about two feet of rope."

"Cam," Jake said, "why the hell would a reporter confide in a fucking low-life like you? Do you expect me to believe you entered a new circle of friends?" Jake's tone was cold.

"Honest, Jake," Baird said, "this reporter buys stuff from me once in a while. We got high and he just started talking about how gruesome the body looked with the rope around her neck. That's the truth, Jake—honest."

"You said you weren't into that shit anymore. Were you lying then, or are you lying now?"

Baird said nothing, looking like a child who had just been caught with his hand in the cookie jar.

Indiscriminate

Jake turned and walked away. He stopped and looked over his shoulder at Baird. "I want you to keep your eyes and ears open. If you hear *anything*, you better call me. Don't make me come looking for you."

"No problem, Jake. You got it." Baird nervously turned and walked away.

Jake returned to his friend and sat down. He lifted his beer and took a long swallow. "It's warm," he said, "I hate warm beer."

"What was that all about?" Dang asked.

"The murdered girl at Gallows Hill," Jake replied, "something's bothering me about this one. I don't know what it is, but I have a nightmarish feeling this is only the beginning."

"Only the beginning?" Dang looked perplexed. "Do you think this is the start of a serial murder spree? What the hell makes you think that? One murder doesn't constitute a murder spree."

Jake held the bottle of warm beer in his hand. It was wet with condensation and large drops of water slowly snaked down the sides. Looking over the railing of the deck and into the water, Jake simply said, "I don't know why. It's just a feeling the nightmare has only begun."

By 8:00 p.m., the Chase House was packed with the regular Friday night crowd and Jake decided it was time to head for home. The thought of the young murdered girl lingered in the back of his mind and he couldn't propel himself into a party mood.

He said goodbye to Dang and left the Chase House. Walking through the parking lot toward his 'Vette, he noticed Bill Stoughton walking toward him. Jake thought Stoughton a bit odd and didn't usually go out of his way to engage in conversation with him.

Stoughton was a consultant to a number of companies on the North Shore. His forte was helping corporations weed out malcontents and he had often been used by the police department for profiling fugitives. "Hey, Jake," Stoughton said, "it's only eight o'clock. Where are you going this early?" His tone was bubbly and annoying.

Jake didn't give him a reason, but asked, "You still doing profiling for the department?"

Jake's question infused a sense of power into Stoughton's manner. He stood tall with his hands folded across his chest as if to say, "Yes, and that makes me important."

"As a matter of fact, I did receive a call from Captain Reins. He wants me to come to his office in the morning to discuss a case. I'm willing to bet he needs my help to find out who killed that girl at Gallows Hill." Stoughton's face beamed with pride. His look suggested he was going to tell everyone the police asked him to help with such an important case. Without saying another word, Stoughton put his hands in his pockets and walked toward the Chase House.

Jake watched as Stoughton walked away. He saw a bounce in his walk and noticed how uninteresting this man actually was. With his white-cuffed shorts, plum-colored polo shirt and brown sandals, he looked even more ridiculous than he actually was. "What a fucking dork!" Jake slid behind the wheel of his 'Vette.

At three o'clock in the morning the nagging ring of the telephone awakened Jake. He fumbled around the night table until his hand covered the alarm clock. When the ringing persisted, he threw the clock across the room. The ringing continued and he realized it was the telephone. Lifting it from the receiver, Jake sleepily answered, "Hello?"

"Jake, this is Dang, were you asleep?"

Jake glanced at the clock lying on the floor on the other side of the room. Squinting his sleepy eyes to read the time, he said, "It's only three in the morning. Of course you didn't wake me. I was in the middle of my fucking yoga lesson. What the hell is so important that you couldn't call at a reasonable hour?"

Dang said, "I know it's early but I just heard something on the radio that bothers me. It's got to do with what you said at the Chase."

Jake rubbed his face into the pillow as if wiping the sleep from his eyes. "You don't listen to WKLB. What the hell would I find interesting listening to the elevator music you listen to?"

Dang's voice became serious and somber. "I heard it on the police scanner—they found another girl's body."

Jake sat straight up, eyes wide open. "Where?" His heart began to throb.

"Mac Park," Dang said, "a couple of lovers pulled in and parked up on the hill around 1:30 this morning. They found the body—same condition as the first."

"What else did they say?" Jake asked.

"The girl's name is Ellen Hayward, nineteen-years-old. She was here on vacation with her parents. Her mother told the police she went to Mac Park with some friends and got separated. The mother called the police about the same time the two lovers reported finding the body. I guess the parents are coming apart. The father identified the body and the mother was rushed to Salem hospital—possible heart attack."

At six o'clock Jake was still awake, his mind running in different directions. He remembered how obsessed he was with the girl that was murdered eight years ago and he could feel that uneasy feeling again. He decided to call his friend and ex-partner, Mark Roads. Mark was a Salem police detective in charge of homicide. He dialed Mark's home phone number and waited until the answering machine came on. "Mark," he said, "this is Jake—"

Before he could leave a message, Mark picked up the phone. "Jake, why the hell are you calling me at six in the morning? Whatever it is, no!"

"Calm down," Jake said, "I don't want anything—just a little information."

"Jake, don't do this to me," Mark said. "If Reins knew I was even talking to you he would shove my badge right up my ass. Christ, he chews me out at least twice a day, just because you *used* to be my partner."

"Mark," Jake said seriously, "I want to know about the body you just found."

"Christ," Mark said, "I feel so bad for the parents. Their daughter transferred from Ohio State College to Salem State two months ago so she could be close to her parents."

Jake was perplexed. "I thought they were here on vacation."

"Jesus, Jake, you know about that one, too?"

Indiscriminate

There was a long pause when Jake asked, "You mean there were two murders last night?"

"You seem to already know as much as I do," Mark said. "I might as well tell you everything we know—which isn't very much."

Jake listened as Mark told him about Ellen Hayward, the nineteen-year-old girl who was found at Mac Park. The body of twenty-year-old Susan Martell was found at Gallows Hill at five o'clock in the morning by two joggers. "There *were* two murders last night, Jake."

"Were these two girls found with rope around their necks?" Jake asked.

"How the hell did you know about the hangman's knot? That information was not given out."

"I didn't," Jake said. "I knew about the rope, but didn't know about the hangman's knot— until now."

"Christ, Jake," Mark snapped, "this is privileged information. No one knows about this. This is the information we keep *out* of the press. You know how it works. If Reins finds out I gave you any details, I'll lose my job, my pension, my retirement. You gotta keep your mouth shut about this."

Jake could feel the concern in the voice of his ex-partner. "Mark, I know how Reins is…I know how vengeful he can be…I won't mention this to anyone."

"Thanks, Jake," Mark said, "I'll talk to you later."

After hanging up, Jake sorted through what had happened in a short time. "Three young girls strangled with a hangman's knot in less than twenty-four hours," he murmured out loud in disbelief.

Two

After showering, Jake sat in front of the television with a cup of coffee in one hand and the channel selector in the other. He searched for the news, constantly changing from one station to another. He was disturbed by the events that had happened over the past twenty-four hours and still harbored the feeling this was only the beginning.

It was nearly nine in the morning when Jake opened the store. He was in no hurry because his real concern was to conduct his *own* investigation into the murders. He fought the urge to contribute his expertise of obtaining information. He knew Captain Reins would do everything in his power to punish him for the slightest infraction and he didn't feel up to another confrontation with the man who was responsible for forcing him to resign from the Salem police department.

As the morning wore on, Jake sat in a chair in front of the store and couldn't shake the three murdered women from his mind. Glancing at his watch every ten minutes made the three hours that had passed seem like three days.

He considered closing the store for the day when Mark Roads walked up and squatted next to him. "Jake, we gotta talk."

"Don't worry. I told you I wouldn't say anything about what you told me." Jake's voice was low and cautious.

"Well…um…that's not why I'm here," Mark stuttered.

Jake looked into the eyes of his ex-partner and saw pure panic. "What's wrong? You're shaking like a bucket of sea worms."

Mark fumbled with his keys as though he didn't know what to do with his hands. "We got two more, Jake. We found them this morning at Palmer Cove. Same as the first three."

Jake sat straight up in his chair. His heart thudded in his chest at break-neck speed. "Two more kids were murdered?"

"Not exactly."

"Well what the fuck *exactly* did happen, Mark?" Jake's tone turned cold.

"They weren't kids," Mark replied in a remorseful and solemn tone. "Rachael Nickels was seventy-three years old. The other was a forty-three-year-old black woman named Sandra Woods. There doesn't seem to be a connection between any of them. Nothing in common…" Mark's voice trailed off.

"Other than talking to that fucking idiot, Stoughton, what is Reins doing?" Jake asked.

Mark lowered his head. "Nothing. There really isn't

anything to go on. We can't find even one common factor between any of the victims. They seem to be random."

"Indiscriminate?" Jake asked.

"That's what it looks like. There is absolutely no connection. At least none we can come up with." Mark stared down Essex Street and focused on the water fountain. "It's inconceivable that something like this could happen here. This isn't the inner-city. This is Salem, Massachusetts for Christ-sake."

"Indiscriminate my ass!" Jake blurted out. "No fucking way this is random. That bottom-feeder is choosing his victims for a reason. I can feel it."

Jake closed his store at two o'clock and drove home to relax before going to Swampscott Beach for the fireworks. After taking off his shoes, he poured himself a three-fingered shot of Labrot & Graham Kentucky Bourbon. Sliding the cork back into the bottle, he marveled at the sleek flat shape of the container. "Marketing and cosmetics," he said out loud, "if you want to sell something, it's marketing and cosmetics."

Jake sat back on the sofa and took a long swallow of bourbon. After turning on the television it wasn't long before his eyes became heavy and he fell asleep.

His eyes popped open to the sound of sirens. He jumped from the sofa and looked around the room as if the sirens came from within. After rubbing his eyes, he realized he was right. There was a police chase, but it was on the television.

"Christ." Jake said out loud as he looked at his watch. It was almost eight o'clock and the fireworks started at nine. It should take ten minutes to drive to Swampscott Beach,

Indiscriminate

but with the holiday traffic he planned on closer to thirty minutes.

Cruising through Vinnin Square, he turned left then right until he came to Humphrey Street. The cars were already backed up for as far as he could see. *If I'm smart*, Jake thought, *I'll park right here and walk to the beach.*

When he finally got to the beach, it was wall-to-wall people. Some were standing while others made themselves comfortable in lawn chairs and patio furniture. Looking out into the water, he could scarcely make out the shape of the flat platform anchored in the harbor. This was the location that launched the fireworks and where everyone's attention was focused.

Looking around at the thousands of people, Jake knew this would be a perfect place for a predator who was looking for an abundance of prey. But in his heart he knew the predator who murdered those five people didn't need to be in a place where there was a large group. He chose his victims with care. He chose his victims for a reason.

The fireworks ended with an unbelievable grand finale. The colors were rich and elicited an excited response from the spectators. The pattern of each and every explosion had its own identity, and Jake watched in awe as the huge display came to an end.

It wasn't until eleven o'clock that Jake was behind the wheel of his Corvette heading north on Humphrey Street. Although this was Saturday night, he couldn't muster a party mood and decided to go home.

He woke at nearly eight o'clock Sunday morning and took a shower. He wanted to visit the police station and offer his help gathering information about the five murders. He knew his effort would be for naught, but he decided to try anyway.

He headed for breakfast at Reds. He felt comfortable and enjoyed the food in the small restaurant. The fact that Reds was located beside the old police station on Central Street added to its appeal.

After finishing two of the largest pancakes found anywhere in the world, Jake sat back to enjoy another cup of coffee.

"You're up early for a Sunday," came a voice from behind him.

Without turning around, Jake smiled. "Sunday? I thought this was Monday. Sit your ass down, Dang."

Jake ordered two more cups of coffee and both men talked for ten minutes before Captain Reins and Bill Stoughton entered the restaurant.

The two men passed Jake and Dang without noticing they were there. They sat at a booth at the far end of the restaurant and Reins had his back to Jake.

"I'm gonna talk to Reins," Jake said to Dang.

"Don't do it, Jake," Dang replied. "Bull Reins hates the ground you walk on, and you know it. I don't know what you did to make him hate you like he does, but whatever it was—"

"That's between me and him," Jake said. "It's been five years and about time to put the past where it belongs—in the past."

"Jake," Dang interjected, "at least be smart enough to realize this is not the place to repair the relationship. For once in your life use your head."

Indiscriminate

Jake stared across the table at his friend and knew he was right. He had always known his hot temper was his worst enemy. It had been proven many times.

Stoughton glanced up and noticed Jake and Dang. He leaned across the table and whispered something to Captain Reins, which caused him to turn and look over his shoulder at Jake.

Jake returned the glance. For a split second he thought the captain would invite him to join him at his table.

He was wrong. Reins' face turned bright red as he glared at Jake with intense hatred. The stare actually caused some of the customers, including Dang, to stop in their tracks and watch. Some patrons paused as their fork shoved food into their mouths, while others sat motionless in the middle of their meal, as if frozen in time.

Jake stepped away from his table as if he were going to walk over and talk to Reins. Dang immediately stood and grabbed Jake's arm.

"Don't worry," Jake said coldly. "Let's get the fuck out of here." He reached into his pocket and pulled out more money than was needed to pay the bill. He tossed it on the table and left.

Both men silently crossed Central Street to the small parking lot behind the fire station.

As they walked Dang noticed fury in Jake's eyes "Why does Reins hate you so much?"

"It's a long story," Jake said. "I'll tell you someday. But not today."

Dang knew Jake had a quick temper and he knew how it surfaced. When Jake was a small boy he was at the park with his mother and father. Three bullies came over and began to insult his mom. His dad tried to talk the three men into leaving them alone, but they were drunk and got even more obnoxious. One of the men leaned over and kissed his mom and that's when Jake's dad retaliated. He grabbed the man by the back and smashed him to the ground. The other two men beat his father severely. That one incident left an impression in Jake's mind so vivid it actually would wake him up from a deep sleep. When Jake turned fifteen years old, he had a reputation as one of the toughest kids in Salem. He never went looking for a fight, but had zero tolerance for bullies. As the years passed, his intolerance escalated into zero tolerance for anyone who took advantage of someone else, especially children. Dang knew this was the driving force why Jake acted the way he did.

After saying goodbye to his friend, Jake drove to his store to take inventory. *'Shit! It's a beautiful Sunday morning and I'm going to spend it taking fucking inventory.'* He parked in his usual space, walked up the ally, and turned left onto Essex Street. His store was less than a block away and when he reached the front door he noticed an envelope sticking out of the mail slot.

He unlocked the door, stepped inside and pulled the envelope from the slot. He didn't take notice of what was written on the envelope because it was pushed into the mail slot with the writing side facing down. Orders for books were often left this way and Jake didn't give it a second thought. Tossing the unopened envelope face down on his desk, he began counting each book he had in stock and logging in the information by title, author and ISBN. Every time he did inventory he fantasized about getting a computer to do the work. *'I gotta get out of the dark ages and buy a computer.'*

After working for an hour he made a pot of coffee. When the machine began brewing, he sat with his feet on his desk and leaned back in the chair. He picked up the unopened envelope and bounced it up and down on the desk while waiting for his coffee. He closed his eyes and thought about the murder of a girl eight years earlier. That case took a huge toll on him and he couldn't help but think about the murders of the past twenty-four hours.

All of a sudden his eyes opened as if his sub-conscious told him to open the envelope. Slowly, he turned his head and looked at the envelope on his desk.

Burnett, was all it said. What gripped his attention was the fact that it appeared to be written in charcoal. Large smudged letters as though a child had written it, but yet something inside told him it wasn't from a child. It was written in charcoal because it's almost impossible to trace. Slowly, and with purpose, he slid the envelope across the desk and opened it.

Staring at what was written on the paper in charcoal and, in the same hand as on the envelope, Jake's face took on a look of complete bewilderment. He read the letter out loud.

"*J.B. STAY OUT OF THIS!*" was all it said.

Jake folded the paper and put it back into the envelope. Totally confused, he stared at the envelope. *I have to talk to Reins. This is something the police have to know. Maybe they have something similar.*

Jake drank coffee until enough time had passed for Reins to return to the police station. Not really enthusiastic about seeing Reins, he reluctantly closed the store and walked to his car.

The police station was less than five minutes away. Jake's Corvette rounded the Riley Parking Plaza and onto Margin Street. He pulled into the impressive parking lot and shut off the engine.

Jake walked toward a side door that was usually only used by police officers. As he reached for the doorknob, the door opened.

Standing face-to-face, Captain Reins and Jake stood silent for what seemed like an eternity.

"Burnett!" Reins snapped, breaking the silence, "this entrance is for police officers only."

Jake held the envelope in the air so Reins could read what it said.

The captain reached for the envelope and Jake snatched it back, shoving it into his pocket. "We gotta talk!"

Captain Reins stood motionless. He did not acknowledge Jake's request. He continued staring coldly into his eyes.

"Captain," Jake began, "let's put our differences aside, at least for now, and maybe between the two of us we can make sense of all this."

Still holding the door halfway open, Reins said nothing. Looking over both shoulders as though he didn't want anyone knowing he was talking to Jake, he motioned Jake inside. "Up the stairs, Burnett," Reins ordered him. "You know where my office is."

Jake walked into the Captain's office and noticed how much it had changed. Rich, deep blue wall-to-wall carpeting made the small room look much larger. A large oak desk sat

Indiscriminate

in front of a window that extended almost the full width of the room. Commendations, plaques of recognition and pictures of Reins with other high-ranking officials covered the walls.

Reins sat behind his desk. Motioning for Jake to sit in the chair opposite the desk, he asked, "When did you get the note?"

"I found it in my mail slot at the store," Jake answered. "Looks like it was written in charcoal, a bit smudged, but still readable."

Reins indicated for Jake to give him the envelope.

Jake removed the envelope from his pocket, but was reluctant to give it to the captain. He knew once it was in Rein's hands, he wouldn't see it again.

This hesitation irritated Reins. "Burnett, this is evidence in a murder investigation, for Christ sake. Give it to me—now."

Jake knew Reins was right. He handed him the envelope. "Captain, I suspect you've received something similar. How far off base am I?"

"Burnett," Captain Reins replied, "I'm neither compelled nor obligated to disclose any information to you. This is a police matter. You are no longer a police officer, or have you forgotten? The slightest interference from you could jeopardize this entire investigation. Any information you can contribute will be helpful. However, conducting your own *maverick* investigation could get the case thrown out of court."

Jake knew this was how the meeting with Reins would be conducted. He knew the captain would insist on all the information Jake had, but there would be no reciprocation. "Captain," he said, "I know I can help with this one."

"You're not part of this investigation, Burnett," Reins barked. "You're not involved."

"Bullshit," Jake snapped. "That sick son-of-a-bitch sent me that note, and he put me right in the middle." Jake paused, then added, "That's right, Captain, I am involved whether you like it or not."

Captain Reins was furious but he knew Jake was right...Jake *was* involved. He also knew if he didn't share the information he had with him Jake wouldn't offer anything further. Jake would probably conduct an investigation on his own—unsupervised.

Maybe that would be a good thing, Reins thought. *Maybe Burnett will do all the dirty work and turn over whatever information he finds.* However, it would have to be without the knowledge of or help from the department. Reins looked across the desk at Jake. "All right, Burnett, you come up with anything else and we'll talk. Until then, keep this to yourself. Understood?"

"Fine," said Jake. "But you still haven't answered my question. Have you received something similar?"

Reins put the note back into its envelope and dropped it into his top desk drawer. "This is not the time for me to divulge whether or not there is another taunting note."

Jake took the captain's evasive answer as a yes, then stood and walked to the door. Before leaving the office he turned. "Captain, this guy isn't finished. Not by a long shot."

He drove to Dang's house on Bridge Street and saw his car wasn't in the driveway. Continuing north he noticed Dang's

Indiscriminate

1997 Chevy van parked in the rear of the 99 Restaurant. Jake smiled and pulled into the parking lot and came to a stop beside Dang's van. He knew his friend liked to sit on the small beach overlooking the Salem/Beverly harbor, and read.

Jake walked around to an opening in the twelve-foot chain link fence and saw Dang sitting in the sand. As he walked up behind him, Dang said, "You should learn from this, Jake. It's tranquil and serene here."

Jake sat in the sand next to Dang. Staring out into the harbor he soberly said, "The killer sent me a note."

Dang closed the book and turned to Jake. "A note? The killer sent *you* a note?"

"Yup," said Jake. "He sent one to Reins, also."

"Let me get this straight." Dang turned to face Jake. "The killer sent you *and* Reins a note? Let me see it."

"I don't have it any more. Reins has it. I went to see him today and he told me the police also received a note. I gave him the one I had and he kept it. He refused to show me the one he had."

"Sounds like you and Reins have kissed and made up."

"Not on your life. He wants anything I have that may help him solve this thing, but he doesn't want me to be involved in the investigation."

Dang turned in the sand and faced the harbor. "The word on the street is that Reins is in bed with Stoughton. He has Stoughton involved in all the meetings surrounding these murders. Word is Bill Stoughton is riding this for all it's worth. He feels that when big business gets wind of how important he's been in this case, he can write his own ticket with the consulting fees."

"Why the hell would someone send me a note telling me to back off?" asked Jake. "I haven't done any digging into this case—well, not very much, anyway. I haven't come up with anything the police don't already have."

"I don't think it was directed to you alone, Jake," Dang said. "You said the police received a note, also. Sounds like this psycho is taunting the police—and you. To randomly murder five people in less than twenty-four hours tells me he's confident in his ability to elude the police."

"I'm telling you, his victims are not random." Jake said. "He's choosing them for a reason that makes sense to *him*."

"There is absolutely no connection between the murdered women," Dang stated. "He chooses his victims because of their availability. He's the predator and they're the prey. It's as simple as that."

Jake focused on the harbor and how tranquil it appeared. Cabin cruisers and sailboats followed the speed limit to open water. Small anchored boats with people fishing dotted the harbor. Without looking at his friend, he said, "I don't know what would be worse."

Dang looked perplexed. He wasn't sure what Jake meant. He didn't know where Jake got his information on how the women were murdered, but knew he had an uncanny way of finding things out. "The women were strangled with two feet of rope tied into a hangman's knot, right?"

Still staring into the harbor, the expression on Jake's face remained unchanged. He simply nodded. Dang continued, "Every one of the victims was left in a place where they would be easily found?"

Again, Jake nodded.

Indiscriminate

"Jake," Dang said, "I'm no profiler like Bill Stoughton, but the way it looks to me is he wants his victims to be easily found. It makes him feel superior to the police. He doesn't want to have *any* connection between them. Look buddy," he continued, "this guy is crazy, but he is definitely not stupid."

Jake clenched his fists. True, it had only been a day, but not enough was being done.

"You going to the fireworks tonight?" Jake asked.

"I thought they were last night," Dang answered.

"Last night was in Swampscott, tonight they're in Marblehead."

"Devreaux Beach?"

"Yup," Jake said, "I'll meet you at the little restaurant, *Flynnies*" He stood and brushed the sand from his jeans. "Eight o'clock, I'll see you then."

As Jake walked away, Dang hollered, "Jake, Reins is right…you're not a police officer any more. You have no right interfering in the case."

Jake didn't respond to Dang's comment. He simply walked to his car.

Per their arrangement, Jake and Dang met at the restaurant on Devreaux beach. As in Swampscott, the beach was wall-to-wall people and the excitement in the children's eyes was overwhelming. With every burst, the colorful firework arrangements seemed to go on for hours. Both men were in awe of the enormous explosions of brilliance that filled the navy blue sky.

The narrow streets in Marblehead swelled with an abundance of traffic. It took Jake almost two hours to travel the five-minute drive into Salem. As he rounded the curve

Howard Olsen

that brought him from Marblehead into Salem, he was finally on Lafayette Street.

As he drove, he continued changing the stations on the radio listening for a broadcast of another murder. *I hope this is a good sign*, he thought. *I hope it's not because they just haven't found another body, yet.*

Monday morning brought another bright and sunny day. At six o'clock Jake opened the blinds in his bedroom and looked out onto Lafayette Street. The traffic was almost non-existent and he pondered opening the store. Because he had bought a winning lottery ticket almost two years earlier, he didn't need the money from Books, but really enjoyed the interaction with customers. He had more money than he could ever spend, but he couldn't just sit back and do nothing with his life, he had to continue working. The bookstore wasn't as exciting as being a police officer, but he enjoyed interaction with the tourists.

"Ah, what the hell," he said out loud, "Maybe I'll just poke around a little and see what surfaces."

After showering Jake drove to Reds for breakfast. Even at seven o'clock in the morning there was a wait for a table. At the door, Jake noticed Captain Reins at a table in the far corner. Contemplating an altercation, Jake decided to have his breakfast at Maria's restaurant.

He turned to leave and heard his name being called. Jake turned around and saw Reins motioning for him to come to his table. Unsure what Reins wanted, Jake slowly walked over to Reins' table.

"Burnett," the captain said, "sit down. Want some coffee?"

Indiscriminate

This was completely out of character for Captain Reins. He hadn't called him to his table just to socialize…he wanted something. Jake was sure the Captain was on a fishing trip to find out if he had any other information—any more notes from the murderer.

Jake sat down and Reins motioned for the waitress to bring another cup of coffee. "Got anything else for me, Burnett?" the captain asked.

Jake took offense to the question. He didn't like being used by anyone, especially Captain Reins. "Captain, I'm not your Goddamn snitch. I came to you because I thought I could help with your investigation. I don't report to you, or anyone else. I know you got a note from the asshole who killed those people and I want to see it." Jake took a sip of his coffee and looked into the Captain's eyes, then added, "I showed you mine—now let me see yours."

Reins face turned red. He didn't want to involve Jake Burnett in this case, or any other. He reasoned that if he could keep Jake just outside the department without any authority or representation from the police, maybe he could dig up something that he could use.

Reins reached into his jacket pocket and pulled out a copy of the note he received from the murderer. Slowly, and with caution, he slid it across the table to Jake. "This will go no further. Understood?"

Three

Jake took the note and placed it in his lap as if protecting it from being seen by anyone else. He unfolded the paper and glanced over both shoulders to be sure no one was watching. Slowly glancing down, he saw it was written in charcoal and in the same hand as the note he received. Jake mumbled the words written on the paper:

C.R. – LOSE YOUR TOP GUN, W.S.
HISTORY REPEATS ITSELF.
IT'LL ALL BE OVER SOON.

Jake glanced up at Captain Reins and noticed an expression of torment on his face. His frustration and anguish were evident. Jake knew he could help with solving the murders, but he also knew Reins held a grudge and wouldn't allow him to be involved with any form of authority. In his heart he knew the Captain was right, he wasn't a police officer and had no right to be involved. But he had an uncontrollable drive to find this murderer.

He knew Bull Reins would do anything in his power to keep him from redeeming his reputation. The only reason Reins let him see the note was because if he didn't reciprocate, Jake would not divulge any more information he might have.

"Captain," Jake said, "the C.R. is obviously you, but who the hell is your *TOP GUN, W.S.?*"

Reins leaned over the table and whispered, "Bill."

Jake looked perplexed. "Bill? Who the hell is Bill?"

"Stoughton," replied the Captain. "You know, William Stoughton, *W.S.*"

Jake blurted out loud, "Stoughton! Bill Stoughton is your top gun?"

Reins looked around the restaurant, nervous sweat beading on his forehead. "Burnett, Bill Stoughton has been invaluable to this investigation. He's seen this note and refuses to back off. He knows his life may be in danger and continues to stay involved. The person who is committing these murders is obviously worried about him and wants him out. Bill had the chance to back away, but decided to stay and help—"

Jake cut Reins off, "Captain, Bill Stoughton is a fucking idiot. He makes his living by handing out bullshit to companies who are having problems with production and don't have the brains to correct the problems themselves. Stoughton steps in and blames some poor working slob and gets him fired. That's all he does, Captain, nothing more. He's a publicity scavenger who is too fucking lazy to hold a real job. This venture to help with the murders is not because he gives a shit, but because of the exposure in the media. His consultation fee will double when this is all over. Christ, he's not even a registered profiler."

Reins' hands clenched into tight fists and he leaned over the table into Jake's face. "Bill Stoughton is putting his life on the line to help solve the murders. He asks nothing in return. You're the fuck-up, Burnett, not him."

Reins' steely gaze said it all. Jake's first impulse was to punch him in the face, but he knew if he wanted to become involved in this case he'd better back off. "Captain," Jake said methodically, "Stoughton is not qualified to profile someone like this. He's not a member of the FBI profile unit. He's never spent a day of training at the FBI Academy in Quantico. He somehow worked his way into the Salem police department without any credentials. Why do you have so much faith in this guy?"

The waitress returned to the table with a pot of coffee. Reins waved her off, indicating he didn't want another cup. She looked in Jake's direction and he shook his head, also.

Reins stared into Jake's eyes, hatred marring his appearance. He looked long and hard as if his mind was searching for something to say in defense of Bill Stoughton. Finally, he said, "You have no clue how valuable Stoughton is to this investigation. He has an uncanny knack of seeing things that we don't. He has already come up with a profile that we're certain will help find this individual."

Jake knew no matter what he said, he was not going to discredit Bill Stoughton. He knew the captain was determined to prove his theory that Stoughton would have

Indiscriminate

some input into the way the murderer thinks, resulting in his capture.

"What has Stoughton come up with so far, Captain?" Jake asked.

"I'm not at liberty to discuss this case any further with you, Burnett," Reins announced.

With that remark, Jake decided it was time to leave. He stood and turned to face Reins, "Don't call me, Captain. And don't hang by your shot hairs waiting for me to call you."

Jake walked out of Red's with an inner feeling Reins would contact him. He knew when the case came to a halt Reins would fish for further information.

Jake started his engine and sped away. Slowing down through the center of Salem Square, he was aware of all the tourists on both sides of the street. They took advantage of the signs that read: *THE PEDESTRIAN HAS THE RIGHT OF WAY.* They simply stepped out into the street and assumed that all vehicles would stop. This infuriated Jake. "Hey, asshole," Jake yelled, "next time I'll run your dumb ass down!"

When he drove past the courthouse, he stopped next to the newsstand that was located just before the overpass. The old man knew Jake always bought the *Salem Evening News* and automatically handed it to him. Jake always exchanged the paper for a dollar and drove off, never waiting for his change.

He inched the 'Vette out between traffic and across to the small rotary. He stepped on the gas and pulled out over the overpass. Feeling the power of his Corvette, he had difficulty controlling the urge to put the pedal to the metal.

Cruising down North Street Jake took the usual shortcut around the Green Lawn cemetery to the Kernwood Bridge, which connected Salem and Beverly. He used this route when the traffic was heavy on Bridge Street and the Salem/Beverly Bridge was congested.

Jake liked to drive while he was thinking. He was deep in thought when he turned onto Route 62. Heading north, he drove until he entered the town of North Andover. *Christ, I didn't realize I'd come this far.* He waited for a break in the traffic, then turned around and drove south toward Beverly.

Route 62 seemed to go on forever. A large grin spread across his face when he thought of his ex-partner, Mark Roads. Mark lived on Poplar Street in Danvers, which was also Route 62. Mark always said, "If Route 62 don't go there, you can't get there from here."

Turning onto Poplar Street in Danvers, Jake decided to stop at Mark's house. He knew the Roads family would be home because Mark always took his vacation during the Fourth of July holiday. He turned into the driveway at 52 Poplar Street.

There was a late morning haze and the humidity made it feel as though it was above ninety degrees. He turned off the engine and heard Mark holler through the kitchen window, "Hey, want a beer?" He pointed toward the backyard.

Jake smiled and gave Mark a thumbs-up, then walked around to the back of the house. He gazed at the backyard of his ex-partner and couldn't help but envy the way Mark lived. He had a lovely wife, Joanne, who understood her husband's dedication to his job, and was very supportive. There have been times when Jake actually thought that Mark, or his wife, were connected to the murders. He would shake his head and think, 'How can I think these things, they are my friends, and after all, Mark is a police officer.'

His thirteen-year-old daughter, Patty, was a typical teenager. Mark described her as thirteen-going-on-twenty. Mark's son and Jake's Godson, Mark Jr., was wise beyond his seven years. In school he was moved from the first grade to the third grade because he was bored with the simplicity of the work. According to Mark, the school commissioner was considering moving him again, this time to the fifth grade.

Jake sat at the picnic table and Mark came out of the house with a cooler full of ice and beer. "Try one of these," Mark said. "I guarantee this is the coldest beer you ever had."

There was a thin layer of ice covering the cans and Jake punched his hand through the top only to find ice cubes floating in water. "Christ," Jake snatched his hand from the water, "this is freezing!"

"Yeah," Mark said, smiling. "Isn't it great? It's so cold it's going to make your forehead hurt if you drink it too fast."

Jake popped the top and took a long swallow. "You're right. This is the coldest beer I've ever had. What did you do, put it in the fucking freezer?"

Mark answered, "As a matter of fact, that's exactly what I did. Joanne's brother stopped by yesterday afternoon with a bag of food for the grill. He had everything you could imagine. We ate until we couldn't eat any more, then started on the beer. "Mark popped the top on his beer and took two short sips. "Jake, I like Jo's brother. He's a great guy…"

Jake looked at Mark and said, "Okay, he's a great guy. But what?"

"Well," Mark said, "He's nice to have around until the fifth beer, then some sort of metamorphosis takes place and he turns into a fucking asshole. I hid the rest of the beer under the sink, but he found it."

Jake was trying not to laugh. With a straight face, he asked, "That's when you put the beer in the freezer?"

Mark shook his head in disgust. "I tried hiding it in the kitchen cabinets, but he found it there, too. So I brought it down to the basement and put it in the meat freezer."

Jake stared at his can of beer trying desperately to control his laughter. "That's why it's so cold?"

Mark glanced in Jake's direction. "Yes, and I forgot about it till late last night. Don't bust my balls."

Jake's expression grew somber. "I talked with Captain Reins this morning." Handing his ex-partner the note Reins had given him, he added, "He wants me to be his fucking snitch."

Mark read the handwritten note. "He gave you this? Christ, Jake, he didn't even let me know about this note." Roads looked at Jake in disbelief, "He asked for *your* help?"

"He's under a great deal of pressure from the media. He wants me to dig into everything—without any backing from the department." Jake's voice dripped with animosity.

Mark set the note on the picnic table. Still staring down at the warning, he said, "It looks like it was written in crayon."

"Charcoal," Jake said.

"Charcoal?" Mark asked, "You mean like, *charcoal?*

Jake nodded and looked at his ex-partner. "Yes," he said, "just like *charcoal*."

"Smart," Mark said, "even trying to trace something written in pen is difficult, this makes it just about impossible. This guy ain't stupid."

"And he ain't done yet." Jake stood up and set his half-full can of beer on the table.

"Why do you think that?" Mark asked. "There haven't been any reports of anyone missing and no bodies have been found. If there was another murder, we would have found the body. This psycho leaves his victims out in plain sight. He wants them to be found. Maybe he's moved on to continue his dirty deeds somewhere else." Mark faced Jake, "There's been talk in the department that Bill Stoughton has made this guy nervous. Maybe he's afraid Stoughton will ID him."

"Stoughton couldn't ID his grandmother in a fucking lineup," Jake snapped. "That asshole is playing this for all it's worth."

"Jake," Mark said, "the word is that Stoughton's life has been threatened by the murderer and he refuses to back off. Does that sound like an asshole to you?"

"It's more complicated than that," Jake said. "There's a lot more to this than what has already happened. I can feel something, but I don't know what it is. Something. Trust me."

At that moment Joanne walked out from the house. "Hi, Jake," she said warmly, "how have you been? How's business at Books?"

"Hi, Jo," Jake responded cheerfully, "everything's fine with me. How about you?"

"Fine," she placed gardening tools on the picnic table, "we're having a cookout this afternoon. Would you like to come, say around, two o'clock?"

Jake smiled. "I'd love to." He tapped Mark on his shoulder, turned and left. He knew Mark looked forward to his vacation and really didn't want to talk shop during this week.

He continued down Route 62 into Beverly and over the Beverly/Salem Bridge. Traffic seemed much lighter than he expected, so he decided to drive through Salem Square. Passing the courthouse on his left, then city hall, he stopped at the intersection in the square. Tourists crossed the street with utter disregard for traffic.

Stopping in the middle of the intersection to look at a map, one couple stood there pointing to all the sights. The man was wearing a *Witch City* tee shirt with khaki shorts. The woman, dressed identically, was giving the orders.

"Hey!" Jake yelled, "How about shooting the shit on the sidewalk?"

The man took offense at Jake's remark. He took two steps closer to Jake's 'Vette and leveled his camera at Jake. "Smile," he said in a sarcastic tone. All the while the woman pleaded, "George, don't!"

Jake smiled tightly, "You should have listened to her, George." He opened the door and started to get out.

Just then a police officer strode into the intersection. "Get out of the street, sir," he barked at the man with the camera. "I don't know how it works where you come from, but around here we don't stand in the middle of the street taking pictures. Move it."

Jake slid back behind the wheel and shut the door. He had never seen this young officer. He must be a rookie.

"Thanks, officer," Jake said.

"Sergeant Burnett," the officer said, "it should be that guy thanking me, not you. He has no clue how close he was to having his ass kicked."

Jake stared at the police officer. He was convinced they had never met. "Do I know you officer?"

"No sir," he responded, "but I know all about you. How you got screwed by the review board. Everyone knows about Sergeant Jason Burnett."

Jake nodded in appreciation and continued through Salem Square. Rounding the Riley Plaza he decided to look for Cameron Baird. He hoped the junkie would have information he could use. He turned onto Peabody Street then hung a right onto Congress Street. This led to one of Baird's hangouts, Palmer's Cove. Being familiar with this neighborhood, he decided to park his 'Vette in the small parking lot of a convenience store with the hopes it would be safe.

As Jake walked toward the park, he noticed many different ethnic groups who lived in this area. White, Black, Hispanic and Oriental all interacted without any problems. As bad as some people considered the neighborhood to be, the crime rate was no higher than any other part of the city.

As he stood by the fence overlooking the park, he thought about what the young officer said. "I know all about you, how you got screwed by the review board." In his heart Jake knew he didn't get screwed by the review board; it was Captain Reins who screwed him. He knew his temper had always put him in the middle of trouble. However, the captain went out of his way to have him removed from the police force and it had nothing to do with his temper. It was a personal vendetta, and Jake knew why.

Across the park he spotted Cameron Baird standing with a group of teenagers. Disgust and anger raged through his veins. The thought of Baird selling drugs to kids infuriated him.

Baird glanced over his shoulder and noticed Jake standing at the fence. As usual, his first reaction seemed to be to run. But he apparently decided against it when he saw Jake motioning for him to come to the fence. He slowly walked toward Jake. When he reached the fence, he nervously said, "S'up, Jake?"

Jake fought the urge to smash his face through the fence. He thought the man standing in front of him was the lowest form of life that ever existed. He needed Baird's knowledge of street crime, and that was the only reason he didn't beat him on a regular basis.

"Talk to me, Cam," Jake said with conviction. "You didn't call me and that really pisses me off. I know you've heard something."

"You mean about the murders, Jake?" Baird asked.

Jake stared coldly into Baird's eyes. "Don't play stupid. I'm not in a good mood."

"Oh yeah, the murders," Cam mumbled. "The only thing I can tell you is that the killer's worried about Bill Stoughton. He's afraid of him, even threatened to kill him if he doesn't back off. But Stoughton's a pro. He won't let go, even though he might get killed.

Indiscriminate

Jake saw how nervous Baird was becoming. "How the hell do you know about that? Have you been talking to your buddy, the reporter?"

Baird nodded. He was reluctant to give any further information until Jake said, "Keep going, Cam, I don't have all fucking day."

"The reporter told me an anonymous phone call was taken at the news desk. The caller said Stoughton would be killed if he didn't back off. The reporter in charge of the murders said he was working on a full-page article about Bill Stoughton. It's going to be on the front page of Friday's paper—pictures and everything."

Jake's thoughts scrambled together. *Did I misjudge Stoughton?* he wondered. Maybe Bill Stoughton was trying to help because he cared, or maybe he wasn't. In either case Jake wasn't going to dwell on him. There were more important things to think about. There were five brutal murders in a twenty-four-hour span and he couldn't dismiss the thought of more deaths on the way.

The teenagers across the park were still standing where they were when Baird was with them. Again, anger formed in the pit of Jake's stomach. "Are you selling poison to those kids, Cam?"

"No way," Baird snapped, "we're just shooting the shit—honest."

Disgust raced through Jake. It was a feeling he always had when he talked to Cameron Baird. Without responding to the junkie's answer, Jake shook his head in repulsion and walked back to his car.

Pulling out of the parking lot, Jake turned onto Congress

Street and headed home. He wanted to stop at the police station and talk with Captain Reins, but didn't want to create another altercation. He knew Reins wanted his input, but he was reluctant to reciprocate.

The day was perfect and Jake wished he hadn't committed himself to Mark's invitation. He would much rather have driven to New Hampshire and toured the coastline. He always found it soothing to drive this route with no end destination.

Driving South on Lafayette Street, Jake pulled in his driveway and stopped. He looked up at the numbers 242 on the front of the house. Remembering the day when he and his father nailed the numbers to the home, he grinned and remembered how proud his father was when the finishing touch was nailed. That was thirty years ago.

After showering, Jake stretched out on the sofa and dozed off. His mind drifted in a flow of tranquility that gently pushed him into a deep sleep.

The telephone rang and brought him back to the present. On the second ring, Jake picked up the cordless phone. "Burnett."

There was a pause on the other end of the phone and Jake sat up straight on the sofa. "Hello?" he said in an annoyed tone.

"Hello, Jake," came the friendly voice of Joanne Roads. "I'm having a hard time hearing you. It's getting a little noisy around here. Are you coming over or what?"

Jake glanced at his watch. Nearly three o'clock. "Holy shit!" he bellowed. "Sorry Jo, I fell asleep. I must have been more tired than I thought. I'll be there in thirty minutes."

Indiscriminate

"Hold on," Joanne said, "Mark wants to talk to you."

Jake heard the loud music and laughter of the people at the cookout. He really didn't want to go, but Mark and Joanne were his closest friends.

"Hey, Jake," Mark voice shot over the noise, "are you coming?"

Jake told him the same thing he said to Joanne.

"Jake," Mark whispered, "the little matchmaker has invited someone she wants you to meet. Her name is Rebecca White. She's really nice, but I wanted you know what you're in for."

Jake closed his eyes and hung his head. "Why does your wife always think *I* need a wife? I like my life the way it is. I don't need someone telling me what to wear, what to think where to go…"

"You're not locked into anything," Mark said. "Rebecca doesn't know about you, either. If you don't like her, don't worry about it. She has no clue that Jo has arranged this."

"Okay," Jake said. "I'm on my way"

Jake dressed in cut-off jeans and a faded gray tee shirt with *Salem Police Athletic Department*, stenciled across the front. He hovered over the sink in the bathroom brushing his teeth. He noticed a small tear on the shoulder of his shirt. When he finished brushing his teeth, he noticed another tear on the front. *Christ, my favorite shirt!* After determining he wasn't going to Mark's cookout to impress anyone, he decided to wear it anyway.

Backing out of his driveway, Jake drove north on Lafayette Street. Before he knew it, he was driving over the Beverly/Salem Bridge and into Beverly. Taking the back roads, he turned onto route 62 and entered Danvers.

As he got closer to 52 Popular Street, Jake noticed the cars parked in Mark's driveway and on both sides of the street. Jake parked his 'Vette two blocks away and walked to the cookout, all the while wishing he had declined the invitation.

He walked into the backyard and into a cookout that was in full swing. There were fifty people standing and sitting holding beer. The music was loud and everyone's voice seemed to be trying to outdo the volume of the stereo. Jake looked around until he saw Mark standing in front of the grill flipping hamburgers and chicken filets.

He walked past the huge picnic table and noticed all the food. There were multiple bowls of everything possible to eat, from potato salad to calamari.

Standing behind Mark, Jake said, "Make mine well done."

Without turning around, Mark smiled and slid a hamburger onto a bun. "Here ya go, Jake. Just the way you like it."

Jake accepted the food and walked over to the stone retaining wall that he and Mark had built. Sitting on the wall he remembered the long hours in the sun he and Mark spent placing each stone.

Before long Mark joined Jake with a hamburger of his own and two cold beers. "This is the cold stuff, Jake, my private stash. Drink it slow, buddy. Remember the brain freeze you got the last time you gulped it down?"

Before Jake could respond Joanne motioned to Mark that he had a phone call. Mark walked into the house.

Jake sat looking at all the people, most of whom he knew.

Indiscriminate

He was looking for a woman he didn't know, but there were at least ten women there Jake had never met. He noticed an attractive woman with shoulder-length auburn hair talking to a man she seemed irritated with. *Probably her husband. I bet she's pissed because he drank too much.* He smiled to himself. *That's just what I need, someone to get pissed every time I open a beer.*

Mark walked back from the house and sat next to Jake. Without saying a word Mark lifted his beer and took a long swallow.

"Hey, remember the brain-freeze," Jake said.

Mark set the beer down and rubbed his forehead. "Christ, that hurts," he mumbled.

Both men sat in silence for a moment when Jake asked, "What's wrong? What happened, Mark?"

Mark stared across the yard, silent.

"Another murder?" Jake asked gravely.

"Almost," Mark responded. "This time the victim didn't die."

Jake's heart pounded as blood raced through his veins. "So, we have a witness this time?"

"No," Mark said, "he was wearing a mask, and he couldn't ID him.

"*He* couldn't ID him," Jake said. "You mean this victim was a man?"

"Bill Stoughton," Mark replied. "He was attacked in his bed at four o'clock this morning. He was strangled with a rope tied into a hangman's knot and left for dead. Somehow he managed to get to the phone and dial 911. He couldn't talk, but the call was traced and the police arrived about five this morning. He was found on the floor of his bedroom with the noose still around his neck. He's in the hospital now."

Nothing more was said about the attempted murder of Bill Stoughton. Both felt guilty because of their badgering of Stoughton. They realized that although they didn't like the profiler, he continued to help the police even though his life was in danger. He did this for no fee or tangible gain.

Joanne walked up to Jake. "Jake, I'd like you to meet Rebecca White."

Jake looked up and was surprised to see the woman he noticed arguing with a man earlier. Standing, he held out his hand. "It's nice to meet you, Becky."

Shaking Jake's hand, she replied, "Rebecca. My name is Rebecca. It's nice to meet you too, Jake."

Jake looked into the most beautiful green eyes he had ever seen. "Jason, my name is Jason."

This brought a burst of laughter from everyone, including Rebecca. Her smile was bright and breathtaking and Jake was instantly attracted to her. His mannerism changed into that of a little boy talking to his first crush. He stumbled over every word.

Joanne was the first to pick up on the attraction. Nudging Mark to let him know it was time for them to leave, they walked back to their other guests.

Engrossed in conversation, Jake and Rebecca talked for almost an hour, mostly about Mark and Joanne, when the man she had been arguing with walked up and sat on the wall next to Rebecca.

"Here," he said, holding out a beer, "this is for you, honey."

Indiscriminate

"No thank you, Bert." Rebecca turned her attention back to Jake.

"Rebecca," the man placed the cold can of beer on the inside of Rebecca's thigh, "how about I take you out of here?"

Without showing any emotion, Rebecca spread her legs just wide enough to let the can of beer fall between them and onto the ground. "No thank you, Bert." Her tone was calm. It was obvious she wasn't easily intimidated.

The man reached down and retrieved the can of beer. As he was about to place it back on her thigh, he asked, "Come on, Rebecca, how about it?"

Jake's face reddened. "Hey, Bert, how about if I shove that can up your ass?"

Rebecca snapped a cold look at Jake. "Jason, don't." She walked away, leaving the two men sitting on the wall.

As she walked away, Jake noticed how tight and athletic she looked in her frayed Levi shorts. Wearing a half shirt, her braless chest heaved as she walked.

"I'm gonna get me some of that," Bert said as he watched Rebecca walk away.

"What you're gonna get, Bert, is your fucking ass kicked," Jake shot back.

Bert turned and put his finger to within one inch of Jake's face, "Who's gonna kick my ass? You?"

With cat-like speed, Jake snatched Bert's finger and snapped it back, breaking it instantly. Bert held his finger in pain and walked toward the house. As he reached the door, Mark walked out. They spoke briefly and Bert went inside.

Mark came to Jake and asked what had happened. Jake

explained what had taken place, then apologized for what he had done. "Is his finger broken?" he asked.

"Yup," replied Mark, "it's definitely broken."

"I'm sorry, Mark," Jake said. "I feel bad about this."

"Don't worry about it," Mark said. "He's an asshole anyway. I'm surprised someone didn't kill him years ago."

Jake smiled and continued looking over the guests at the cookout.

"Looking for someone specific, Jake?" Mark asked in a sarcastic tone. Jake let Mark's taunting remark pass.

Mark began to return to his guests when he said, "She left."

"She left?" Jake said. "Did she say anything?"

"As a matter of fact, she asked me to give you this." Mark handed Jake a piece of paper with Rebecca's phone number written in pink ink.

Jake smiled and shoved the paper into his front pocket. After saying goodbye to everyone, he left.

As he drove home, his thoughts were of Rebecca White. He was infatuated with her and this feeling was not normal for him. The sight of her bright smile lingered in his head. He couldn't get her out of his mind.

All at once a vision of Bill Stoughton lying on the floor with a hangman's noose around his neck took over Jake's thoughts. *I hope he makes it.*

Four

That night Jake decided to call Rebecca white. He felt as nervous as a high school kid as he dialed the number. On the fourth ring, Rebecca answered.

Jake stammered, "Hi Rebecca, this is Jake – I mean, Jason Burnett…"

Then he heard Rebecca's voice continue, "I'm sorry I can't get to the phone right now, but please leave a message." He realized he was talking to her answering machine.

His mind stumbled for something intelligent to say when Rebecca picked up the phone. "Hello, Jason, you caught me getting out of the shower."

A vision flashed through Jake's mind as he shook his head and smiled to himself, "Sorry," he said, "Do you want me to call back at a more convenient time?"

"No, when I gave Mark my phone number to give you, I was hoping you would call. I wanted to apologize for leaving the cookout without saying goodbye. I know it was rude, but

I saw what was happening and I didn't want to be the cause of a fight."

"I didn't want to fight, either, but that guy was obnoxious," Jake replied.

"Jason, I'm a big girl. I can take care of myself. I don't like violence. I *always* stay clear of that type of behavior."

Jake was ashamed of his childish behavior and told her so. He realized she was right and didn't want her to think that mindless violence was a part of his life. "Rebecca," Jake said, "I'm sorry. I promise to control my temper in the future." He knew he could control his temper under normal circumstances; he simply had a hard time overlooking obnoxious and ignorant behavior.

Rebecca was happy with Jake's answer and began talking about Mark and Joanne. "I've known Joanne since high school," she said. "When I got married, I moved to California with my husband and lived there for the past ten years."

Jake listened to Rebecca tell him everything he wanted to know about her life: How she met her husband, about her wedding, the move to California and how her husband evolved into a violent man. She didn't realize the signs and overlooked many of his outbursts until his violent temper was happening every day and beat her on a regular basis. Jake knew this was why she became so upset at the thought of a fight.

They talked for more than two hours about everything and nothing. Jake felt like a new, young man when they finished the call for the evening. They made a date for Friday night at the Chase House and Jake's mind abandoned the murders—at least for the moment.

Indiscriminate

The week flew by and Rebecca stopped in at Books almost every morning. She sat with Jake and helped with questions from the customers. On Friday morning she met Dang and his girlfriend, Mary.

When Rebecca invited them to come along with her and Jake to the Chase House that evening, Jake was happy and disappointed at the same time. He wanted to be alone with her, but he also enjoyed Dang and Mary's company.

"Well," said Rebecca, "if the four of us are going to the Chase house tonight, maybe I should call Mark and Jo. I'm sure they'd love to come, too."

Jake closed Books at five o'clock and went home to shower. Rebecca was handling all the arrangements for the triple date at the Chase, and Jake wanted to relax before the night began. Thoughts of the murders faded from Jake's mind as he showered. Instead, his thoughts were of Rebecca.

At seven-thirty, Jake drove to Rebecca's house. He knew her address but had never been to her house. Driving down Marlboro Road he turned right onto Rockdale Avenue, up a hill and around a sharp curve. He was searching for number 24 when he saw Rebecca sitting on the front steps of a beautiful little one-story ranch house. As he pulled into the driveway he noticed how well kept the lawn and shrubs were. "Very nice, who's your gardener?" he hollered.

Rebecca smiled and walked toward the car. "You're looking at her."

Jake backed out of the driveway and waited his turn to enter the mainstream on Marlboro Road. Turning left onto Highland Avenue, they headed to the Chase House.

As usual, Jake parked in the parking lot away from

the Chase to avoid having his Vette bumped by another car. He knew parking in this lot was no guarantee that his car wouldn't be touched, but it was the safest place in the area.

Jake and Rebecca walked into the Chase House and out onto the deck. As they approached Dang and Mary, Jake heard an angry voice. "What the hell was that, French?"

Jake looked in the direction of the angry voice. A man stood with a beer in his left hand and had his right finger stuck in Dang's face. Jake surveyed the situation and noticed there were three other men standing with the man who was picking a fight with Dang.

Dang noticed Jake standing to his left and indicated for him not to interfere. In a soft tone, he said, *"Ich weise zu in eine Schlacht des Verstands mit einem unarmd Mann geht ab."*

"I'll ask you again little man," the antagonist demanded, "are you talkin' French?" He shoved a callused hand through his unruly dark hair.

Dang faced Jake and smiled, then turned back to the obnoxious man standing in front of him. "No, that was German," then added, *"Je refuse à entre dans un combat d'esprits avec un homme de unarmed."* He took a step backward. *"That was French!"*

Jake walked over to Dang and placed his hand on his shoulder, "Got a problem, buddy?"

"Jason!" Rebecca's irritated voice rang out. "Let's sit down."

As Jake turned to walk away, the man said, "You better listen to your bitch. She just saved you a whole lot of pain."

Jake's arm tensed in anger. He turned and faced the man

who had been pushing for a fight, when Rebecca pulled him back. "Jason, I don't like fighting."

Jake looked into her eyes and saw how serious she was. Without looking back at the man, Jake ushered Rebecca to a table and waited for Dang and Mary.

Within minutes Mark and Joanne walked in and sat at the table. With the good conversation and a light-hearted atmosphere the night flew by without further incident from the man who tried to instigate a fight. Finally, the waitress walked between the tables and announced, "Last call for alcohol."

Jake looked around and watched all the heavy hitters try and order two drinks with the hopes the evening would not come to an end. They were wrong. On the last call of the evening only one drink per person could be purchased.

As the waitress cleared the table, Jake stood and everyone followed his lead. Walking out the front door, Dang looked over his shoulder in the direction of the man who had earlier tried to pick a fight. He was staring at Dang, but obviously wasn't about to leave before finishing his drink.

As they walked across the parking lot, Dang heard footsteps hurrying behind them. He turned around and saw the man from the bar. He was only ten feet from Dang and was aggressively moving toward him. Dang knew he wouldn't be able to talk his way out of a fight. This man, for some reason, was obsessed with wanting to fight with Dang.

Jake saw the man approach Dang. Standing with both hands at his side, Dang apparently still hoped he could talk his way out of a fight. He was wrong.

The man charged forward and Dang sidestepped and

let the man stumble and fall against a car. "What's your problem?" Dang asked the man. "I don't want to fight with you. Please, leave me alone."

In an attempt to put an end to the confrontation before it escalated out of control, Mark held his badge in the air and announced he was a Salem police officer. He ordered the man to leave or he would be arrested.

"We're gonna kick your fucking ass, too," the man barked at Mark.

In a show of force, the other three men stepped up and let their intentions be known.

Once again Rebecca squeezed Jake's arm. "Jason, please, I don't like fighting."

Jake looked into her eyes and saw fear. He knew violence of any kind terrified her and she would do anything to avoid it.

"Rebecca," Jake said, "I can't stand here and do nothing while four men are assaulting my friends. I hope you can understand that."

Rebecca saw the look in Jake's eyes, and it frightened her because in her heart she knew he was right. She let loose of Jake's arm and walked to Joanne and Mary.

Rebecca watched the man she had known for less than a week step up and stand beside his friends. At that moment she realized how much she cared for him. She knew Jason Burnett would defend his friends regardless of the odds against him. The three friends stood side by side in front of the four would-be attackers. The expression on their faces was hard and cold and they made no attempt to hide their intentions to defend themselves.

Indiscriminate

The man who had been the instigator in the beginning suddenly changed his tone to that of a coward who had been put in a position to fend for himself. "Hey," he barked and pointed at Dang, "my fight is with you, not with your friends."

Dang studied the man standing in front of him. What he saw was nothing more than a close-minded bigot who couldn't bear the thought of an Oriental man with a white woman. Dang stepped back. "I don't want to fight with you, but it's going to end here." He motioned for Jake and Mark to back off, and squared off against the antagonist. The man also motioned for his friends to back off.

Rebecca turned to Jake and Mark, "That man is much bigger than Dang. This isn't a fair fight. Please stop them."

Jake turned to Mark and said sarcastically, "She's right, Mark, this isn't a fair fight. What do you think we should do?"

Without turning his attention away from the up-coming fight Mark said, "Well…we could always let two of his asshole friends help him. At least that will make it a little more fair."

Rebecca stared at Jake and Mark with a puzzled expression. "You're saying we should allow *three* of them to gang up on Dang?"

Jake looked at Mark, and with an emotionless tone said, "She's right, Mark, that isn't fair. Maybe we should let all four of them take a crack at Dang."

"Jason, stop it!" Rebecca barked. She turned her attention back to the fight as the man lunged at Dang. It was then she realized what Jake and Mark were saying. Dang sidestepped the attack and slammed his open hand under his assailant's throat, straightening him up then sending him to the ground. It was over in less than one second. The other three men stood motionless as Dang looked in their direction. Holding their hands in front of them in a passive gesture, everyone knew it was over.

Jake drove Rebecca home and he knew she was upset. The violence her ex-husband put her through had taken its toll. He could understand why she was against violence, but hoped she could understand why it couldn't be avoided this night.

Not a word was spoken during the ride to Rebecca's house. When Jake pulled into her driveway and stopped the car, Rebecca opened the door and got out immediately. She began walking to the front door of her house, then stopped and looked back at Jake. She turned around and walked back to Jake, kissing him passionately. "Please stay the night with me, Jason. I don't want to be alone."

The night was spent making love to an elevation of passion neither of them had ever thought possible. From the moment their lips met he knew he wanted Rebecca more than he realized.

At nearly seven o'clock in the morning Jake got dressed and went home, leaving Rebecca in a deep sleep. He knew she would call him at Books.

Jake showered and got dressed in his usual jeans and tee shirt, and drove to downtown Salem. He parked his Vette and walked up the alley to the bookstore. This time he had a bounce in his walk that made him feel unbelievably happy and carefree.

Indiscriminate

At nine-thirty Rebecca entered the store carrying two large coffees and a dozen doughnuts. "I hope you're hungry." She leaned down and kissed Jake lightly.

Jake felt as though he had known Rebecca White his entire life. When they were together it was a comfortable feeling that he hadn't known in years.

"Jason," Rebecca said softly, "I can't explain why I acted the way I did last night. It's way out of the norm for me. I know this will sound like an old story…but I've never done that before…ever."

Jake looked into her eyes. "You have nothing to apologize for. We were both there, remember?"

"I know. It's just that I haven't been with a man since I left my husband. Plus, after witnessing your temper…who would have guessed I would have been with you? You know how I feel about violence."

Jake smiled and gently kissed her forehead. Feelings stirred in the pit of his stomach for Rebecca and this was new to him.

At nearly eleven o'clock Rebecca said she had to leave and finish a promotional article for a company she had contracted to write an ad for. When she walked out the door, she poked her head back through the doorway. In a playful tone she said, "Being a freelance writer working out of my home allows me a lot of free time, but I do have to work, too."

The next three weeks went by fast, and August rolled in before Jake knew it. The weather was exceptionally hot and humid, but neither Jake nor Rebecca seemed to care. They spent almost every night together and their relationship escalated to heights previously unfamiliar to either of them.

Howard Olsen

On Monday, August second, Mark walked into Books at nine-thirty in the morning. His face wore a somber and heavy expression and Jake knew something was wrong. Jake excused himself from a customer and walked up to Mark. Before Mark spoke Jake said, "You found another body."

Mark said nothing, but held two fingers in the air.

"Two bodies?" Jake asked. "You found two more bodies? Where?"

Mark waited for the customer to leave the store, and then said. "At a construction site off of Marlboro Road. They were murdered somewhere else Sunday night and dumped at the site so they would be easily found. It's starting all over again, Jake," Mark said. "I thought it was over. I thought this sick motherfucker had moved on."

Jake's thoughts returned to Rebecca. She lived off of Marlboro Road and Jake knew the construction site was less than a half-mile from her house. He immediately picked up the telephone and called her. On the fourth ring, Rebecca answered.

Jake felt immediate relief. Not wanting to upset her, he told her he had errands to do and he would be closing the store early.

"It must be nice to just stop working whenever you get the urge," Rebecca said playfully. "Is your important business at the beach?"

Jake reassured her it was important, and hung up the telephone. He put receipts into his top desk drawer then looked up at his ex-partner. "Who were they?"

"Gary Banos, a forty-eight-year-old salesman. He was here on a business trip. The second body was identified as

Indiscriminate

Marie Chapman. She was a thirty-two-year-old housewife from Beverly. Her husband identified her body early this morning. They have two children—he's in bad shape.

Jake continued to stare at his desk. "What about the rope?"

Mark nodded. "Hangman's knot, just like the others."

"These serial murders have put the city into a state of panic," Mark continued, "and it's only gonna get worse if we don't find this son-of-a-bitch."

Mark told Jake about the meeting in Captain Reins' office and how Bill Stoughton had profiled the murderer. "Stoughton had profiled him as extremely intelligent with the ability to out-think the police. "He said the only way we're going to catch him is by trickery and he was capable of anything and shouldn't be underestimated." "Don't underestimate him!" Mark blurted out, "The son-of-a-bitch murders seven people in less than a month, and Stoughton says, *don't underestimate him!*"

Jake looked at his ex-partner. "What about Reins? Is he going to let me help?"

"Bull Reins is a fucking asshole," snapped Mark. "The first thing out of his mouth was that he didn't want *ex-police officer* Jason Burnett, involved in any part of this investigation. He made it clear that if anyone fed you information about the murders, they would lose their badge."

"You're taking a big chance talking to me, Mark. I don't want you to get into trouble."

"Don't worry about that. Reins is running around in a million different directions at once. Christ, he even has twenty-four-hour protection for Bill Stoughton. Stoughton is walking around like a sheik with an entourage. He's becoming a legend in his own fucking mind. He insists he will only allow the protection for one week. We can't force him to accept it, and after this Friday he will not have anyone to protect him if this sick son-of-a-bitch decides to finish the job with him."

Jake didn't want to talk about Bill Stoughton and dismissed Mark's comment on how Stoughton was acting. He knew his near-death experience must have been terrifying and could understand why Reins had given him around-the-clock protection.

Mark confessed to Jake that both victims had a hangman's knot around their necks and it was definitely done by the same man who murdered the other five people. "We can't find a connection among any of the victims," Mark said. "We fed every scrap of information into the computer and gave the printouts to Stoughton for him to analyze. We believe these murders are committed at random from someone who moved to this area within the past three to five years.

Christ, there are over 300 names from Salem alone and we're expecting to have over ten thousand names from the whole North Shore."

Jake shook his head in disgust. In his heart he knew the murders weren't random. He had no proof or reason for this deep-rooted feeling, but somehow he knew there was a purpose when the murderer selected his victims.

"What about a note?" Jake asked, "Were there any more notes?"

"I don't know for sure, but Reins referred to *several* notes at the meeting. I know about the notes that you and Reins received, but mentioning that there were *several* notes leads me to believe in addition to the first note he received, he got at least two, maybe more."

Jake hadn't thought of the murders in almost three weeks and he felt guilty about not digging into the case. He knew the captain wasn't going to turn up anything working by the book and he decided to go to the police station and talk to Bull Reins.

It was ten o'clock when Mark left and Jake closed the store. He walked down the alley to his Corvette, and with every step his anger increased. He couldn't understand why Reins wouldn't allow him to contribute to solving the murders. *Reins knows I'll be able to get information that the police can't.*

Driving the familiar route around the Riley Parking Plaza and onto Margin Street, Jake pulled into the parking lot of the police station. Knowing the side door was for police officers only, Jake stood just outside the door and waited for someone to come out. When an advocate walked out, Jake walked in. He walked up the stairs to Captain Reins' office and entered without being announced.

The captain looked up from his desk at Jake and became furious.

Before Reins could say anything Jake said, "Hold on, Captain, I know you're still pissed at me, but I can help you with this investigation."

Reins stared at Jake with hatred. "What the hell are you doing here, Burnett? I don't remember inviting you. Get the hell out of my office. If you want to speak to me, call my secretary and make an appointment."

Jake walked to the door. Instead of closing it behind him, he shut the door from the inside and turned back to Bull Reins. "You're an unforgiving son-of-a-bitch! You've been carrying a sick hatred for me for five years and it's eating you alive. You wouldn't listen to the truth five years ago, but you're gonna hear it now—whether you like it or not."

Reins darted across the room toward Jake. His 240-pound frame moved with amazing speed and grace.

Jake sidestepped and pulled the captain's tie, causing him to stumble against the wall and fall on the sofa.

Reins looked up at Jake in bewilderment. He never expected Jason Burnett to retaliate against his attack and couldn't believe that he actually had.

Straightening his tie, Reins reluctantly said, "Okay, Burnett, you have one minute."

Five

Jake looked down at the man who was solely responsible for him leaving the Salem police force. For five years he had wanted to explain the events that led up to the night Captain Reins and his brother, John, broke into the motel room where Jake was spending the night with a woman. He wanted to clear the air and, at the very least, let Bull Reins know what actually happened.

The captain rose from the sofa and sat behind his desk. Staring down at some papers, he said, "Well Burnett, let's hear it."

Jake saw how uninterested Reins was with his plea to clear the air. He knew that no matter what he told the captain about the events of that night, it would make little difference to the vengeful man sitting in front of him.

Realizing his attempt to make things right was futile, Jake turned and walked to the door. Opening the door, he looked over his shoulder. "Did you receive another note?"

Howard Olsen

The captain's manner changed immediately. He discarded the animosity he held for Jake and asked, "Did you?"

Jake closed the door. "I asked you first, Captain."

Reins' tone was cold and calculating. There was no misunderstanding his feelings toward Jake. "Burnett, I don't like you. I never have. The only reason I'm even talking to you is because of the murders. I realize I have to put my personal feelings aside and put an end to this murder spree. But keep in mind when this is all over my feelings toward you won't change. I didn't like you then, I don't like you now, and I will never like you. Are we clear on that?"

As odd as it was to Jake, this characteristic of Reins was the only part of his personality that Jake respected. The fact that Reins made no attempt to sugarcoat his feelings toward anyone was something Jake could relate to. "At least everyone knows where they stand with you."

Reins opened the top drawer of his desk and removed a piece of paper. Holding it flat on the top of his desk as if to hide it, he said, "For the record, I don't want you involved in *any* aspect of this case." He slid the folded piece of paper to Jake.

Jake slowly picked up the note and unfolded it in front of Reins.

"For Christ-sake sit down, Burnett," Reins snapped. "Show some professionalism."

Jake looked at the brown leather chair to his left, but sat on the corner of Reins' desk instead.

"Burnett!" Reins barked and motioned to the chair.

With a grin, Jake slid off of the desk and into the chair.

Jake read the note written in charcoal:

Indiscriminate

*CR, I TOLD YOU TO LOSE YOUR
TOP GUN. HE WAS LUCKY ONCE.
HE WON'T BE LUCKY A SECOND TIME.
MAKE HIM BACK OFF. THIS WILL
ALL BE OVER SOON.*

Jake looked up at Reins with disbelief. "I don't understand what he means by, *it will all be over soon*. Do you make any sense from it, Captain?"

Reins sat with a perplexed expression on his face. "I have no clue what that means. Maybe it's some sort of deadline."

"Jesus Christ," Jake snapped, "the death toll is up to seven! How many more people will have to die before this sick son-of-a-bitch is finished?"

"Burnett, for the record, you're not officially part of this or any other investigation. If you bull your way into something, outside the law, the department will not back you up. I have the authority to solicit help from outside the department, but you're not my first choice. The only reason you're part of what's going on now is because of the note *you* received. If your means of investigation brings you outside the law, I will come down on you—hard. Is that perfectly clear?"

Jake folded the note and placed it back on the captain's desk. He knew he would have no support if anything went wrong, and he didn't need this vindictive man explaining that fact to him. He looked at Reins and indicated that he understood the rules. At the door he turned and faced his ex-boss. "When this is all over, we're gonna sit and talk, whether you like it or not."

Without looking up at Jake, Reins motioned with his

hand for him to leave his office. Jake left without saying another word.

As Jake drove home the third note played over and over through his mind. *This guy's real nervous about Bill Stoughton,* Jake thought. *Maybe he's getting too close. Maybe he* is *worth having on the team.*

The second week of August came and went without any further news about the murderer. Jake wondered why the murders would come in spurts, then stop for a short time. He pondered the murderer as a possible truck driver or salesman who only passed through Salem on occasion. He dismissed this thought immediately because in his heart he was convinced the victims were selected for a reason and not by chance.

Jake was spending more time with Rebecca and was enjoying his newfound love. He had trouble admitting it to himself, but he *was* falling in love with her. They talked on the telephone every morning before and during work. At night, if they were not together, they would talk on the telephone for hours before going to bed. The feeling building inside was a feeling he hadn't felt in many years, partly because as a police detective he never found the time to commit to a relationship, and partly because his job always came first.

It was Friday, August 20th and Jake looked forward to going out to dinner with Rebecca. They talked about it all week, and with the week being extremely hot, they were both anxious to go out and relax.

When Jake stepped out of the shower he heard the telephone ring. He scurried to the phone, still dripping wet. "Hello?"

Indiscriminate

There was a pause on the other end of the phone.

"Hello?" This time, he was annoyed.

"Burnett, I need you in my office in thirty minutes," Reins demanded.

Jake recognized Reins' voice immediately. "Captain, can't it wait until tomorrow?"

"If it could wait until tomorrow, I would have called you tomorrow," Reins snapped back. "Thirty minutes. Don't be late."

Dripping wet, Jake held the receiver to his ear and mumbled, "Reins, you're a pain in the fucking ass." He called Rebecca and told her he would call her as soon as possible. It was evident in his voice he was disappointed.

Rebecca responded, "I understand. I'll wait for you to call." Rebecca White was unlike any other woman he knew. Her ability to understand his situation only added to her attraction.

Jake dressed and left for the police station. The short drive seemed longer than usual as his mind ran through what had happened thus far. "Seven murders within a month," he said out loud. "I hope Reins isn't going to tell me there's another one."

Circling the rotary he was on Margin Street and pulled into the police parking lot. This time he walked through the front door of the police station and told the sergeant on duty that Captain Reins was expecting him. The sergeant buzzed Jake in through the impressive oak and glass door. As he walked up the stairs and through the detective squad room, for an instant he felt as though he had never left the department.

Howard Olsen

The detective's lair was completely empty except for sergeant Moran who was sitting behind what use to be Jake's desk. Moran and Jake never got along when he was on the police force and nothing had changed.

"What the hell are you doing here, Burnett?" Moran asked in a tone laced with animosity.

Jake saw this as a chance to provoke Moran without causing any aggravation to himself. He stopped and faced the sergeant. Holding his middle finger high in the air, he said nothing and kept walking toward Bull Reins' office.

Moran bellowed, "I'm talking to you, Burnett. Where the hell do you think you're going?" Moran caught up with Jake, then stopped short when he saw Lucy, Captain Reins' secretary, greet Jake with a smile and a pleasant voice.

"Hello Jason," she said, "the captain is expecting you." With a bright and approving smile she added, "Go right in."

Lucy Madden was an icon with the Salem police department. She has been the secretary for the last three captains and knew more about procedure than anyone. At the tender age of sixty, her appearance and the masterful way she carried herself were second to none.

Jake shot a wide and friendly smile at Lucy, and then walked toward Reins' office, all the while holding his middle finger at Moran. Jake's defiant gesture toward the sergeant brought a giggle from Lucy as Jake walked past.

Reaching for the door, the thought of sergeant Moran's anger flashed through Jake's mind. Smiling to himself he thought, 'He's an asshole anyway!'

Jake opened the door and walked into Reins' office. As he shut the door behind him everyone turned and stared with

Indiscriminate

amazement that Jake was invited to this meeting. Even Jake was amazed at the fact that he was invited. He looked around the room and the first person he saw was his ex-partner, Mark Roads. He walked over and sat in a chair next to Mark.

"Burnett," Reins began, "I believe you know everyone here except Mr. Grant. He is Mayor Sweeney's right-hand man, and is here to represent the mayor's office."

Grant waved his hand at Jake from across the room and Jake reciprocated by nodding his head.

In addition to Mark and Mr. Grant, there were three detectives, three sergeants of detectives, and the medical examiner, Doctor Granger, from the Holyoke medical examiner's office, and Bill Stoughton.

"For the record," Captain Reins began, "I want to make it clear that I am against Jason Burnett attending this, or any other meeting, conducted by this office." Reins stared hard at Jake. "Mayor Sweeney did not order me to invite Burnett, but suggested it. Burnett is here with no authority or backing from the Salem police department."

After Reins said his opening statement, Jake looked around the room and noticed all eyes were focused on him. He tried not to show his discomfort.

Reins continued, "The first things we will address are the four notes the murderer sent."

Jake interrupted, "Four notes, Captain? I thought there were only three."

Reins didn't acknowledge Jake. He stood from behind his impressive desk and walked to a large bulletin board and turned it around so that it faced everyone in the room. Pinned to the board were enlarged pictures of all murder victims with rope marks around their necks. There were also blow-ups of the four notes that were sent.

Jake scanned the notes and immediately recognized the first three. The fourth note he hadn't seen but instantly knew who it was meant for. It was written in charcoal and in the same hand as the first three notes.

WS, STAY OUT OF THIS OR YOU WON'T BE AS LUCKY THE SECOND TIME!

Jake glanced at Bill Stoughton and saw a sheepish expression on his face. He wore a short-sleeved dress shirt buttoned all the way to the top and a silk scarf around his neck. Stoughton's choice of dress looked out of place in the ninety-degree weather. Jake soon realized why.

"The fourth note was sent to Bill Stoughton," Reins said. "This crazy son-of-a-bitch doesn't want Bill working up a profile on him. I, for one, would like to take this opportunity to express my deepest appreciation to Bill Stoughton for his help in trying to solve this case. He hasn't been deterred by the death threats. Even after he was brutally attacked and left for dead, he still insists on helping this department."

Everyone looked in Stoughton's direction and Jake detected a hint of embarrassment in his expression. He never liked Bill Stoughton and thought of him as an opportunist, but after looking at the faces of the murdered victims, Jake realized how traumatized and frightened Stoughton must have been when he was attacked.

Stoughton removed the scarf from around his neck and displayed the pinkish-red impression of a rope burn. He sat

Indiscriminate

still in the chair for almost a minute and allowed everyone to look at his injury. Then, as quietly as he removed it, Stoughton tied the scarf back around his neck.

The next person to speak was Doctor Granger. "As you can see from the photographs, the trauma to the victims' necks was substantial. It took a lot of strength to inflict that much damage to the internal organs. Enough force was used to actually pull the neck organs and tongue into the back nasal cavity."

Everyone's attention focused on Doctor Granger as he divulged the gruesome details of how the victims' lives were so brutally taken. The thought of the brutality used to take a human life lingered in everyone's mind. Jake knew very well what type of man it took to inflict this kind of terror, but he still couldn't conceive it happening in Salem.

"The victims' hands were bound behind their backs with duct tape," Granger continued. "Unfortunately, it's just about impossible to lift fingerprints from duct tape. The man we're looking for is strong and very smart. He leaves no evidence we're able to use. Even after ten victims, we can't find a clue or a common factor anywhere."

Jake was perplexed. As far as he knew, there were seven murders, not ten. Before the doctor could continue, Jake snapped, "There were *ten* murders?"

"Yes," replied Granger. "Twenty-nine-year-old Greg Jennings, a widower with a four-year-old daughter. He was from Danvers and worked at Triple S Machine Shop. Beside his body was fifty-two-year-old John Price. He was divorced and has a son attending the Berkley School of Music. He was recently retired from General Electric due to heart problems. Both bodies were found at a soccer field in Salem."

Jake stared at Doctor Granger with a stone-hard glare, "And the tenth?" Jake asked, his teeth clenched.

Granger thumbed through his notes. "The tenth victim was sixty-four-year-old James Wilson from Peabody. He was a semi-retired cook from the Hill Top Restaurant and was found one day later, August 19th, at the rear parking lot of the Ninety-Nine Restaurant in Salem. The last three victims were bound in the same manner as the first seven—with duct tape."

Jake's mind ran through a marathon of events surrounding what happened in less than six weeks. He didn't know why a medical examiner from Holyoke was in charge of this case when the chief of staff, Doctor Kessler, was based in Boston. Jake wasn't questioning Doctor Granger's ability to do a good job; it was simply that Jake thought of Kessler as the best forensic scientist that ever took a breath. He didn't want to create a scene by voicing his opinion in front of Granger. With this in mind, Jake decided to wait until he could talk to Captain Reins alone.

The meeting wore on for almost an hour. Jake became annoyed at the repeated comments on all the evidence they *didn't* have. Jake wanted to hear something positive and voiced his opinion.

"With all due respect," Jake began, "all we've discussed are the things we *don't* have. Is there anything we *do* have?"

This comment brought a burst of anger from Captain Reins. "Burnett!" Reins shouted, "this room is filled with professionals, except for you. You ask for hard evidence, but you have no clue of how to obtain it! Your idea of a good investigation is to beat a confession out of a suspect, and I

Indiscriminate

don't consider that to be professional investigation. I fulfilled my promise to the mayor and invited you to this meeting. For some unknown reason he thinks you may have something to offer. I told him you were a disgrace to law enforcement, but he asked for this favor. I granted him this courtesy and invited you because of his position, and now I'm telling you to leave."

Jake reeled in disbelief at Reins' outburst. He always knew Bull Reins wouldn't allow him any backing from the department, but hoped that the animosity would be set aside until the murderer was caught. He couldn't have been more wrong.

Without another word, Jake rose from his chair and slowly walked to the door. As he opened the door, he looked back at Bull Reins and saw the expression in his eyes. It was an expression he had seen before and he knew there was nothing left to say. Reins needed all the help he could get, but would not acknowledge anything that Jake could offer.

Jake walked out of the captain's office without looking back. He realized Lucy had heard everything that was said and felt a surge of embarrassment. Not wanting to make eye contact, Jake attempted to exit without talking to her.

"Jason," Lucy said, "he's under a lot of pressure from all directions. He didn't mean those things."

Jake looked at the secretary who had been his friend for many years. She had always liked him and he knew it. "I wish that was the case, Lucy, but he was wrong five years ago, and he's wrong now."

Lucy managed a slight smile and winked at Jake, "It will all work out, Jason. Just be patient."

Jake walked through the detective squad room and

noticed Moran sitting behind his desk thumbing through a stack of paperwork. He obviously heard the captain's outburst because he had crooked smile and wide-eyed expression. This look of arrogance confirmed Jake's observation.

"Looks like you're not as welcome as you thought," Moran said in an arrogant tone.

Without looking back at the sergeant, Jake said, "I notice *you're* sitting out here, Sergeant *Moron*."

Moran instantly jumped up from behind his desk. Doing so, he knocked over a cup of coffee, spilling it all over the files on his desk. "Shit!" Moran bellowed as he opened his desk drawer and pulled out a roll of paper towels.

Looking over his shoulder, he became even more enraged when he saw Jake shrug his shoulders in a manner that said, "See what I mean, Sergeant *Moron*?"

Jake looked across the squad room directly at Lucy, who had both hands covering her mouth in an obvious attempt to muffle her laughter. Jake smiled back at her, then left the police station. He walked to his car in confusion about the meeting. He couldn't understand why the Holyoke coroner's office was used instead of the Boston office. Not that Doctor Granger was incompetent, but the fact that Doctor Kessler was the best made more sense with such a high profile case.

Jake started the powerful engine of his Stingray and drove out of the parking lot. When he reached the Riley Rotary, he decided to return to the police station and wait for Reins to leave. He wanted to confront him in private and ask why he was invited to the meeting and then asked to leave so abruptly.

Jake pulled into the lot and parked in the rear. He didn't

Indiscriminate

want anyone to notice him waiting for Reins. Within two minutes, he saw Mark, Doctor Granger and Bill Stoughton walk out and get into their cars. As they drove away, Grant walked out into the sunlight and a limousine pulled in and stopped. He opened the rear door and climbed inside. When the limo sped away, Reins opened the door and walked to his car.

Jake shifted into first gear and sped toward Reins. He pulled into the space right beside the captain's car and stopped.

"Burnett! What the hell are you still doing here?" Reins snapped. "I thought I made myself perfectly clear that I didn't want you around!"

Jake said nothing. He opened the door of his Corvette and walked around to face Reins.

"Captain, you're gonna talk to me now, or talk to me later—through the press." He glared into Reins' eyes. "It's your call."

"Through the press?" Reins asked. "What the hell is that supposed to mean?"

Jake took a step closer. Within six inches from his face, he said, "What that means is that maybe if the press asks you these questions, you will have an answer. You come to me for help, then go to the extreme to alienate me from everything. I want to know where I stand."

The expression on Reins' face said it all. Hatred oozed from every pore, and he made no attempt to conceal it. The only reason he talked to Jake was because of the first note. He thought he could squeeze information from the ex-detective without endowing him with any authority. He wanted to use

Jake and still have the ability to degrade him. Jake was aware of Reins' intentions, but would never allow it to happen.

"You're putting me in an awkward position, Burnett," Reins said. "What exactly do you want to know?"

Jake saw something in the captain's eyes that he never saw before. He saw a plea for help that was pushed aside by pride—and a five-year-old grudge. "I don't want to discuss our personal differences – at least not now. I know you're taking pressure from the mayor's office and every place in between, especially the media. I think I can help put this sick son-of-a-bitch away, but you won't let me. You're allowing your personal hatred for me get in the way of your judgment. Let's set aside our differences and work together."

Jake knew Reins could feel the sincerity in what he said. He felt he had finally hit the nerve that Reins had covered and protected for the past five years, and he wanted to clear the air.

Bull Reins leaned against his car and stared at the ground. Jake saw the veins pulsating in his forehead as his train of thought had been channeled into the direction that Jake was hoping to find. "You're wondering why I have the Holyoke M.E.'s office involved, instead of the Boston office," Reins said. "You're wondering why I didn't bring your buddy, Doctor Kessler, into the case, right, Burnett?"

Jake instantly realized that the vision of his help being accepted was only in *his* mind, and not in Reins'. He saw the animosity and hatred run much deeper than he had thought. "Doctor Kessler is the best and we both know it." Then he softly added, "Let's get him involved."

"Burnett," Reins began, "when we found the first body,

Indiscriminate

the Boston office was buried with work so we sent it to Holyoke. At that time we had no reason to believe we had a serial killer in Salem. Then a second body—and a third, then a fourth…" The captain's voice faded and fell silent as he continued to stare at the ground.

Jake had never witnessed this type of behavior from Reins. The captain always had to have the last word and was uncompromising when giving it.

"Captain," said Jake, "There's something else and I can feel it. There's another reason you don't want Kessler involved. What is it?"

Reins clinched his fists and gritted his teeth. "All right, Burnett, I'll tell you why. I'll tell you why I don't want Kessler involved, and you're not going to like it!"

At that moment, Jake realized the captain's reason was more than just the Boston office being overworked. Inside, he knew Reins didn't want Kessler involved because of a personal reason, and he also knew the captain was right—Jake wasn't going to like it.

Jake leaned against the Stingray, putting his hands in his pockets. Peering into the captain's eyes said, "Okay, Captain, let's hear it."

"I'm not gonna sugar-coat anything. I'm gonna tell you *exactly* the way it is, and I don't give a shit if you like it or not. I owe you nothing—no reason—no explanation, and certainly no apology for my discussions."

Jake knew what he was about to hear was going to sound ludicrous to him and everyone else—everyone except Bull Reins. He knew he wasn't going to like what the captain had to say, but knew it had to be said.

"What I told you about the first victim being sent to Holyoke was true. The Boston office was overwhelmed with work and couldn't handle another case at that time. There was no reason to believe there would be more murders of this kind and we didn't think it would make any difference where the body was sent." Reins put his hands on his hips and sighed. "When the second body was discovered we knew we had a serial killer on our hands. Lucy called Doctor Kessler without my permission, or my knowledge, and that's when the shit hit the fan. Kessler showed up at my office the following day with a suitcase full of theory."

Jake listened to everything the captain had to say, but couldn't see any reason why the Boston office wasn't handling the case.

"Captain," Jake said, "I don't see what the hell you're getting at. You had Kessler here. Where the hell is he now?"

Reins fumbled for words. He began kicking the toe of his shoe into the blacktop pavement, as if searching for something to say.

"Come on," Jake said, "what the hell is going on?"

"Well," Reins began, "Kessler just showed up one morning without my knowledge. He walked into my office and began laying out photographs and documents all over the place. I asked him what the hell he was doing and he responded by telling me that I was in trouble and *he* was here to help. For Christ sake Burnett, how does that make me look to my detectives? My secretary calls in some *heavy-hitter* to bail me out? Bullshit!" Reins snapped, "I know you and Kessler worked a lot of cases together, but I don't need someone coming in here with visions of taking over. This is *my* town."

Indiscriminate

Everything became clear to Jake. He had always known that Reins was in the habit of running the show, but never thought the captain's vision of grandeur would interfere with a case as important as serial murders. He stared at Reins in disbelief. With squinted eyes, he cocked his head in the direction of where the captain was standing. "Are you telling me that Kessler is not involved in this case because you're afraid he may get some of the credit?"

"No! When he told me he was asked by *my* office to help, I flew off the handle and called Lucy into my office. It was then that I found out she called him. I reprimanded her in front of Kessler and he snapped at me in her defense. The good doctor went into a fifteen-minute debate about how I should treat my staff with more respect than I displayed with Lucy, then stormed out in a huff."

It was evident to Jake that Reins' pride blocked his judgment, and this was the sole reason he wouldn't call Kessler. Jake could also see that Reins wanted Kessler involved, but didn't know how to apologize.

The expression on the captain's face was filled with frustration and disappointment. He was a proud and stubborn man and had extreme difficulty in admitting when he was wrong. He was in the habit of always being in the driver's seat and was unable to relinquish it to anyone.

"Captain," Jake began, "I wasn't implying that Doctor Granger couldn't handle it. I was simply asking why we didn't bring in Kessler, also."

The captain's demeanor changed in a fraction of a second. He spun around and faced Jake, "What the hell do you mean, *we* should bring in Kessler? Who the fuck do you think you are? You are no longer a police officer, Burnett, or have you forgotten?" The intensity in Reins' voice rose to a level that traces of saliva formed in the corners of his mouth. .

"I don't know why I let you get involved as much as I already have," Reins bellowed, "but I guarantee you one thing—you're out for good! You will never be allowed to interfere again and I don't give a shit who wants you here! Get the hell out of here and don't ever come back!"

Reins opened his car door and started the engine. Before Jake could respond to the captain's outburst, Reins stepped on the gas and sped out of his parking place, almost hitting Jake.

The ex-detective stood in astonishment as Reins disappeared around the Riley Parking Plaza. He was invited to attend the meeting, but was treated as though he was not wanted. He knew Mayor Sweeney suggested he be there, but that was no guarantee he would be welcome.

"Fuck him," Jake said out loud. "I wouldn't help that son-of-a-bitch now if he came begging on his fucking knees."

Jake left the police parking lot and drove to Rebecca's house. He hoped she would take his mind away from Bull Reins.

He pulled into Rebecca's driveway and saw her standing in front of the bowed picture window. She wore a wide smile and was waving like a child does when she sees Santa Claus. He was immediately taken with her vision, and the hope Jake had earlier had come true. Reins' outburst and threats seemed to be a thing of the past. At least for the moment.

Six

Jake and Rebecca enjoyed a remarkable late afternoon drinking wine and making love. They spent their quality time together lounging around in her central air-conditioned home and the thoughts of the murders and Bull Reins faded into the background.

When the sun bleached into the horizon it was time to go out to dinner. Since it was Friday, they both knew the restaurants would be busy and the wait for a table would be close to an hour or more.

When Jake pulled out onto Marlboro Road, he realized they hadn't decided on a restaurant. It didn't seem important where they had dinner as long as they had it together.

"The Wardhurst," Rebecca said clutching Jake's arm and breaking the silence, "let's go to the Wardhurst."

Jake smiled and pulled into a driveway to reverse his direction.

He turned into the Wardhurst parking lot and shut off

the engine. As he started to open the door Rebecca pulled him close and kissed him hungrily.

"If you do that again," Jake said, "You can forget about dinner because we're going back to your house."

Rebecca pulled away, smiling. "Let's eat first."

The early evening had turned into night when Jake and Rebecca left the Wardhurst. They drove to Rebecca's house and spent a night that Jake could only describe as perfect.

At seven o'clock in the morning Jake got dressed and kissed Rebecca as she slept. He quietly left through the front door and drove home. As he drove, the thought of Captain Reins returned and crushed the pleasant memory of the night with Rebecca. The captain's arrogance and unwillingness to accept his help infuriated Jake. *Christ,* he thought, *is his vision of grandeur that important to him?*

Jake took a shower and decided to spend the day doing nothing. He lounged on his sofa and watched television for the entire day. Feeling as though he should get out on the street and dig for information about the murders, Jake let the feeling pass. He knew his efforts would be met with arrogance and he wasn't going to subject himself to another outburst from his ex-captain

The last two weeks in August came and went without incident. There were no murders, and Bull Reins was the last thing on Jake's mind. Most of his time was spent with Rebecca and an occasional double and triple date with his friends, Mark and Dang. Jake tried putting a distance between himself and the brutal tragedies that had taken place all around him. He fantasized about the murders being

Indiscriminate

over and the murderer being caught, but that was short-lived.

On Saturday, September 4th Jake was awakened by the nagging ring of the telephone. As he fumbled for the receiver he noticed the time: four-thirty. Jake knew a call this early on a Saturday morning was not going to be good news, and he hesitated. On the fourth ring he lifted the receiver to his ear, apprehensive of who the caller might be and what he had to say.

"Hello," Jake mumbled.

"Jake," came the frantic voice of Mark Roads, "get down to the station right away. Don't bother taking a shower. Get down here now."

Jake sat straight up in his bed. "Mark, what the hell happened?" In his heart he already knew there was another murder. He felt a pounding in his chest and knew the latest victim was someone close. Someone close enough to Reins to have him swallow his pride and order Mark to call him. "Who was it this time?"

"This time it was a fourteen-year-old kid," Mark spouted. "A boy named Gary Cronin was found crushed to death under a car. His body was found next to the transfer station on Swampscott Road about an hour ago."

A surge of sorrow raced through Jake. He didn't know this boy, but thought of the pain that awaited the boy's parents. This was something that every parent had nightmares over. "Who told you to call me?" Jake asked, though he knew what Mark's answer would be.

"Reins," replied his ex-partner. "He called me immediately after he was notified. I just got off the phone with him."

Jake was confused. Why would Reins tell Mark to call him? Reins had made it clear he didn't want Jake involved in this case. "There's something else you're not telling me. What is it?" Jake paused. "If the body was found under a car, why couldn't it have been an accident? You didn't mention anything about being strangled."

"Jake," Mark said in a low voice, "the kid's hands were bound behind his back—with duct tape."

"I'll be there in fifteen minutes." Jake leapt to his feet and groped for his jeans. "If Reins blows up at me this time, I'm gonna smash his face through the fucking wall."

Jake finished getting dressed and was on his way to the police station within five minutes. As he drove, he knew something was different about this murder—something more than the victim *not* being strangled. Bull Reins wouldn't call him to the station unless he was pressured from someone much higher up in the food chain.

When Jake pulled into the police parking lot, it was crawling with vehicles from every media source within fifty miles. The parking lot was completely filled with cars, most of them belonging to off-duty police officers that had been called in to help control the crowd. The mayhem led Jake to believe the latest victim was someone who was well known in the community.

Jake walked toward the police entrance he had used many times in the past. This time, reporters rushed toward him shouting questions: "Did you know the boy who was murdered? Are you back on the police force? Did Mayor Sweeney call you?"

The last question caused Jake to stop and turn to face the

reporter. "Mayor Sweeney? What the hell makes you think the mayor would call me? As you probably already know, I'm no longer a police officer."

Before the reporter could respond, Mark Roads opened the door and ushered Jake inside.

"What the hell is going on?" Jake asked. "You've got a cluster-fuck going on out there and I seem to be in the middle. This victim is close to someone, someone important. Who the hell was this kid?"

Mark walked up the stairs and stopped. "Mayor Sweeney's nephew. The boy was the Mayor's sister's only son… her only son."

Jake stopped and looked up at his ex-partner. The expression on Mark's face was a combination of fear and grief.

Before Jake could respond, Mark said, "Reins doesn't want you here. This time he was ordered to bring you in and he's not in a good mood about it." Mark paused. "Walk softly, Jake. Control your temper and keep your big mouth shut."

Again, Jake could sense the sincerity in Mark's voice and knew he was right. "Don't worry. I won't start any trouble with Reins."

As Jake walked through the detective squad room he noticed Moran sitting behind his desk. Police officers scurried past one another at a frantic pace and no one noticed Jake walk in. He cruised past Moran and nodded. Moran acknowledged Jake's greeting with a nod of his own.

Jake followed Mark into Reins' office and recognized the same faces that had been at the previous meeting, with the exception of Mayor Sweeney. The mayor sat behind the captain's desk and glanced at Reins. He knew Reins had taken offense at being rousted from his position in this meeting.

With the exception of ruffling papers and photographs, the office was completely silent. No one spoke and anxiety hung thick in the air as Jake sat on the arm of the sofa. He felt uncertain and didn't want to be the first to speak. He suspected the mayor would be unyielding in the way he conducted this meeting, and Jake didn't want to be singled out again.

The silence finally broke when Mayor Sweeney said, "You all know why you're here. You all know what happened early this morning."

Everyone's attention was focused on the mayor. The tension was as thick as a rain cloud.

"I know the efforts from this department have been extensive, but after eleven murders you aren't any closer to solving this case than you were two months ago."

Sweeney's voice was authoritative and unquestioning. "I've been contacted by other agencies who have offered to contribute their expertise and manpower if I thought we needed it. Captain Reins convinced me his department would step up its efforts and bring this crazy son-of-a-bitch down. I'm giving the captain another week to make an arrest, and if it doesn't happen, the FBI will take over."

The mayor paused and looked at Jake. "I've brought in ex-detective, Jason Burnett because of his ability to extract information from the street. We all know why he's an *ex*-detective, and as much as we're against his methods, I feel we have no other choice."

The meeting lasted for over an hour and everyone had a

chance to contribute his own ideas and theories. The concept of the murderer being a truck driver, a salesman, a transient or even someone who came to the Salem area from another state just to commit the murders, was discussed.

Jake listened to everyone's input about the random selection of the victims, but in his heart he knew each victim was selected for a reason. He just didn't know what that reason was.

At nearly six-thirty, the mayor dismissed everyone from the meeting. As they filed out the door Sweeney bellowed, "Burnett, I want to talk to you."

Jake glanced at Mark as he walked past. With a slight grin, Mark winked. "If you need a partner…"

Jake walked back and sat down in front the man who had taken charge of the meeting. He knew Mayor Sweeney had no authority over him, but wanted to assure him that any help that was needed would be readily given.

"The boy who was murdered last night was my nephew," Sweeney's voice quivered. It was obvious he was on the verge of tears. "He's my *only* sister's, *only* son." The mayor's eyes filled with tears and his tone faded as though he couldn't continue.

This was a side of Mayor Sweeney no one had ever seen. Jake was overwhelmed with sadness and compassion for the man who had always displayed the strength and ability to control his situation as well as his emotions.

The mayor looked at Reins then stared at Jake. "I realize you have no responsibility to extend your hand to this department, but I'm asking for your help." The mayor folded his hands in front of him, and pleaded, "Jason, he was only fourteen years old…"

Before Sweeney could continue with his plea, Jake responded, "I will do everything in my power to help find this son-of-a-bitch. But there's going to be a few things I'll need." He glanced in the captain's direction and noticed the perturbed expression on his face—an expression of anger, hatred, disgust and animosity all rolled into one. He knew Reins wasn't happy with what Mayor Sweeney said, but knew there was nothing he could do about it.

"What the hell do you mean?" Reins bellowed. "You're not a police officer. I'm not going to open the department to your every whim. You can feed information from the street, nothing more." Reins hesitated a moment then added, "Do you understand what I said, Burnett? You get nothing from this department."

Before Jake could respond to Reins' flare-up, the mayor barked, "He'll get whatever he thinks he'll need to help solve these murders." Sweeney paused and looked Reins in the eye. "If he wants his gun permit back, you'll see that he gets it. If he wants a partner, you'll see that he gets that, too. And if he asks you where the reinstatement forms are, you'll get it. Do *you* understand, Captain?"

Reins' expression transformed into that of a whipped puppy, along with a combination of disbelief, shock, frustration and betrayal.

Continuing his stare into Reins' eyes, The mayor continued, "The more I think about it, the more I'm convinced that Burnett would be more effective on the street if he had a badge. In other words, Captain, he *will* be reinstated."

Mayor Sweeney turned his attention to Jake, "Tell me what you need *Detective* Burnett."

Indiscriminate

The atmosphere in Bull Reins' office hung heavy with animosity. Reins had been put down and humiliated in his own office and Jake could feel his embarrassment. He could feel the knot that was building in the pit of the Captain's stomach—the same knot that Reins had so eagerly twisted in Jake's stomach at the last meeting.

Jake walked to the window. Looking out at the cluster of reporters in the parking lot, he said, "The only way I would consider working with the department would be if Captain Reins was in total charge of the investigation. He's thorough in everything he does, and he's the best there is when it comes to pulling information from the street."

Jake didn't turn around to look at either man, but could feel their look of bewilderment burning in his back. Reins hated Jake Burnett, and Sweeney knew it.

"Burnett," Sweeney began, "I'm well aware of the bad blood between you and the Captain. I don't think it would be a wise decision to have you working directly under Reins." Pausing, he added, "I suggest using someone in between, someone you would *both* report to. You know what I mean. A buffer, so to speak."

Jake turned and faced the mayor, "Negative, Mr. Mayor, you told me I could have anything I needed to help solve the murders, and I need…" Jake corrected himself, "What I mean is *we* need the captain's expertise. He's the best there is, and not having him spearhead this investigation would be a mistake."

Reins regained his composure after hearing Jake's comments to Mayor Sweeney. He sat straight up in his chair and donned a look of appeasement. The man who had been on the receiving end of his hatred for the past five years had insisted he would be in charge of the investigation. He didn't know why Jake Burnett was in his corner, but wasn't about to question it in front of Mayor Sweeney.

The mayor nodded and acknowledged Jake was right. He knew the Captain was a good police officer, but he also knew of his stubborn and vindictive side.

Jake glanced at Reins, then back to the Mayor. "I want Doctor Kessler from the Boston M.E.'s office. We've worked together on many other cases and I know he will be a great asset."

This request brought an immediate response from Reins. "If we bring in Kessler, what do I tell Granger? It would appear as though we didn't think he could handle it, as though we didn't think he was good enough."

Sweeney studied Reins' face and said, "He's right, Detective Burnett. Replacing Granger now would cause animosity between the Boston and Holyoke offices."

Jake looked at Reins and knew his request wasn't because of any animosity that might be caused between the two offices, but rather his pride had reared its ugly head. He knew Reins didn't want to call Kessler and apologize for their last meeting. An apology from Reins would be an indication of him being wrong. It would be admitting he made a mistake, and that was something Reins had difficulty dealing with.

In a low voice, Jake said, "Mr. Mayor, you said I could have anything I thought would be needed to help solve these murders." Jake sat on the corner of the desk and added, Kessler is essential."

"What the hell am I supposed to tell Granger?" Reins

snapped. "Am I supposed to tell him we don't think he's capable of doing the job?" Reins' voice was loud and indignant.

Jake's first reaction was to lash out at the captain. He wanted to say everything that had plagued his mind for the past five years, but decided to rationalize what had just happened. "In no way was I suggesting Dr. Granger was incompetent. What I'm suggesting is that we bring in Kessler to *help* with the investigation."

Before Reins could respond, Jake added, "I'll call Kessler and Granger and explain everything. There will be no ill feelings from either man. I give you my word."

The thought of not having to apologize to Dr. Kessler brought a favorable response from Reins. "If you can explain our situation to them, I don't have a problem with bringing in Kessler."

"Concerning being reinstated and your gun permit," Sweeney began, "I think you would be more effective on the street if you had the authority of a police officer. But, I can't guarantee this will be permanent."

Jake felt uncomfortable and had a sense of uncertainty in the pit of his stomach. He knew he was being used, and the thought of Mayor Sweeney dangling a carrot in front of him made him wary. This feeling was immediately squelched by his overwhelming urge to put an end to the murders.

"I'm going to need a partner," Jake said. "I want Mark Roads."

"Detective Roads has a large case load," Reins said. "His plate is full. I will assign Moran as your partner."

"No way," Jake blurted out, "Moran has the intelligence

of a fucking hammer." Turning his attention toward Mayor Sweeney, Jake said, "I've worked with Mark Roads for years. We work well together."

The mayor looked at Reins. "Is there a problem with Moran?"

Reins fidgeted in his chair. "Mr. Mayor, John Moran is a sergeant with the Salem Police department. He's a good detective and there is no valid reason he shouldn't be partnered with Burnett."

Jake saw indecisiveness in the mayor's eyes. He didn't want Sweeney to make his decision based on what Bull Reins had said. He knew that once the decision was made, it would not be reversed.

"Mr. Mayor," Jake began, "Mark Roads and I have always been on the same page. I mean we complement each other's strong and weak areas. We're familiar with each other's way of doing things. This compatibility would be essential in this, or in any other case."

Sweeney sat silent. He continued staring at the photographs of the eleven victims, distress written all over his face.

Jake drove the final nail home. "You said I could have what I needed, and I know you're a man of your word."

The expression on Sweeney's face said it all. Jake knew it, and so did Reins.

Before another word was spoken, Reins leaned over and pressed the button on his intercom.

"Yes, sir?" came Lucy's friendly voice.

Reins simply said, "Send in Detective Roads."

Mark walked into Reins' office and sat next to Jake. He

Indiscriminate

knew something had happened and suspected it was good news. He wasn't disappointed.

"Detective Roads," Reins pointed at Jake, "you have a new partner."

Mark sat silent as Reins told him everything that had taken place since he left the meeting. He went on to say that being partnered with Jason Burnett was only temporary, and not to get used to this arrangement.

"I'd like to have my old desk back, Captain," Jake said. "I'll feel more comfortable in familiar surroundings."

Reins knew Jake wanted his old desk back because it was now being used by Moran. He knew Jake didn't like Moran and this was just one more act of defiance to aggravate the other detective.

Before Reins could respond to Jake's request, Sweeney said, "I'm sure Detective Moran won't have a problem moving his things to another desk."

Mark knew Jake's request for his old desk was only to aggravate Moran. Mark missed the subtle way Jake would do things to upset the other detective. He knew Jake didn't do these things to be mean, but rather as a joke. In the beginning, Jake and Moran would do things to taunt each other, but Moran always took it much more seriously than Jake did. It seemed the more upset Moran got, the more things Jake would do to keep him that way. It was an ongoing contest between them, and Mark knew this was only the beginning.

"I still have my Beretta," Jake said. "I don't carry it anymore, but I keep it in my store. I'll need my gun permit."

"I'll give you a written permit to use until your official permit comes from 10-10 Commonwealth," Reins said.

Howard Olsen

Sweeney, with his eyes still fixed on the photographs of the murder victims, said, "How long before you can get him his badge?"

Reins paused, a look of embarrassment and pride etched on his face. Reaching across his desk he opened the top drawer and pulled out Jake's old badge. "Here," Reins tossed the badge to Jake and shrugged. "I don't know why I kept it."

Jake caught the badge and held it tight. The gold shield in his hand was something he worked very hard to get, and when it was taken away it had left an empty feeling in his heart. As Jake looked down at his badge, a feeling of pride raced through him. He knew the feeling was only temporary, but relished the sensation of the void in his heart being filled. At least for the moment.

Mark announced he would inform Moran to relocate to another desk. He walked to the door and left the office. Jake knew that Mark wanted to be the first to see the expression on Moran's face when he was told he had to give up his desk to Jake.

There was an intense quiet in the captain's office that hung as an eerie silence. Sweeney continued to stare at the photographs while Reins' eyes fixed on the window, trance-like.

Jake broke the silence. "I'll call Dr. Kessler and bring him up to speed on everything." Jake knew Reins was not looking forward to inviting Kessler to join the investigation, and by offering to make the call he would put the captain at ease. He was right.

Bull Reins stood and announced, "Good, you take care of calling Kessler and Granger." He paused. "Burnett, I don't

Indiscriminate

want any ill feelings between the Boston and Holyoke offices. Be diplomatic. Understood, *Detective?*" Reins' tone was sharp and laced with animosity and sarcasm. What was worse, Reins was unable to override any directive that came from the Mayor.

Sweeney walked to the window. Looking down at all the activity in the parking lot, he said, "Captain, I'd like to speak to Detective Burnett—alone."

Jake felt the hatred racing through the captain's body. Reins said nothing as he turned and walked out the door.

Jake sat silent for what seemed to be an eternity. He had mixed feelings of why the mayor wanted to talk to him alone, but knew it was something that he didn't want anyone else to hear.

"He was only fourteen years old," Sweeney began. "He played football, baseball and basketball and had his sights set on being a professional athlete. Even at fourteen he knew he was destined to be an athlete." The mayor's voice cracked with pain.

Jake walked to the window next to Sweeney. He saw the reflection of the mayor's face in the glass, and the expression of heartache was unmatched by anything Jake had ever seen before.

"I know you have ways of extracting information from the street," Sweeney said softly. "I'm aware of your reputation of beating the answers from a suspect."

In a friendly gesture, Jake placed his hand on the mayor's shoulder. "Mr. Mayor, you have my word that I will do everything by the book this time. I won't deviate from police procedure."

"Bullshit!" Sweeney barked. "I want you to do whatever it takes to nail this son-of-a-bitch. Your tactics may not be legal, but they're effective. I will back you to the hilt, Burnett. You have my word on that."

Jake felt the plea for help in the mayor's voice and could do nothing but imagine the pain he felt.

"I'll do whatever it takes, Mr. Mayor. There are going to be times when I may have to overstep my boundaries. We're gonna draw a lot of flack, and the question is: Are you prepared to handle it?"

Sweeney continued to stare out the window. Slowly he turned and faced Jake. "I gave you my word, Detective. Now I'm telling you to nail that motherfucker—and nail him hard."

SEVEN

Jake left the office and called doctor Kessler from Lucy's phone. As he talked to Kessler, Captain Reins walked past wearing a tired and frustrated expression. He wasn't happy with the turn of events and made no attempt to hide it.

Jake gave Kessler the short version of what had taken place that morning. He informed him he was temporarily back on the force and in charge of this case.

The good doctor said he had to attend a meeting and would be tied up for several hours, but would call Jake at noon. His tone of voice let Jake know he was excited about working with Jake again. "How is the captain handling this?" Kessler asked.

A low chuckle rumbled from Jake's throat as he said, "I've seen happier faces at an autopsy."

"Have they removed the duct tape, Jake?" Kessler asked, and then added, "If they haven't removed it yet, tell them to leave it alone. I want to check it for fingerprints."

"Doc," Jake said, "you're really grabbing for straws on that request. We both know that even if he wasn't wearing gloves it would be almost impossible to lift prints from duct tape."

"Hold that thought, Jake," Kessler said. "I've developed something that's going to impress the living hell out of you. Just make sure no one touches the tape."

Jake acknowledged the doctor's request and made a phone call to inform anyone working with the body to leave it intact. He learned they were about to remove the tape and undress the boy, but they hadn't done it yet. They agreed to wait for Doctor Kessler.

There were a few things Jake had to take care of before he could actually begin working with Mark. He told his partner he would be back in two hours and then left the police station.

Jake drove to Books and opened the door. He stood in the doorway looking at the books that were scattered all around. *This is my new life,* he thought, *I'm not sure I want to give it up.*

The first thing he did was call Rebecca and tell her everything that had happened. She was excited about Jake's reinstatement, but he heard a hint of uneasiness in her voice. He didn't tell her the reinstatement was only temporary because he wasn't sure if he wanted it to be. He was torn between his new life with Books and his old life as a police officer.

Jake opened the bottom drawer of his desk and took out his nine-millimeter Beretta. Other than cleaning and adding a drop of oil, he hadn't touched the weapon in five years. He opened the small broom closet in the back of the store and took out his shoulder holster. After strapping it on, he took out the windbreaker jacket he used during the summer months. It was dark blue, and since it was made from a material called banlon, it was extremely lightweight and wasn't too uncomfortable in the heat.

Sliding the Beretta into the holster that hung under his arm, Jake stood motionless in front of the mirror. The weapon felt foreign and heavy, almost awkward.

He scribbled something on a piece of paper and taped it on the inside window of the front door facing out. It read: *ON VACATION*.

He closed and locked the door behind him and walked to his car, all the while wondering if he was doing the right thing. He wanted this in the beginning, but was unsure if he wanted to be involved as a police officer.

The first thing he wanted to do was talk to Cameron Baird. He knew Baird would be hanging around wherever there were teenagers, and he wanted to let him know he was watching.

Jake drove past Palmer Cove where he had seen Baird on their last meeting, but he wasn't there. He continued driving to all the hangouts the junkie frequented, but Baird was nowhere to be found.

Almost ready to return to the police station, Jake drove around the Salem Common. Not expecting to find Baird there, he completed the circle and was about to leave when he noticed three men sitting on the steps of the gazebo located in the center of the Common. Jake pulled into the parking lot behind the Hawthorne Hotel and walked toward the three men. The Common was bustling with tourists and local joggers and Jake used the abundance of people as camouflage. Baird didn't notice Jake until he was within five feet of him.

When Baird finally noticed Jake, panic spread across his face. Not wanting a confrontation with Jake, Baird stepped back and tried to blend with the people that were scattered all around. It didn't work.

Stepping up with a shaky smile, the junkie said, "Hi Jake, whatcha doin here?"

"Looking for you, Cam." There was no emotion in Jake's voice.

One of the men Baird was standing with stepped up and challenged Jake. "Hey, Burnett," he said angrily, "hit the road. You ain't a cop no more.

Jake turned his head toward the second man. He didn't know his name, but had frequently seen him with Cameron Baird. He knew he was a drug dealer but wasn't interested in him at the moment. *Your time will come*, he thought. Jake motioned with his finger for Baird to come to him. He didn't want to make a scene in front of all the tourists, but he wasn't going to leave until he talked to Baird.

Baird decided it would be wise to obey Jake's command and began walking in Jake's direction.

The other man stepped in front of Jake. "Hey, you ain't got a badge to hide behind no more. Leave now, or I'm gonna kick your fucking ass."

Jake looked directly into the man's squinted eyes. He had saliva pooling in the corners of his mouth and Jake took a step backwards in an attempt to avoid his bad breath.

The man took Jake's retreat as a sign of weakness. "Hold

on, Snake," Baird said. "Jake only wants to talk to me. It's okay, I'll talk to him."

Baird's statement only added to the man's false sense of superiority. Taking a step closer, he said, "You're lucky this time, Burnett. The next time I see ya, I'm gonna teach you a lesson you won't ever forget."

Without warning, Jake slammed his fist into the bridge of the man's nose in a downward motion. The sound of Jake's fist hitting the man's flesh was unmistakable. He shattered his nose without effort.

He dropped to both knees and clutched his face. With blood streaming through the fingers of both hands, he screamed, "My nose! You broke my fucking nose!"

Jake leaned over the downed man and said, "I'm a real slow learner, Snake. You want to *teach* me that lesson again?"

Turning his attention to Baird, Jake motioned with his finger for him to come to where Jake was standing. "Have you talked to your reporter buddy?"

Baird shifted nervously as he stood with his hands in his pockets. Jake knew there was more to the junkie's nervousness than what had just happened to his friend. He knew Baird had information about the murder of the boy, but wasn't sure how important it would be.

"Cam," Jake began, "you know why I'm here. I want information about last night's murder. I know you're an information sponge on the street, and I want to know what you know."

Baird continued nervously shifting his weight from one foot to the other. It was obvious he was high. "The only thing I know, Jake, is the kid was placed under a car and then someone kicked out the jack. The poor kid was crushed to death."

Jake heard what he expected to hear. He knew Cameron Baird didn't have any substantial information, but was hoping he had something he could use. As he walked away, he said, "Keep your ears to the ground. Understood?"

Baird nodded and watched Jake disappear into the crowd of tourists.

As Jake drove back to the police station, he thought about how he was looking forward to working with Doctor Kessler again. The downside was the brutality of the murders. Jake had worked a dozen homicides with Kessler, but this case was far more unnatural than anything he had ever seen. He parked in the rear of the police parking lot and walked through the reporters toward the police entrance. His light-blue jacket was unzipped and his gold shield was visible on his belt.

"Mr. Burnett," one reporter shouted, "I notice you have your badge back. Are you back on the force?"

Jake said nothing and continued to walk toward the door.

Two more reporters stepped in front of him. One of the reporters pushed a microphone in his face and said, "Is the department going to turn its head when you use violence to obtain information?"

Jake stopped and looked at the man standing in front of him. He wanted to show this man what he thought of his question, but decided to let it pass.

Before Jake could open the door, the same reporter asked, "Is the department willing to give up a person's constitutional rights because of your methods, just to solve this case?" He held his microphone in Jake's direction.

Jake walked up to the reporter and snatched the microphone from his hand. He ripped the cord from the back of the microphone and said, "I won't dignify that question with an answer." Then with a smile he added, "Your microphone doesn't work, anyway."

Jake went into the police station and walked up the stairs to the squad room. He stood in the doorway and looked at all the activity in his old domain. For an instant, he felt as though he had never left. It was though he had been on vacation, and now he was back. He walked over to his desk and sat down and was staring at the pile of folders when Sergeant Moran approached and said, "Burnett, it's good to have you back."

Moran's tone was not sincere and it was obvious. Jake looked up and saw the sergeant standing with his hand extended in an indication he wanted to shake Jake's hand. Jake stood up and shook hands with Moran.

Mark was standing at the door of Captain Reins' office and motioned for Jake to come in. As Jake walked toward the captain's office he noticed a smile on Mark's face.

When he walked into the office, Reins met him halfway across the room and handed him a temporary gun permit. "Go downstairs and have your picture and fingerprint taken for the permanent permit. You'll have it from 10 10 Commonwealth Ave. in about two weeks." The captain's voice was flat and authoritative.

Jake nodded and left the office with Mark.

Mark's desk was located adjacent to Jake's desk and the men were facing one another.

"Christ," Jake blurted, "when I first walked in here this morning I felt as though I never left. But now I feel as though I don't know where to begin." He looked at the stack of folders on his desk. "Is all this shit for me?"

"This is all from the serial murders," said Mark. "Some information could be useful, but most of it will be worthless."

Jake started reading the first report on his desk when Moran said there was a call for him on line one. A feeling of déjà vu filled his mind. Not only did Jake feel comfortable being there, but it also appeared as though the other detectives felt the same way.

Picking up the phone from his desk, Jake answered, "Burnett." It felt natural. Police work was his only passion when he was growing up. His parents were extremely proud of him when he graduated from the police academy and were even more proud when he got his gold shield.

"Detective Burnett," came the voice of Doctor Kessler, "it's nice to hear your voice again. I cleared my calendar and I'm at your disposal. When do you want to meet?"

"I'll be there in an hour," Jake replied. "I had the boy's body transported to the Boston office. I want to be there when you examine him."

Mark heard everything Jake had said, and made a gruesome face. He never liked being present at an autopsy and would always find an excuse for Jake to drive to the medical examiner's office without him. This time he knew he had to be there.

Jake winked at Mark and stood. "Okay, partner, let's hit the bricks."

Indiscriminate

"I guess we're taking my car," said Mark, "I know you don't want the Vette in Boston. It might get scratched."

Mark took route 128 south then turned onto route one. Within thirty minutes they were in the medical examiner's parking lot searching for an empty visitor's parking space.

Mark shut off the engine and looked at his partner. "I hate this place."

Being anxious to work with his old friend again, Jake looked at Mark and smiled. "Come on, Mark, this is going to be like old times."

Jake got out of the car and walked up the stairs to the lobby of the medical office. As he walked, there was a bounce in his stride that Mark hadn't seen in five years. "It's nice to have you back, partner." Mark hurried to catch up with Jake.

The two detectives walked into the lobby and found Doctor Kessler waiting for them. A wide smile spread across Kessler's face when he saw Jake and he stood to greet him. As Jake walked up to his friend and Chief of Staff for the state of Massachusetts, he noticed his rugged frame hadn't changed in the past five years. Kessler was a big man, well over six feet tall and weighing over 220 pounds. His salt-and-pepper hair matched his neatly trimmed full beard. His bright gray-blue eyes added to his impressive Sean Connery appearance.

The two men shook hands and what felt like a catcher's mitt engulfed Jake's hand.

"It's great to be working with you again, Jake," Kessler said.

"Ditto, Doc," Jake replied. "Do you remember my partner, Mark Roads?"

Kessler shook Mark's hand. "Yes, I remember Mark." The doctor held onto Mark's hand and added, "You're the one that gets queasy, then vomits, right?"

Mark's face took on an uneasy glaze as he attempted a fake smile. "That would be me."

"I have the boy's body ready to be autopsied in room three," the doctor said. "Follow me."

The three men took the elevator down to where the autopsies were performed and walked into room three. Everything was as Jake remembered—sterile, frigid and unsettling. When they walked through the door, Mark stopped and stared at the 130-pound frame of Gary Cronin lying on the stainless steel gurney. He turned away and rubbed his forehead in an attempt to chase the vision from his mind.

"Jake," Mark said, "I'll wait for you in the car."

Jake looked at his partner and knew the feeling that was racing through his mind. He knew the pain that Mark was dealing with, and simply nodded.

Doctor Kessler performed the autopsy as he had thousands of times, all the while verbalizing his findings into a microphone that hung in front of him. Jake noticed how thorough Kessler was, and as usual, did not ask any questions until the autopsy was completed.

When the autopsy was finished, Kessler put his hands on the edge of the gurney, closed his eyes and hung his head.

"What's wrong?" Jake asked. "You've done more than you're share of autopsies and this is the first time I ever saw you this way…" Jake paused. "What's so different about this one?"

Indiscriminate

Kessler removed his face shield and then his rubber gloves. He tossed them into a bucket on the floor and walked to his desk without saying a word. His demeanor was a mixture of sorrow, compassion and anger.

Jake watched as the doctor filled out paper work and forms at his desk. Saying nothing, he sat next to Kessler and witnessed his friend attempt to regain his composure.

When he finished writing, Kessler stared at Jake, his eyes filled with sadness and disbelief. "In all the years I've been doing this I've never seen anything this brutal or merciless."

Still remaining silent, Jake stared at the doctor and waited for him to explain his findings. He knew the distress that Kessler's job demanded, but also knew that Kessler existed with the purpose of finding information that would apprehend murderers in the future, and this was why he devoted his life to his job.

The doctor told Jake that he had previously removed the duct tape from the boy's hands and performed a procedure that he and a colleague had developed. "It's a test that will allow us to lift fingerprints from the sticky side of tape," Kessler said. "We lifted two perfect latents. You'll have them before you leave."

Jake sat in awe as the doctor explained how the procedure was performed. "In the past we used a liquid solvent to loosen the tape from the victim. This procedure caused the tape to become gummy, and it was almost impossible to lift any fingerprints." Kessler walked to the coffeepot and poured himself a large cup. "With the new procedure, the tape is placed in liquid nitrogen, which is more than 240 degrees below zero," Kessler explained. "It's held there for three to five minutes, then removed and left to thaw at room temperature."

"That's it?" asked Jake

"Yes," Kessler shrugged, "all that remains is to dust the tape with fingerprint powder. The print becomes perfectly clear and ready to have its picture taken. In fact, many times we don't even need to use the powder."

"It sounds too simple to be true," said Jake.

"Well, it is true," the doctor said. "The procedure is remarkably accurate and is now being introduced to the FBI lab. It will become standard procedure with all agencies."

Jake stepped back and donned a look of embarrassment for insinuating Kessler's technique didn't work. "I didn't mean it didn't work, what I meant was—"

Doctor Kessler cut him off, "I'm sorry, Jake. I didn't mean to snap at you like that." He hung his head. "The boy on the table…I've never seen anything this crul in all the years I've been doing this."

Jake knew the good doctor had seen it all – he had seen the destruction and death that human beings were capable of inflicting on each other, but this time it was different. This time it was far more callous than he had ever seen before.

"Talk to me, Doc," Jake said. "Tell me how the boy he died."

Kessler's face turned to stone. He cleared his throat and looked at Jake. "The official cause of death was suffocation at the hands of another."

Jake knew this answer was true, but not complete. "When the jack was kicked out from the car, did the impact of the

Indiscriminate

car hitting his chest…" Jake paused. "What I'm trying to ask is did the boy die immediately?"

Kessler said nothing. He folded his hands and looked up at his friend sadly. Jake had never seen this side of Doctor Kessler. He had never seen anything other than pure factual explanations and behavior, until now.

"The small red dots in the boy's eyes and on his face are called petechiae hemorrhage, and that tells me he died from suffocation." Kessler's voice was slow and monotone. "With the rope burn around his neck, I was hoping he died *before* the car was lowered onto his chest." He paused, and then said, "I was wrong."

"Lowered?" Jake asked. "You're telling me the car was *lowered* onto the boy's chest?"

The doctor explained everything that the boy endured before his death. The brutality of the murder was incomprehensible.

Before Jake could speak, Kessler continued, "The ribs tore into his lungs and heart, and the tiny fractures surrounding the actual break in the ribs tell me the car wasn't dropped. It was lowered, slowly."

"Jesus Christ!" Jake barked, "Are you sure?"

The doctor didn't respond to Jake's question and Jake knew why. Kessler wouldn't have made the statement if it were not a fact.

"Jake," Kessler said, "it took the boy three or four minutes before he was rendered unconscious. He was aware of everything that was happening to him, and in my opinion, the murderer stayed and watched him die. He enjoyed the struggling efforts of his victim as he attempted to cling to life. He watched until he heard the boy's final gasp."

Jake's legs felt weak and he leaned against the wall. How could anyone could commit such a heinous crime?

"I'm not in the habit of sugar coating my findings," Kessler said, "but, there is no way I'm going to tell the whole truth to this boy's parents. My official report will state that the boy was unconscious when he died, and felt nothing."

Jake looked perplexed. "Doc, you're gonna falsify the report?"

"Of course I'm not going to falsify the report…I was just doing some wishful thinking out loud."

"If he had a rope burn around his neck, isn't it possible he was strangled *before* he was placed under the tire?"

"No," Doctor Kessler responded, "the rope burn around the boy's neck was caused by being dragged by the rope. Someone used the rope to drag the victim to where he wanted him to be found. All the rope did, in this case, was to make it easier to move the boy, nothing more."

"Is this consistent with the other murders?" Jake asked.

"I haven't seen any of the other victims," Kessler replied.

Both men remained silent. Jake's eyes opened wide and the doctor seemed to know exactly what Jake was thinking.

"I'll have my office contact the families of the other victims and request permission to exhume the bodies," Kessler said. "At least we'll know for sure if the rope burn on the boy is consistent with the other victims."

Doctor Kessler reached for the telephone to make arraignments for a court order of exhumation, when an

Indiscriminate

assistant to the staff photographer walked in and placed several large photographs on the corner of Kessler's desk.

Jake picked up the photographs and stared. "These are perfect. How the hell did you lift prints this clear from duct tape?"

"I told you the technique was damn-near perfect." Kessler's voice was laced with pride. "All you have to do is feed these prints into the computer and hope this sick son-of-a-bitch is in there."

Jake stared at the doctor with an expression of bewilderment.

"Jake," Kessler said, "We've come a long way since you've worked a case. The FBI has developed a program that takes all the work out of matching fingerprints. I forget what they call it, but if this guy has ever been fingerprinted for a past crime, it will be in the computer. If he's in there, you'll know his name in minutes."

Jake was excited about the new technology and wanted to get back to the station to process the fingerprints. "Will you call Doctor Granger?" he asked. "I have orders from Captain Reins, *not* to offend the Holyoke office, and Reins has doubts about my diplomacy."

"I can understand his concern about that," Kessler said. "I'll handle it."

Jake turned and left without saying goodbye. He was halfway down the hall when he turned around and walked back into room three.

"Let me know when you get the okay to exhume the bodies," Jake said. "I want to know what you find, as soon as you find it." Then with a half smile, he added, "See ya later, Doc."

Howard Olsen

Jake left the building and walked to Mark's car. He slid into the passenger's seat and tossed the photographs to his partner. "Check these out."

Mark looked at the photos of the fingerprints with amazement. "These prints were lifted from the duct tape?"

Jake assured Mark that they were the prints on the duct tape and asked him if he knew how to feed the photos into the computer for a match.

Mark smiled and said, "Absolutely! If he's in there, we'll find him."

Mark started the engine and drove back to the Salem Police Station. Jake wasn't the only one excited about the new evidence.

EIGHT

When the two detectives returned to the station, they immediately went to work scanning the fingerprints into the computer. Jake felt out of place as Mark began pounding away on the keyboard. He had no clue what his partner was doing. He was familiar with NCIC, the national crime information computer, because this system has been in place since the mid-sixties.

He was also acquainted with TRIPLE I, interstate identification index, and BOP, border probation check. But AFIS was something that only the state police had and it was implemented just as Jake left the police department five years earlier.

"Mark," Jake said, "It's been a long time for me. I don't know what the hell you're doing, but I hope it's gonna work."

"Trust me. If that son-of-a-bitch is in here, we're gonna find him." Mark hit the last key and sat back in his chair. "All we have to do now is wait for AFIS to do its job. It should take between ten and twenty minutes."

"AFIS?" Jake asked. "What the hell is, AFIS?"

"Actual Fingerprint Image System," Mark answered, "the only way we can find him through his fingerprints is if he was caught doing something in the past. AFIS is relatively new and they're adding fingerprints every day. It will take some time before all the felons are entered. There's a fifty percent chance he'll be in here."

Jake reported to Captain Reins and filled him in on the new evidence they discovered. He let him know everything Doctor Kessler was doing and told him he would keep him up to date with the re-autopsies.

The new evidence seemed to inspire a feeling of progress in Reins. He had been at a complete standstill with information until now, and finding out about the fingerprints infused him with a small spark of optimism. "I want to know about the fingerprints immediately, Burnett," Reins said. Then, in a cold and calculating tone he added, "I want to be the *first* to know what AFIS finds. Understood?"

Jake recognized contempt in the captain's eyes. There was a mixture of satisfaction for finding new evidence, and then a festering of hatred that had been consuming him for the past five years.

Reins looked intently into Jake's eyes waiting for a response. Jake knew the Captain's behavior was for *his* benefit, but also to solidify Jake's position in the food chain. Reins spearheaded this investigation and he wanted that fact made perfectly clear to his new detective.

Jake acknowledged the order with a nod and left the office.

Indiscriminate

He knew the captain's contempt for him still outweighed his urge to accept Jake as one of his own. But in time he hoped that feeling would pass.

Mark's eyes were still focused to the computer screen when Jake sat at his desk. He knew Mark well enough to read his facial expressions and the look on Mark's face said it all: No matches.

Mark slowly looked up at Jake. "Nothing, partner, absolutely nothing."

"Run it again," Jake said, "maybe it missed it the first time."

"Jake," Mark stated, "if his prints were in here, AFIS would have matched them. He's not in here. I have trouble believing that this sick son-of-a-bitch has never been arrested in the past, but it looks as though he's been clean until now. Well, at least he has never been caught before."

Jake looked at Mark, puzzled. The fingerprints on the duct tape were the only lead they had and Jake had hoped this important piece of evidence would identify the murderer. "I can't believe this is the first time this crazy son-of-a-bitch has done this. With all the computer shit you have on your desk, isn't there something else we can do?"

Mark didn't answer. Instead, he tapped the keys of his keyboard. As he pounded away, he mumbled, "Time for plan B."

Jake watched as Mark fed information into the computer. His gaze was intense and fixed to the screen as though he was watching a movie.

"What are you doing?" Jake asked, but the only response he heard was, "Shhhhh."

Jake's telephone rang. "Books—I mean, Burnett."

"Make up your mind, Jake."

Jake smiled. "Dang, haven't you got anything better to do than bust my balls?"

"Well, I heard you were back on the force, but I had to confirm the rumor."

"It's a long story. I'll explain everything later."

"Are we all going out Friday night?" Dang asked.

"I can't commit to anything right now, Dang. I just don't know when I'll have any free time. Sorry, buddy."

The two friends chatted a while, then hung up. Dang knew Jake had a lot of work in front of him and wasn't too disappointed about not going out to dinner.

Jake returned his attention to his partner, who was still engrossed in entering data into his computer. The suspense about what Mark was doing was beginning to wear thin on Jake's nerves, partly because he wasn't involved, but mostly because he had no clue *what* Mark was doing. Being distant from the new technology for the past five years made everything appear alien.

As frustration set into the new detective, Mark tapped the final key and said, "Come on, CAIN, do your stuff." Mark was oblivious to everything around him, including Jake. He didn't notice the restrained expression on his partner's face.

"Mark!" Jake snapped, "what the hell is, plan B and who the hell is CAIN?"

"Plan B *is* CAIN."

By this time Jake couldn't hold his temper any longer. He felt like an outsider and inferiority hung on his shoulders like a clinging vine. He was not in the habit of being kept in the dark about what was happening all around him. This feeling irritated him to say the least. "Mark!" Jake snapped.

"Okay, Jake," Mark began, "plan B is CAIN. You know—C-A-I-N—Crime Artificial Intelligence Network. It's a database that is connected throughout the country and will call us back with any similar crimes that have been committed somewhere else. We may be able to connect these murders to similar murders in other parts of the country, or in some cases, in other parts of the world."

"How long will this take?" Jake asked irritably.

"It's difficult to say. It could take a few minutes or it could take a week. We'll get a hit on every murder that's close to this M.O., but most of the hits will be useless to this case. It's a crap shoot."

Jake's thoughts were torn between learning how the new technology worked, and the old-fashioned way of doing police work. Going out on the street and mingling with the people was Jake's way, but it certainly was faster through the computer. "I gotta get out of the dark ages and buy a computer."

The two detectives spent the rest of the day reading the files that had accumulated over the past six weeks. Mark was right; most of the information in the files was useless.

The day came and went and nothing new was added to the case. When fingerprints were discovered, hopes of identifying the murder escalated, but the feeling was short-lived. Tired and disappointed, Jake and Mark called it a day. They went home and tried to enjoy their personal lives, but the thought of Gary Cronin's murder lingered in their minds. The thought of such a young life being taken so brutally, so cruelly, held an image in Jake's mind of what the murderer might look like. Although he knew the murderer could look like anyone else, he couldn't dismiss the notion of him being freakish in appearance and would stand out in a crowd. The thought of something in the murderer's appearance identifying him was nothing more than a fantasy that was immediately dismissed. *That son-of-a-bitch looks like anyone else*, Jake thought.

The next few days went by with nothing new being added to the case. Mayor Sweeney grilled Jake daily and he had nothing new to tell him. The fourteen-year-old boy had been buried and the feeling of grief engulfed everyone. Even people who weren't involved in the case couldn't dismiss the grief and heartache of this brutal murder.

On Friday, September 10th, Jake received a call from Doctor Kessler. Kessler told him he had a court order for the exhumations of the first victim, Sally Grogan, and the third victim, Susan Martell. "I'll have both bodies here this weekend and I should be finished by Monday morning," Kessler said. "If you want to be here for the autopsies, I'm starting at 8 a.m. tomorrow."

Jake's heart throbbed at the thought of new evidence being uncovered. He wanted to be there when Kessler found it. "What about the second victim, Ellen Hayward?" Jake asked.

"Her body was shipped back to Ohio for burial. I have the M.E.'s office out there trying to get a court order to exhume the body. I've already talked to the chief of staff in Ohio and he will perform the same tests that we do."

Indiscriminate

Kessler paused. "He wants to wait until I've finished the two autopsies here."

That evening Jake drove home from his shift and looked forward to a good night's sleep before the meeting with Kessler in the morning. He pulled into his driveway and noticed Rebecca's car parked all the way in the back. He hadn't seen much of her in the past week and the thought of her spending the night made him feel light-hearted. When Rebecca was around, he always found the ability to extinguish the evil thoughts of everything around him.

Jake walked around to the back of his house and saw Rebecca sitting on the swing. Her eyes were closed and her hair gently lifted and fell as she swayed back and forth. He slid around to the back of the swing and gently pushed it higher and higher. Noticing her eyes were still closed, he pushed a little harder.

Smiling, and without opening her eyes, Rebecca said, "Take me into the house and *I'll* show you how to push."

The out-of-character statement from Rebecca brought a burst of laughter from Jake. He knew what she meant, and he was a willing partner.

They spent the evening drinking and making love. The tragedies surrounding Jake disappeared when he was with Rebecca. She made him feel whole and complete.

Jake woke at 6 a.m. and took a shower. When he came out of the shower Rebecca was at the kitchen table with two cups of coffee. He kissed her lightly on the top of her head and then sat down. "I have to be in Boston before eight. I don't know how long I'll be there, but I'll call you when I get back."

Howard Olsen

Rebecca knew why Jake was going to Boston and she could feel his discomfort about doing so. The re-autopsies were something that was uncomfortable to everyone, but they had to be done.

The traffic was light on Saturday as Jake drove south on I-95. He turned onto Rt. 1 South and within fifteen minutes pulled into the medical examiner's parking lot.

Jake walked up the stairs to the front office and was told to go to autopsy room three. He stepped into the elevator and pushed the button for his floor. When the elevator's doors opened, Jake noticed how quiet and empty the building was. He walked down the hall and into autopsy room three where Doctor Kessler was sitting at his desk drinking coffee. He looked at the empty autopsy table in puzzlement, but before he could speak Kessler said, "Get yourself a cup of coffee and sit down. I already finished with Sally Grogan and I'm just waiting for them to bring in Susan Martell."

Jake walked to the coffee pot and mumbled, "Christ, Doc, you said eight o'clock, it's only seven."

"I couldn't sleep." Kessler continued filling out paperwork. "It's just as well, because if the findings with the second victim are consistent with what I found with Sally Grogan, I'll be even more confused than I was when we started.

Jake didn't ask Kessler what he meant, he just sat and waited until the doctor finished with his paperwork.

Kessler signed his name at the bottom of the form and slid it across the table. He picked up his coffee cup and noticed Jake's baffled expression. "Relax, Jake. I'll tell you my findings when I finish with Susan Martell."

The doctor's assistant wheeled in a gurney with the body

Indiscriminate

of Susan Martell on it. Although covered with a sheet, Susan Martell's body declared its presence as though it wanted to be there, almost as though she knew she could help find her murderer.

In the past Jake always stood at the table when Doctor Kessler worked. He always watched as the doctor made the Y incision and used the electric circular saw to inspect the most personal parts of a human being. This time he couldn't watch. *I'm getting old*, Jake thought. *I just can't take this case as impersonally as I used to.*

The doctor examined and photographed every area of Sally Grogan's body. Two hours after he began, Kessler was finished and called his assistant to come in and wash and disinfect the body, table and everything around it. Autopsy room number three was filled with an eerie silence that added to its unfriendly atmosphere.

Kessler scrubbed his hands and walked back to his desk. Sitting and facing Jake he said, "Before I make any determinations of my findings, I'd like you to wait here until the photographs are developed. I want you to help me interpret what the hell they mean."

Jake nodded and poured himself another cup of coffee. "How long before we have the photographs?"

"Thirty minutes," Kessler said. "There are similarities that tell me it's the same murderer in all three cases, but there are also some inconsistencies."

"Inconsistencies?" Jake asked. "You mean it's possible there may be more than one murderer?"

"It's possible, but I don't think so. I'm reasonably sure it's the same man, but I can't figure out why he deviated from his M.O. We'll know more when we get the court order to exhume the other bodies."

The more Jake learned about this case, the more confused he became. When Kessler found the fingerprints, Jake was convinced the new evidence would lead him to the identity of the murderer. He was wrong, and the mixed emotions from Doctor Kessler only added to his confusion.

When the photographer's assistant brought the photographs to Kessler, the good doctor snatched them from his hands and spread them out across his desk. "Can you make me larger blow-ups of this area?" Kessler asked as he circled an area in the picture of the ring around Sally Grogan's neck. "I need them right away."

"No problem, Doc," the assistant said. "You'll have them in fifteen minutes." He scurried out the door and down the hall.

Jake slid his chair close to Kessler and they both stared at the pictures of the victims. The cold expression on the victims' faces cut into Jake like a sharp knife. He felt the pain these people suffered during their last minutes of life. He couldn't shake the visions from his mind. But the vision of the boy bothered him the most.

Kessler pointed to the rope burn around the necks of the two women, then pointed to the rope burn on the neck of Gary Cronin. "They look the same, but they're not. Look at the burn on the women, then look closely at the burn on the boy."

Jake leaned forward and studied the photographs. He noticed a thin line in the middle of the rope burn on the women, but not on the boy. "What the hell is that, a different rope?"

Indiscriminate

"No, the rope burns on all three victims seem to be made from the same type of rope," he pointed to the burns around the women's neck, "but there's something in the middle of these burns that doesn't appear on the boy. We may be able to see it better in the blow-ups. The tissue has decomposed too much on the women to actually see it with the naked eye, and I'm hoping the enlargements will give us a better look."

Staring at the pictures of the victims, Jake said, "I can see something different, also. What the hell could it be?"

"Electrical cord," Kessler said in a low tone, "I think they were strangled with an electrical cord, but I'm not positive, yet."

"What about the rope burns?" Jake asked.

"I think the rope burns were caused by the victim being dragged by the rope. I think he used the rope to make it easier to move the body." Kessler paused. "The other thing I believe is that he uses the rope as some sort of symbol, a symbol that relates to something in *his* mind."

Jake stared at the photos of the rope burns. "I think it's also left as a clue. A meaningless clue for us to spend time chasing our asses in a direction that leads nowhere."

"I don't think so," Kessler replied. "I don't agree with Stoughton's profile of the murderer being extremely strong. I think he's weak, average at best."

"It would take someone pretty strong to cause the damage that Granger described. I mean, it was extensive."

"True," Kessler admitted, "but Stoughton did his profile on the information that was handed to him. He didn't have all the evidence."

Jake was perplexed and didn't understand what the

doctor was insinuating. "Are you saying Stoughton was right, half-right, or dead-ass wrong?"

"I'm not saying anything until I see the blow-ups of the scars on the victims' necks. Hopefully they will be clear enough for identification."

Jake didn't want to push the doctor until he saw the photographs. He knew Kessler was painstakingly meticulous with his conclusions and would not speculate. He always made sure he had all the evidence before giving his opinion of the findings.

Forty-five minutes passed and Jake became restless. Several times he stepped into the hallway and glanced in each direction as though he expected to see the delivery boy with the photographs.

"You're beginning to annoy me." Kessler picked up the telephone and dialed an extension. "Sit down and relax."

"What the hell is taking so long with the photographs?" Jake asked.

The doctor hung up the telephone. "The photos are on their way."

Within two minutes the delivery boy walked in and placed the photos on Kessler's desk. "You're gonna like these," he said. "They're perfect."

Kessler ignored the comment and immediately spread out the photos. The boy was right, they *were* perfect.

"Well," Jake sat next to the doctor, "what do you see?"

Kessler's expression was intense. He stared at a photograph and pointed to a dark line in the middle of the rope burn around Sally Grogan's neck. "This is what killed her," the doctor said, "not the rope. It was done with electrical cord."

Indiscriminate

Jake couldn't understand how Kessler knew it was electrical cord. He could see a dark line in the middle of the rope burn, but didn't know how the doctor could identify it as being caused by an electrical cord, or anything else. "How can you be so sure it was caused by an electrical cord?"

Kessler reached into his top desk drawer, removed a large magnifying glass and handed it to Jake. "Do you see the two thin lines in the middle of the dark ring?"

Jake nodded. "Yes, but how the hell—"

Kessler cut him off, "An electrical cord is thin and very flexible. It has small ridges running down its entire length. When enough pressure is applied, this is the impression it leaves on the skin."

"Wouldn't it take a tremendous amount of force to do this much damage?" Jake asked.

"Absolutely," Kessler said, "and this is definitely the weapon used to kill these two women."

Jake looked at the doctor. "Well, it looks like Stoughton was right, the murderer is very strong."

"No," Kessler said, "I don't believe the murderer is strong."

"Doc, I'm really confused now. You tell me it took tremendous force to inflict this much damage, then you tell me the murderer is a fucking weakling..."

"Jake, these two women were murdered with a garrote, an electrical cord that had a dowel or peg tied to each end. This type of weapon was used by the commandos in Korea, and also by professional assassins. Once it's wrapped around the victim's neck, it will quadruple a man's power."

"The victim would thrash and roll all around," Jake said,

"I know *I* wouldn't just lie there while some crazy son-of-a-bitch wrapped a wire around *my* neck."

"The coagulation of blood," Kessler said, "that's the bruise on the victims' backs, and it was caused by the murderer's knee." Kessler held an expression of disgust. "He had his victim's hands duct taped behind their backs, and they were lying face down. With his knee jammed into their backs to help hold them still, he strangled them."

The doctor's interpretation of his findings sent cold chills down Jake's back. It was difficult to believe anyone could be that merciless to another human being. As inconceivable as it was, Jake knew the doctor was right. Remembering what the murderer said in his notes about it being all over soon, Jake also knew if he didn't find him soon, he never would.

NINE

Jake scanned the screen until he saw the location of the previous murders. "Salem, India?"

"Yup," Mark mumbled, "five years ago there were four murders using this identical MO—even the notes to the Indian police were written in charcoal and in English."

"A connection—there's gotta be a connection with our guy," Jake said. "What were the names of the victims?"

Mark continued to read the report that CAIN was transmitting, but no names of the victims were documented. "It just says that four women were found in open areas with their hands taped behind their backs with duct tape. They were all strangled and found with a rope tied around their necks, tied into a hangman's knot."

Mark printed out the entire report from Salem, India and made two copies. Jake immediately took the copy to his desk and began studying it. He was scribbling notes on a piece of paper when Captain Reins and Bill Stoughton walked in. As they approached his desk, Jake slid the paper with his notes into a folder and closed it to conceal the information.

"Have you turned up anything, Burnett?" Reins asked in his usual arrogant tone.

"No, sir," Jake responded, "but we're working on it."

Mark's excitement of the new evidence was quickly squelched when he heard Jake's answer to the Captain's question. Without knowing why, Mark slid his copy of the report from India into his top desk drawer. He didn't know why his partner was concealing the new evidence, but he was going to question Jake's reasoning in front of Reins and Stoughton.

Bill Stoughton leaned against a desk; his demeanor was that of a whipped puppy. He had a non-athletic appearance, and his clothes only confirmed this observation. Jake thought Stoughton was a sissy who always tried to blend in with the guys, but who was never accepted as one of them.

The captain stepped closer to Jake's desk and asked him questions about what he was doing with the case. Jake let Reins know some of the facts that Doctor Kessler found but omitted most of the findings. "Captain, I want to verify all the information and the only way to be completely sure, is to wait until the medical examiner in Ohio completed the autopsy on nineteen-year old, Ellen Hayward."

Reins gazed toward Jake as if waiting for him to continue. Finally realizing that Jake had no further information at that time, he slowly turned and walked into his office.

Jake walked to the coffeepot and poured himself a large mug of coffee. While he was stirring in the sugar, he overheard Stoughton ask Mark about the fingerprints. A twinge of anger raced through him when he thought of the captain divulging the new evidence to anyone outside the department. This feeling quickly softened when he thought of the profiler lying on the floor with a rope around his neck.

Walking back to his desk, Jake stopped and asked, "How ya feeling, Bill?" His sincerity was obvious.

"Much better, Jake, thanks for asking," Bill answered Pausing a moment, Stoughton removed the scarf from around his neck and displayed the fading rope burn.

Jake stared at the pinkish scar that completed a perfect circle around Stoughton's neck. He felt empathy for the man whom, for long as Jake had known him, had commanded and yet had received no respect.

Before Jake could walk back to his desk, Stoughton pulled down the collar of his polo shirt and displayed the entire scar. "See, Jake," As he turned completely around so that Jake could see the impression of the full circle extending from the front of his throat to the back of his neck. "It's healing pretty good. I should be back to normal in a week or so

Jake stared at the aftermath of an attack that was brutal and unyielding, and had difficulty verbalizing his compassion. He had never felt any respect for Bill Stoughton until he was attacked and left for dead.

Reins walked toward his office and motioned for Stoughton to follow. Like a puppy in obedience school, the self-proclaimed profiler followed the captain into his private domain.

When Stoughton walked into the office and shut the door behind him, Mark sat quietly for a moment. Then, in a whisky-tenored whisper, he asked, "What the hell was that all about? Why did we hide the new evidence from the captain?"

Jake said nothing, but continued staring at the captain's closed door. He had no valid reason to withhold the information, but something inside told him to keep the information concealed until it could be weighed and examined.

"Never mind," Mark held his hands in the air, "I don't want to know."

"Mark," Jake said, "check with the FBI, Interpol and customs and immigration. I want to know who had an active passport five years ago."

Mark looked at Jake with disbelief. He couldn't understand his partner's request for names that would undoubtedly number into the thousands. In a sincere and pleading tone, Mark asked, "Do you know how many people fall into that category?"

"Mark," Jake said with conviction, "I'm not looking for a global listing, just the people in Essex County."

Mark acknowledged Jake's instructions with a nod and reached for the telephone. Before he dialed the number for the FBI, Jake interrupted, "I need the name of the detective in charge of the case in India, and his phone number."

Mark was offended at the way Jake took over and barked orders. He was the veteran, not Jake.

"For Christ-sake, Jake! I'm not a fucking rookie and I don't like the way you bark orders at me!"

Considering the situation for a moment, Mark realized Jake was trying to do a good job and make an impression on Captain Reins. He knew Jake wanted his badge back permanently but was simply overzealous in the way he went about it.

Jake saw the expression on Mark's face and realized his demanding manner was out of place, and certainly not warranted.

"Sorry, partner, I don't mean to bark orders at you. It's just that I'm between a rock and a hard place. I don't know a damn thing about any of the new computer systems and I feel as though I've been left in the dust. It's frustrating."

Mark felt the sincerity in Jake's voice and immediately dismissed his own anger. "Why don't you go home and relax? I'll call you as soon as I find out anything."

Jake retrieved the folder from his desk and spread out the blow-ups of the scars on the necks. He knew there was something in the photos that would cast a light on the murderer, but he couldn't find it. He couldn't erase the feeling that the missing piece was right in front of him, and that was an emotion Jake had trouble dealing with.

Mark studied the intense expression on Jake's face as he examined the photographs. He knew his friend better than anyone, and he could see the emotions that were coursing through his veins, a combination of ecstasy, turmoil and animosity. As tough and strong-willed as Jake is, Mark could see he was having difficulty dealing with so many emotions all at once.

Jake looked up at his partner and blurted, "I'm spinning my wheels, Mark. I've looked at all the scars from the victims over and over and they're all the same, nothing different on any of them. "He closed the folder and stood up, "Okay, Mark, I'm going home and try to figure this out. Let me know when you find the name and telephone number of the detective in India."

Jake left the station before Captain Reins could grill him more on the new evidence. He wanted to check everything out and confirm or eliminate its value before telling Reins, or anyone else. He especially didn't like divulging evidence in front of non-department personal, namely, Bill Stoughton. The self-proclaimed profiler had barely survived an attack that had already killed ten people and Jake didn't want to put him at more risk by keeping him in the loop with information.

Jake turned into his driveway and noticed Rebecca's car hadn't moved. She was still there and that vision brought him a feeling of comfort. He needed the department in his life, but found he needed more—Rebecca White. At one time his only desire was to be back on the police force, but now that one desire had doubled.

He walked into the house to the aroma of roasting beef. Rebecca was standing over the stove preparing the vegetables, still wearing one of his old scanty tee shirts.

"Mark just called," she said without turning around, "he wants you to call him as soon as you get home."

Jake's blood pressure tripled. He didn't think Mark would have the information about the Indian detective this soon. He snatched the telephone from its receiver and pushed the speed dial for the station. On the second ring he heard Mark's voice, "Homicide, this is Detective Roads."

"Mark, did you get the name and number of the detective in India?"

"Hi honey, what's wrong?" was Mark's response.

Indiscriminate

For a moment Jake thought he dialed the wrong number, then realized someone was there with Mark. In a playful voice, Jake said, "Is there something about you that you're not telling me?"

"Okay," Mark said, "I'll pick up the Liquid Plumber on my way home. I'm leaving now. I'll be there in fifteen minutes." He hung up.

Jake knew the information Mark had found would be helpful, and was pleased with the way his partner hid it from the prying eyes of whoever was there with him.

"Dinner will be ready in about two hours," Rebecca said. "It would be nice if you called Dang and Mark and invited them over."

Jake studied Rebecca and marveled at her perfect outline in his old tee shirt. "Okay, I'll invite them for dinner," Jake said playfully, "but are you going to get dressed or are you going to continue to walk around dressed like that—and drive me crazy?"

With a bright smile she told Jake she was going home to shower and change and would be back in an hour, then scurried off into the bedroom, got dressed, and left.

Mark walked in as Rebecca was leaving and they talked briefly before she left. She told Mark that he and Joanne were invited for dinner along with Dang and Mary.

Mark inhaled the aroma of the roasting beef, "That smells great, Rebecca, we'll be here."

Mark walked into the living room and handed Jake a piece of paper with the name of the detective in charge of the murders in Salem, India, along with two telephone numbers.

Jake studied the note and reached for the telephone. "I hope this detective can shed some light on *our* guy. What are the two numbers for?"

"The first number is for the police station in Salem, India and the second is his home phone."

Jake began dialing the first number when Mark told him the detective was not at the station. "Jake, the time difference in India is about ten hours ahead of us. That means it almost eleven o'clock at night there. I don't think you should call him now."

"He's a police officer," Jake said. "He's on call 24-7."

"This is exactly why people think of you as a pain in the ass." Mark helped himself to a cold beer from the fridge.

Jake dialed the number. On the fourth ring an answering machine answered and delivered a message in Indian. Disappointed that he didn't get the opportunity to speak to the detective in person, Jake said, "I'm sorry to call you at this hour, but I'm trying to locate Detective Manjit Patel. I'm a police officer from the USA and I need some information about a case you worked on five years ago."

Before Jake could leave his telephone number, a groggy voice answered the phone, "Hello, this is Detective Patel." The voice had a heavy Indian accent and Jake hoped the language barrier would not be too much of a problem.

Mark sat on the sofa opposite his partner and listened as Jake explained everything to the Indian detective. Jake repeated everything he said twice, and it was obvious to that the two men were able to communicate, despite the language barrier.

"Well, actually, Detective Patel, I really need the prints

Indiscriminate

right away—if it wouldn't be too much of an inconvenience…" Jake hesitated a moment, then added, "(978) 555-5632.

Jake glanced in Mark's direction with a wide smile. Mark heard Jake give Detective Patel the station fax number and knew what his partner's reaction meant. Somehow, Jake had talked the Indian detective into getting out of bed in the middle of the night, going to his station and faxing him the prints. Jake hung up the telephone and looked at Mark. "We'll have two prints in about an hour."

"Everyone has been right all these years—you're a real pain in the ass. How the hell did you talk that poor son-of-a-bitch into getting out of bed in the middle of the night?"

Jake explained that Detective Patel worked the case for two years without any luck. "He said the four murders came in a span of only two weeks and ended as fast as it began. He said they found two perfect fingerprints on the driver's side window of the fourth victim's car, and the murders stopped. He believes that the discovery of the prints scared the murderer into leaving the area."

"Jake," Mark said, "you know what *that* means!"

"Yeah, there's a good chance that sick son-of-a-bitch will pack up and leave here, too."

"I looked up Salem, India on the Internet and found it to be a large city," Mark said. "For some reason I assumed it would be a small village, but the population is three hundred and sixty-four thousand. They're heavily involved in manufacturing—everything from chemicals and electrical products, to brass and handloom weaving. That means there are a lot of large companies in that city and the murderer could become invisible to everyone around him. With the hustle and bustle of that much industry being conducted from one city, he could blend in without anyone knowing. Christ, he could have been a worker in one, or more, of those companies."

The possibilities were endless and Jake had a bad feeling about the murderer moving on. The murders stopped when they found his fingerprints in Salem, India, and now they had his prints in Salem, Massachusetts.

"I just thought of something, Mark." Jake walked to the window and looked out onto Lafayette Street. "If we got a hit on CAIN with the similarities of our MO, why weren't the prints in AFIS?"

Mark explained that CAIN was implemented long before AFIS. "It's gonna take a long time before AFIS is implemented world-wide, and there will be a lot of police departments that won't have access to it. It's a very expensive system to get connected to." He finished his beer and walked to the refrigerator for another. "Want one?" he hollered to Jake over his shoulder.

Jake didn't answer. He was heavy in thought about the fingerprints that were going to be faxed.

Mark returned with two bottles of beer. He handed one to Jake a beer and sat down. "Why don't you want Reins to know what the hell we're doing?"

Jake looked at the bottle of beer with an intense stare. Mark could see the concentration in his partner's eyes and waited for an answer.

"I don't trust the captain. I know that sounds ridiculous, but there's something inside that's telling me there's a rotten apple in the department." Jake's voice trailed off.

Indiscriminate

"You think Captain Reins is the murderer? Christ, Jake, just because of the bad blood between you and him is no reason to think he's a murderer. You're going off the deep end." Mark stood and walked back into the kitchen. "You're out of your fucking mind."

Jake said nothing and continued his unwavering stare at the bottle of beer. He knew the statement he made to his partner sounded biased because of the bad blood between him and the captain, but there was something inside that told him to be wary.

Mark walked back into the living room. "You're not serious."

Slowly, and with conviction, Jake looked up at Mark, "I'm as serious as a heart attack," Jake replied.

"The captain?" Mark asked sarcastically, "Why couldn't it be Moran…Stoughton…or how about the fucking mayor?"

Jake found himself defending his accusation. "Moran is a idiot, but he doesn't have the makeup to be a murder…Unless he hides it very well. He has never been involved in anything more serious than a trespassing case. Bill Stoughton doesn't have the aggressiveness to do anything this violent." Pausing, Jake added, "Besides, Stoughton is lucky to be alive. And the more I think about it, where the hell has Reins been every time he goes on vacation? No one ever knows where he goes. Christ, he could have been in India! And of course, the Captain's brother! He's a loose cannon, for sure!

Mark stared at his partner and saw the passion in his eyes. Jake had a suspicion that the captain was somehow involved in the murders, and Mark only hoped Jake's suspicion did not escalate the hatred between the two men. "And the mayor?"

Jake looked at Mark, annoyed. "It ain't the mayor, Christ, Stoughton, Moran or Dang would be a better candidate than the Mayor! My mind is working overtime with suspicions and at one time I even thought that *you* could have done it! Mark, I know how ridiculous this sounds, but it's someone who is close to the department, and I'll bet it was someone close to the department in India, also."

Puzzled and frustrated Jake said, "I don't believe Reins was the murderer, but for some reason I don't trust him with any new evidence."

He glanced at his watch. "Time to go." He called Rebecca and told her he had to go to the station, but would be back shortly.

"I called Mary and invited her and Dang to dinner, and they would be at Jake's house at three o'clock. Jake, please make sure you're back by three o'clock."

"I promise I will be back by 3:00…Trust me."

"Mark, let's get the fax before anyone else sees it."

Mark shrugged and they both walked out the door. Mark's Chevy van was parked behind the Corvette and Mark slid behind the wheel. "Come on, Jake, leave the Vette."

Within minutes they turned into the police parking lot. Jake noticed Captain Reins' car parked in its usual spot. "Christ!" Jake snapped, "I hope Patel hasn't already faxed the prints."

Mark parked the van and Jake was out of the vehicle faster than a cat on a hot plate. "Wait for me," Mark said in a muffled tone.

Jake swung open the door and raced up the stairs, two

Indiscriminate

at a time. He walked into the squad room and glanced at the fax machine. It was empty.

A combination of relief that Patel hadn't sent the fax yet and the fear of it already being sent and Reins having it raced through his body.

"What the hell are you doing here? Looking for a little overtime?"

Jake looked up and saw Moran sitting at his desk. He walked to the detective's desk. "I'm expecting a fax, anything come through?"

"Only one thing came over the fax today, Jake, the captain has it. He's in his office with Stoughton."

An uneasy feeling engulfed Jake. He didn't know how to ask Reins about the fax. He knew he couldn't simply walk in to the captain's office and ask if he received a fax from India. He had already told Reins there wasn't any new evidence. He sat at his desk and pondered the situation. The only answer he could come up with was to walk into Reins' office and ask about the fax.

Sitting at his desk across from Jake, Mark said, "Jake, you can't just walk in there and ask for the fax. You already told him there was nothing new."

Before Jake could respond to his partner's statement, Reins opened the door and motioned for Jake to come in.

"The shit's going to hit the fan, now," Jake mumbled as he got up and walked toward the captain's office.

As Jake approached, Reins stood in the doorway holding a piece of paper. When Jake reached the captain he noticed his irritated expression. He handed Jake the paper and said, "What the hell is this, Burnett?"

Jake slowly retrieved the paper from the captain and began reading it.

"This department is not for your personal use," Reins bellowed. "I don't want to see any more of this nonsense coming through the department. Understood?"

"Yes, sir." Jake said humbly, and walked back to his desk.

Mark sat quietly and stared at Jake. When he didn't get an explanation, he asked, "Well? Is it from Patel?"

Jake smiled and tossed him the paper.

Mark began reading it out loud, "Dear Mister Burnett, I've tried reaching you at your book store but haven't had any luck. I was told you were a Salem police officer and I thought this would be the easiest way to contact you. I would like to order a book titled…" Mark's voice trailed off. "A book order? Someone sent a fax to the police station to order a fucking book?"

Before Jake could respond to his partner's sarcastic question, the fax machine rang. Both men looked at each other, then back at the machine.

"This has gotta be it." Jake walked to the fax machine.

Standing in front of the machine waiting for his request, Jake saw the captain's door open and Bill Stoughton walking toward him carrying an empty coffee cup.

The coffeepot was located to the right of the fax machine and he knew Stoughton would see the fingerprints as they slowly came out of the fax.

"Coffee's stale, Bill," Jake announced in an attempt to discourage Stoughton from coming over to the fax, "I'll make a fresh pot. I'll let you know when it's done."

Stoughton continued walking toward Jake. "That's okay, I like it strong."

The document from detective Patel began to slowly emerge from the bottom of the machine. Jake glanced at his partner with an uneasy expression.

"Hey, Bill," Mark said with a smile as he held a piece of paper in the air. "Take a look at this."

Stoughton turned and walked to Mark's desk. Leaning over Mark's shoulder, both men began mumbling and laughing as Jake stared at the document being transmitted. *Hurry up, you son-of-a-bitch,* he thought.

Stoughton tapped Mark on the back and walked to the coffeepot just as the fax was completed. Jake snatched the paper from the tray at the same moment Stoughton arrived.

Attempting to see the paper in Jake's hand, Stoughton nervously asked, "What's that, new evidence?"

Jake could see the curiosity on Stoughton's face. He knew if he showed him the fax Stoughton would run into Reins' office and blurt out everything.

"No," Jake responded immediately, "Just a list of street people I want to talk to."

Stoughton poured his coffee, "Have you found anything new?" His eyes drifted from side to side as if looking for something he could find and tell Reins.

"The fingerprints turned out to be a complete dead-end. We've come to a standstill, but we're still working on it."

The smug expression on the profiler's face was as though he already knew the case had come to a halt, as if he wanted Jake to fail. If the Salem police department couldn't solve the murders, maybe Stoughton thought *he* could step in and be the almighty messiah.

Stoughton finished pouring his coffee and strolled back to the captain's office. Jake returned to his desk, pointed in Stoughton's direction and said, "If I ever walk like that you have my permission to fucking shoot me."

Mark chuckled and held out his hand, motioning for Jake to give him the fax of the fingerprints.

Jake handed Mark the fingerprints. "I don't know how long I'll be able to sit here and wait for AFIS to come up with an answer."

"I don't need to use AFIS this time, partner," Mark said as he looked at the fingerprints through a magnifying glass. His eyes lit up and he reached into his desk and retrieved the prints from Doctor Kessler.

Jake watched as his partner looked at one set of prints, then the other. The more he looked at one, the harder he stared at the other.

"For Christ-sake, Mark, what the hell do you see?"

Mark set the magnifying glass down on his desk and looked at his partner. In a low whisper, he said, "Bingo!"

Adrenaline raced through Jake's body. The thought of the murderer leaving his fingerprints at two different crime scenes, in two counties, told the detective that he wasn't as smart as everyone thought. He stood up and approached his partner. Standing behind Mark Jake leaned over his shoulder. "You completely sure?"

"There's no doubt, Jake. See the small faded circle in the middle of this print?"

Jake lifted the magnifying glass to the fingerprint and

saw exactly what Mark described—a small faded circle. When he looked at the second set of fingerprints he saw the same identifying mark. "What the hell is it?"

"My guess is a burn of some kind, maybe from a cigarette. In any case it's been there for a long time."

Jake immediately called Doctor Kessler at home. Being Saturday he knew the doctor wouldn't be in his office.

On the second ring Kessler answered, "Hello, this is Saturday and I'm not coming into work."

"Hi, Doc, this is Jake."

"I know who it is, and I'm still not coming into work."

Jake heard activity in the background and realized his friend was in the middle of cookout. "I hate to bother you at home," Jake explained, "But I need you to verify something for me."

"Okay, Jake, you have two minutes. What can I do for you?"

"I'm going to fax you a fingerprint and I need to know about the scar in the center. Mark believes it's some sort of a burn, but we don't know for sure."

Kessler gave Jake his fax number and Jake wrote it down and slid the number to Mark. It's being faxed to you right now. I'll hold."

"Jake, you're a pain in the ass," Kessler said as he set the telephone down.

In less than a minute the good doctor was back on the telephone with Jake. "Your partner's right. This is definitely a burn, probably from a cigarette."

"How old is the scar?"

"That's hard to determine without actually seeing the

person's finger, but I'd say it's been there since the he was a small child."

"Thanks, Doc, you've been a great help. Go back to your party and have a good time. I'll call you at your office on Monday."

Ten

The two detectives drove back to Jake's house, all while talking about the fingerprints from India and how they could put a name to them.

"We need someone to do the referencing and cross-referencing of all the people who either have, or have applied for, passports," said Mark. "I don't have the time to sit at the station day-in and day-out following up on every name."

Jake agreed and stated that they needed someone who never left the station. "We need someone who spends his whole career at his desk. Someone who's good with paperwork and meticulous enough to sort through hundreds of names."

Mark squinted as he drove and Jake recognized this expression as being deep in thought. "Okay, partner," Jake asked, "what's on your mind?"

"We need someone who enjoys digging through miles of paperwork, right? We need someone who knows all the ins and outs on how to obtain information that has been left through a paper trail, right? We need someone who knows *who* to talk to and how to procure the information we're looking for, right?"

"Mark," said Jake, "What the hell are you trying to say?"

"Moran fits the bill."

"Moran! Moran is a fucking nitwit."

"Moran may be an nitwit, but he really knows how to dig into paperwork and come up with answers. He spends his whole life in that squad room cross-referencing everything from the names of people who had their licenses revoked to people who have moved to Salem within the past ten years. He'd do a good job."

"Maybe," Jake said, "but will he be able to keep his mouth shut about what he finds?"

"Moran would do *anything* to be involved in a murder case, *especially* this one."

Jake sat silent for the remainder of the short ride back to his house. Mark was right about Moran and his paperwork, but could they trust him to keep his findings hidden from Captain Reins? or anyone else. Moran was a tattletale

Mark dropped Jake off at his house and told him he and Joanne would be back shortly. "My mother-in-law is visiting and she'll watch the kids for us."

Once inside, Jake pondered his partner's suggestion. He didn't dislike Moran but was apprehensive if he could be trusted. There were times Jake did things that were against department policy and he had reservations about Moran being part of them. He poured himself a two-finger glass of Labrot & Graham and sat on the sofa. "Ah, what the hell," he said out loud, "It won't hurt to feel him out." He picked up the telephone and dialed the number to the squad room.

"Detective John Moran," came the familiar voice "Hey, John, do you have any plans this afternoon?"

There was a long pause, "Is this you, Jake?"

Jake knew Moran would be suspicious about coming to his house for dinner and didn't believe the detective would accept the invitation. "Hey, John, we're having a little dinner here at my house and I was wondering if you would like to come."

"Is this another one of your put downs, Jake?" Moran asked sarcastically.

"No, John, I think it's about time we put all that crap aside… don't you?"

"Christ, Jake, I hope this is not another one of your pranks. Okay, I'll be there in an hour."

Jake understood why Moran was suspicious about being invited to dinner at his house after the way he had treated him in the past. He also knew the squad room detective would go to extreme measures to be accepted as a field officer. But, before he actually brought him into the investigation, he wanted to be sure he could be trusted with the information that was uncovered.

Before long Rebecca drove into the driveway, quickly followed by Mark and Dang. Jake told Mark that he invited Moran to dinner to feel him out, but would not divulge any information until he was sure Moran could be trusted.

"How the hell are you going to be sure?" Mark wanted to know. "Are you just going to ask him to cut the captain from the loop and put his job on the line—just like me?"

Howard Olsen

There was a touch of animosity in Mark's voice. Jake knew departmental procedure and polices as well as anyone, but during a tough case he had problems adhering to it.

The women were in the kitchen putting the finishing touches on dinner and the men sat in the living room talking about the case. John Moran hadn't arrived yet and Jake was tossing around ideas as to how to approach the squad room detective.

"The first thing you have to think about is how the hell you're going to get Reins to agree to this," Mark said. "I don't think the captain will go along with losing his only squad room detective, especially knowing how you two are consistently at each other's throats."

"That may be a small problem," said Jake, "but, if I play it right, I'll get around it."

The doorbell sounded. Jake knew who it was. "I'll get it," he announced and walked to the front door. He opened the door and greeted Moran with a cheerful smile. "Hello, John, I'm glad you could make it."

Moran stood in the doorway holding two bottles of wine. He didn't know how to react to Jake's pleasant attitude, but returned the greeting with a nervous smile. "I didn't know what we were having for dinner, so I brought a bottle of white and a bottle of red. I hope that's all right."

For the first time Jake saw a side of John Moran he didn't know existed. *This* John Moran was polite, thoughtful and gracious. The obnoxious detective Jake had known in the past had been left in the squad room.

The dinner went well and everyone seemed to enjoy each other's company. The conversation was pleasant and that

Indiscriminate

sent a signal to Moran. He knew Jake's reputation for being a prankster first hand, and deep inside he felt this was the reason Jake invited him to dinner.

Moran drifted off alone and sat at the picnic table in the backyard. He watched a cat stalking an unsuspecting bird in a tree and didn't notice Jake walk up behind him. As the cat was about to pounce on the bird, Jake tossed a pebble at the bird, causing it to fly away.

Moran looked over his shoulder and saw Jake staring into the tree. "Cats eat birds, Jake," Moran said softly. "It's an instinct. It's nature."

Jake sat beside Moran. He knew the detective had reservations about why he was invited to dinner, and thought this would be a good time to test Mark's theory about Moran. "The cat wasn't hungry. He wanted to kill the bird because he likes to kill. The cat enjoys the feeling of the superiority he has over the bird, and his final high is when he violently snuffs out the life of his inferior victim."

Moran glanced into the tree at the cat, and then turned his attention back to Jake. "Then brings it home and leaves it where someone can find it."

Moran's voice harbored a hint of animosity and Jake felt it was directed toward him. He understood why the detective would be apprehensive about the reason he was invited to Jake's house, but didn't understand why he accepted the invitation.

Both men stared into the tree as though watching a movie. The cat had obviously realized he lost his chance to kill, and slowly turned and climbed down.

Moran asked, " Jake why did invited me for dinner. I

know you don't like me and I feel the reason I'm here is for you to insult me—again."

Without hesitation, Jake said, "We're in a situation just like that cat and the bird. We have someone out there who enjoys killing and leaves his victims where they will easily be found. He kills because he likes it, and if we don't stop him now, he *will* continue killing."

Moran could actually feel the sincerity in Jake's voice. "What does that have to do with me? I'm well aware of what's going on with the serial murders, but that still doesn't explain why you invited me to your house."

Jake looked down at his bottle of beer and nervously peeled at the label. He wanted to ask the detective for his help, but didn't want to commit to bringing him in without knowing for sure what to expect. Jake broke the silence. "I'm looking for someone to join the team—someone who I can trust to keep his mouth shut and say *nothing* without clearing it through me. I need someone who knows all the ins and outs when it comes to following and deciphering a paper trail."

Moran's demeanor immediately changed. His hands had a slight nervous shake, and Jake knew the detective understood why he was invited to dinner. He shifted nervously in his chair to face Jake. "Are you asking me to join you and Roads on the serial murder case?"

Jake didn't want to commit to the request without knowing for sure that Moran could comply with the way he did police work. He knew Moran was in the habit of telling the captain everything he did, from turning on his computer at the beginning of his watch, to how many times he went to the bathroom.

Indiscriminate

"John," Jake said, "you're aware of the way I do things. You know how I get things done, and many times it's completely against departmental policy."

"Everyone knows how you work. That's what makes it so exciting," Moran said. "Most of the detectives, including me, ridicule your methods, but deep inside wish we had the courage to do it."

Jake saw his chance to bring the subject into the open without making it look as though it was his idea. "Are you asking me to be a part of this case?"

"Yes, and I'll do a good job," Moran said. "All I'm asking for is a chance to prove myself. I've thought of nothing else since you were reinstated, but I didn't think you had any respect for me, as a detective."

The sincerity in Moran's voice was unquestionable. Jake dismissed the timid remarks and the doormat way Moran conducted himself in the past. He realized those actions were entirely meant for *his* benefit and was not the way the detective actually was. He was looking for a chance to be part of something important, and the thought of Jake giving him that opportunity refined the way he presented himself.

"John," Jake began softly, "I don't know if you can function *out* of the system. You're a by-the-book kinda guy, and I'm just the opposite."

"I don't think you could talk the captain into assigning me to this case," Moran said, "but if you could..."

As his voice trailed off, Jake said, "Don't worry about Reins, I'll handle him. Are you interested?"

"Damn straight, I'm interested. And you don't have to

worry about *anyone* finding out what I uncover. You have my word."

Jake stood and faced Moran. Holding out his hand he said, "Okay, John, welcome aboard."

Moran snapped to his feet and shook Jake's hand with the energy of a marathon runner. His face beamed with excitement at the thought of working with the man who, at one time, was his biggest tormentor.

"I'll bring you up to speed after I talk to the captain," said Jake. "Until then, keep this between you and me."

"What about Mark?" Moran asked.

At that moment Mark walked across the yard and asked, "Did I hear my name?"

Jake explained everything to Mark while Moran sat with the expression of a father whose son just scored the winning touchdown. Pride engulfed his entire being as he listened to Jake tell his partner how valuable he would be to the investigation.

At nearly seven o'clock everyone had left except Mark and Joanne, who had mentioned several times that it was time for them to leave, also.

"How much are we going to tell Moran?" Mark wanted to know.

"Nothing until we're sure he can be trusted," said Jake.

"Captain Reins will never agree to this."

"I have a meeting Monday morning with Reins and the Mayor. It will be solidified then." The self-confident tone in Jake's voice was evident, and Mark knew Jake well enough to know that when he put his mind to something, it got done.

Mark and Joanne left and Rebecca stretched out on

Indiscriminate

the sofa. She pushed the button on the remote control and a movie started on the television. "I rented this movie last night, but haven't had a chance to watch it."

Jake slid behind her on the large sofa and began watching the movie. "The Horse Whisperer?" he asked.

Rebecca looked over her shoulder and said, "Shhh, you're going to love this movie."

When the movie ended Rebecca asked, "Well? Did you like it?"

Jake looked into her eyes, "As usual, you're true to your word. I loved it."

Sunday came and went with the speed of a humming bird and Jake and Rebecca talked on the telephone several times during the day. At eight o'clock that evening she told Jake she had to deliver a package to a client and would talk to him in the morning. Jake fell asleep on the sofa and didn't wake up until he heard the telephone ring at 5:30 in the morning.

"Jake!" blurted the excited voice of John Moran, "you better get down here right away. We have another body."

Jake drove into the police parking lot ten minutes after the call from Moran. It was only 5:40 a.m. and the police parking lot was unusually empty. As he pulled into his parking space, he noticed John Moran's car. "Christ," he said out loud, "doesn't this guy ever go home?"

He walked into the squad room and Moran immediately rushed to greet him. "Jake," he said nervously, "We have another one—number twelve."

Jake's heart sank and he leaned against a desk. The thought of another person being tortured and murdered took over his entire body.

Howard Olsen

Moran began reading from the report; "Her name is Molly Chrisp, twenty-eight years old. She was a first-grade teacher at the Carlton School and was found at 1:00 a.m. this morning at the Collins Cove Park. Jake, this time there was a witness, but they don't know if she's going to make it. She's in the I.C.U. at the Salem Hospital."

Jake's forehead creased and the veins bulged in his neck. His emotions were a mixture of hatred, fury and anger, while compassion for the victim raced through his mind.

"What's the name of the witness," Jake asked, compassion for the victim mixing with the anger and hate swirling in his mind.

I don't have the name, only that it was a woman who stopped to help another woman whose car had a flat tire."

Jake scrambled to his desk and called Mark. He told him what happened and to come in right away. Mark agreed and said he would be there in twenty minutes.

"Captain Reins and Mayor Sweeney are on their way. They'll be here any minute." Moran's voice was filled with concern. "What are you going to tell them?"

Jake didn't answer Moran's question, but asked, "Where's the body?"

"The Salem Hospital," Moran said dryly.

Jake snatched the telephone from its cradle and dialed the number for the hospital. John Moran stood and listened as Jake barked orders to whoever was on the other end of the telephone. "I don't want the body touched," he said firmly. "I want it transported to the Boston ME's office, right away."

Just as he hung up the phone, Captain Reins and Mayor Sweeney stormed into the squad room. "You better have something positive to tell me, Burnett," Reins hollered, "and it better not be, '*I'm working on it.*'"

Jake knew the time had come to divulge the information he had gathered, but was apprehensive about doing so. The captain would only accept a detailed explanation of everything he had. Jake went to his desk and retrieved a folder, then motioned in the direction of the captain's office and opened the door. Holding the door open for the captain and Sweeney, Reins walked past and grumbled, "This better be good."

Reluctantly, and in detail, Jake told Reins and Sweeney about everything he had discovered in the past week. He told them about the fingerprints from Salem, India and how they matched the prints from their murderer. He told them about the autopsy that was being conducted in Ohio on the second victim, and he was waiting for the findings.

"At least you're making progress," said Sweeney. "This evidence is a hell of a lot more than we had a week ago."

The mayor's compliment to Jake didn't sway Reins' feeling about being kept in the dark. "Why is it that I'm finding out this information now, Burnett? I told you I wanted to know everything as it happened."

Jake saw this as an opportunity to recruit Moran. "I realize this information has been slow coming, Captain, but there are only two of us working full time on this case."

"What are you saying? Are you suggesting some sort of a task force?" He slammed his fist onto the desk. "That isn't going to happen. If you can't handle it, then step aside."

Jake cleared his throat, "Captain, Detective Roads and I have been like shit in a barn—we're all over the place. All I'm asking for is one other person to take care of the paperwork, and do the follow-ups internally."

Not wanting to jump over Reins' head and ask the Mayor directly, Jake waited for the captain's response.

Reins said, "The only detective I could spare would be Moran, and I *know* how you feel about him." The captain sat behind his desk with an overconfident expression. "It's Moran or no one."

Jake walked to the door and slowly opened it. Looking back over his shoulder, he confidently said, "Sergeant Moran is a *fine* detective. He will be a great asset to us."

He walked into the squad room, leaving Captain Reins with a confused expression He looked at Moran and Mark, who had their eyes glued to the captain's door. As Jake walked past he smugly said, "That was easy, *too* fucking easy."

"I'm in?" Moran eagerly asked.

"You're in," Jake said. "Now get to work and get me the name and condition of the witness."

Moran darted to his desk and began making phone calls. His enthusiasm was indisputable.

Mark stared at Jake with a blank expression as if to say, "How the hell did you pull *that* off?"

Before Mark could ask the question, Jake said, "All I had to do was make Reins think he was screwing me over. Once he thought that, the rest was a snap."

He called Doctor Kessler at home and told him everything that happened that morning. He told him the body of Molly Chrisp would be at his office within the hour and asked his friend to do the autopsy immediately. Kessler acknowledged the request and hung up the telephone.

Indiscriminate

Jake glanced at Moran and shrugged, indicating he wanted to know what he found out.

Moran sat on the corner of Jake's desk. "The two officers who responded to the call and found the body and the witness are on their way here. I tried getting information about the witness, but it was hectic and noisy in the background so I asked them to come to the squad room instead of filling out their report downstairs."

Jake nodded. "Good job."

Two other detectives came into the squad room and went to their desks. Each had his own caseload and hardly acknowledged what was happening all around them.

Jake opened the folder that held the information about the serial murders and pulled out the telephone number for the police station in India. He began dialing the number when the two officers who responded to the murder call walked in and were immediately greeted by John Moran. He recognized one of the officers as the young rookie who told the tourist with a camera to get out of the intersection. Both men exchanged greetings with a nod, and Jake hung up the telephone before anyone answered. He stood to join Moran and the two officers when his phone rang. Motioning toward Moran, Jake said to Mark, "Make sure he asks the right questions."

Mark went to assist Moran and Jake answered his telephone. It was Doctor Kessler.

"Jake," the doctor said, "I was still half asleep when you called earlier. Tell me everything again."

Jake went through what happened again and answered a handful of questions that Kessler neglected to ask when they talked the first time. While the two men talked, Mark and John were asking the officers questions and scribbling notes on a pad of paper.

Before Jake finished talking to Kessler, the two officers finished answering the questions Mark and John had to ask. They walked past Jake and the rookie tapped Jake on his shoulder in an obvious friendly greeting. Jake acknowledged the greeting with a wink.

Still on the phone, Jake glanced at his two partners and noticed their expressions of fear and remorse. Both detectives looked at Jake and began whispering to each other.

The more Jake looked at the two detectives, the more he knew something was wrong. It was something more than finding another victim. Mark turned his back to Jake and leaned on a desk with both hands, hanging his head. John Moran stood with both hands at his side. His head was hung, also. Jake's hands trembled as he witnessed his partner's behavior. Something had happened, and in his heart he knew it was going to affect him personally. He nervously hung up the telephone without saying goodbye to Kessler. He walked to where Mark and John were standing and looked into their eyes. Tangled and intertwined like a ball of yarn, he saw the emotions of compassion and fear on the faces of both men.

"What is it?" Jake's voice was solemn.

Mark slowly handed Jake the notepad and walked to his desk. Jake watched his partner and friend sit with his head cradled in his hands.

Slowly Jake's eyes returned to the notes and he read aloud, "The victim's name is Molly Chrisp. She was found at 1:00 a.m. this morning at Collins Cove playground. Another

Indiscriminate

woman was found unconscious and is in serious condition. She was strangled with the same weapon as the others, but the killer was interrupted when a man hollered from his window from across the street. She was taken to Salem Hospital, and if she lives, is considered to be a possible witness."

Jake looked at Moran, then back to Mark, who was still sitting with his head buried in his hands. He returned his attention to the scribbled report and read the last notation. "The second victim's name is Rebecca White."

Eleven

Jake's heart sank. He couldn't accept that the second victim was Rebecca. He read the paper over several times as if believing the name would change. It didn't. Rebecca *was* the second victim.

Without saying a word Jake walked to his desk and dialed the number for the Salem Hospital. As the telephone rang, he half-heartedly hoped no one would answer. *Maybe it's a mistake,* he thought.

A crisp, professional voice answered, "ICU, this is Nurse Cole. May I help you?"

Jake listened to the compassionless voice of the male nurse who sounded as though he answered the telephone so many times that there was no emotion He sounded aggravated at having to answer the telephone.

Jake identified himself as a Salem police officer and asked to speak to the doctor who was handling Rebecca's case.

"I'm sorry, sir," came the unconcerned voice of the nurse,

Indiscriminate

"I can't give that information over the phone. You'll have to come in and register in the morning."

"I'm a Salem police officer and I need to talk to the doctor in charge of the women who was brought in early this morning," Jake repeated.

"What part of *no* didn't you understand?" Cole barked, "You will have to report to the office in the morning."

As Jake spewed out his badge number, the nurse hung up. He slammed the phone onto its receiver so hard that the cradle shattered and flew on the floor. He stood and kicked the chair across the room. "I'll be at the hospital." He stormed out of the squad room.

Jake jumped into his Vette and sped out of the parking lot. Taking a left on Jefferson Avenue, he turned right onto Jackson Street and reached the lights as they turned red. Without slowing down he stepped on the gas pedal and sped through the lights onto Highland Avenue.

The hospital was less than one-quarter of a mile from the police station and Jake turned sharply into the entrance. He slammed on the brakes and slid to a stop directly in front of the emergency room.

Leaping over the closed door of the Corvette, he ran into the emergency room and raced down the hall to the elevator. He stepped in and pressed the button marked five.

When the doors opened Jake stepped out and was standing in front of the nurse's station. He looked to his right, then to his left, seeing no one. He was about to begin searching for Rebecca when a nurse stood up from behind the counter.

Standing with several papers she had obviously

dropped, she greeted Jake with a friendly voice. "May I help you, sir?"

"My name is Detective Jason Burnett," he said calmly. "I'd like to speak to the doctor in charge of the woman who was brought in early this morning."

"Certainly, Detective Burnett." The nurse picked up the telephone and dialed the doctor's extension.

Jake listened as the nurse told the doctor there was a police officer there to see him. After speaking to the doctor, she hung up the phone and turned to Jake. "Doctor Shaw will be with you in a minute, Detective. Is there anything else I can do for you?"

"As a matter of fact there is," Jake said. "Earlier I talked to Nurse Cole. Is he here?"

"Yes, he's here," she said. "Do you want me to get him for you?"

"Not yet," replied Jake coldly, "I'll say *hello* to him after I talk to Doctor Shaw."

Jake leaned against the nurse's station and waited for the doctor. He looked down the hall and couldn't help but imagine the pain and suffering emanating from every room. His heart ached at the thought of Rebecca being part of this catastrophe.

The doctor approached and told Jake he would be with him in a moment. Turning his back to Jake and facing the nurse, he said, "I just called it. Log in the exact time of death and notify her relatives." Pausing a moment the doctor added, "I have a hard time accepting the senseless death of someone so young. The person who did this should be put away for the rest of his life."

Indiscriminate

Jake's legs trembled and lost all their strength. His heart pounded so hard he felt as though it would burst through his chest. He listened as the doctor gave the nurse instructions about what he wanted done, and then told her to have the body moved to the morgue.

Jake could barley breath and he began to hyperventilate. As he attempted to suck air into his lungs, the doctor turned and helped him to a chair.

"I want to see her," Jake gasped.

"Are you a relative?" asked the doctor.

Jake couldn't speak; his throat was dry and constricted. He simply held open his jacket and displayed the badge that was clipped to his belt.

The doctor solemnly nodded and helped Jake to his feet. "Follow me, Detective."

Jake walked down the corridor barley able to support his own weight. His hands had lost all feeling and he felt as though he would pass out.

The doctor stepped into the room and motioned for Jake to come in. He stepped into the room and stood silent while looking at the covered body of Rebecca White. Remorse overwhelmed him and his eyes filled with tears.

Doctor Shaw held Jake's arm in an effort to prevent him from falling. Jake didn't move. He stood motionless, staring at the women he had grown to love. His legs feeling like stone, Jake shuffled to the bed where Rebecca was covered with a sheet. He slowly pulled the sheet away from her face and looked down.

"There should be stiffer penalties for drunk drivers,"

stated Doctor Shaw. "The man who did this has been convicted four times in the past for drunk driving."

Staring down at a woman he'd never seen before, Jake fell to his knees and cried. The dead woman was not Rebecca White.

Jake clutched the corner of the bed and pulled himself to his feet. His hands shook nervously as he wiped the tears from his eyes. "I'm very sorry, doctor," his voice cracked. "I'm looking for Rebecca White."

Doctor Shaw escorted Jake to another room where Rebecca lay unconscious. "She's in critical condition. We don't hold much hope for her recovery."

Slowly, Jake approached the bed and looked down at Rebecca. He scanned the needle, tubes, and wires that were connected to her body. A feeling of endearment took over his entire being. Rebecca White had induced an emotion in Jake he had never felt before. He'd accepted the fact that he was in love with her, but didn't realize how much, until now. He held her hand gently. "Don't do this to me, Rebecca. Don't leave me. I love you."

Doctor Shaw left Rebecca's room and returned to the nurse's station. He was reviewing Rebecca's chart when Jake walked over and asked, "How long will she be unconscious?"

The doctor seemed to detect the tone of optimism in Jake's voice and obviously didn't want to encourage a feeling of false hope. He knew her chances were minimal, at best. He closed the metal chart and placed it gently on the counter. Looking into Jake's eyes, he explained, "Detective, she is in *very* serious condition. The person who did this used some

Indiscriminate

sort of wire and attacked her from behind. Enough force was used to partially collapse the esophagus, causing a loss of oxygen to her brain. At this time we don't know how much damage has been done. If she doesn't regain consciousness within seventy-two hours, there isn't much hope that she ever will."

Jake stared down the hall as if expecting Rebecca to walk out of her room. He knew the doctor's prognosis was correct, but he had difficulty accepting it. He couldn't bring himself to embrace or to acknowledge losing Rebecca. He reached into his shirt pocket and handed the doctor his card. In a positive tone, he said, "Please call me as soon as she wakes up."

Doctor Shaw nodded in agreement and put Jake's card in his pocket. As he walked to his office he remarked out loud, "Maybe a positive attitude *will* help."

Jake walked to the elevator and pressed the down button. As he waited for the elevator, the nurse said, "Detective Burnett, Nurse Cole is here." He turned around as Cole walked up to him.

The nurse was a big man who wore a look of confidence and conceit. "You wanted to talk to me?" he arrogantly asked.

Jake stared into Cole's eyes and detected a man who was on a power trip. His demeanor suggested he wanted to be the person who everyone had to report to and follow *his* instructions. Jake stepped closer and coldly said, "Take a good look at my face."

The big man didn't understand what Jake meant. With squinted eyes he asked, "What for?"

Jake drove his fist into the nurse's face, sending him

tumbling backwards into the wall. He bounced from the wall back at Jake and was met by another punch into the center of his chest. This proved to be the final blow. He slumped to the floor. "The reason I told you to look at my face is because I wanted you to know who did this to you. If you want to press charges, my name is Detective Jason Burnett."

Cole lay sprawled on the floor, bewildered. It was obvious he was not used to receiving such a beating. "What the hell was that for?"

The doors of the elevator opened and Jake stepped inside. Before they closed he said, "The next time a police officer calls and asks you for information, you better answer his fucking questions."

Jake returned to the squad room and went directly to Moran. "John, you said there was someone who hollered out a window and scared off the murderer. Who was it?"

Moran skimmed through the notes he took from the two officers that responded to the scene. Not seeing the man's name, he called downstairs and asked the patrolman.

He heard the rustling of paper, and then the officer responded, He looked up and turned to Jake. "His name is Walter Rollins. He's on his way here now."

Moran told Jake what the patrolman said, then sat at his desk. Noticing the expression on Jake's face, neither he, nor Mark, asked about Rebecca's condition.

Jake dialed the number for Detective Patel and talked to the officer who answered the phone. The Indian police officer had difficulty understanding Jake until he slowly said, "Manjit Patel—Detective Manjit Patel."

Indiscriminate

"Ah," he responded, then almost inaudibly, "one moment, please."

Within thirty seconds, Detective Patel answered. "Detective Burnett, was the fingerprint I sent you helpful?" For some reason his English was almost perfect, or at least much more understandable than the first time they had spoken.

"Detective Patel, I have some more questions if you have the time."

"No problem, Detective, what can I do for you?"

"We've found a fingerprint with a distinctive scar and it matched the print from the murderer you were looking for. I was hoping you could fax me everything you have on the murders in India

"Detective Burnett, I have compiled a large folder of notes that spanned a two-year investigation, but they are written in Sanskrit. I will have them transposed into English, and then fax them to you. It will take three days."

Patel's voice was enthusiastic and Jake sensed this case consumed a large part of Patel's life. He could feel the churning in the Indian detective's mind as Jake relayed the information he had uncovered.

"This case is officially closed, but I would transpose the notes personally. This is an evil man," Patel said, "I will do everything in my power to help you find him." He paused a moment, and in a dark and solemn tone, he added, "This man is the devil's servant. Do not underestimate him."

"I will take head of your warning, Detective Patel, and between your police department and mine, we'll get this son-of-a-bitch."

Howard Olsen

Mark stared at Jake from across the desk and Jake knew what was on his partner's mind.

"She's unconscious," Jake said, his voice cracking with emotion. "She's real bad, Mark."

Before Mark could respond he looked up and saw an elderly man standing in the doorway of the squad room. He motioned to Jake with a nod, and when Jake looked over his shoulder, he knew it was Walter Rollins.

Jake rushed to greet him and ushered him to his desk. Without hesitation, Jake asked, "Did you see the man who attacked the woman?"

"Nope," Rollins replied confidently.

Jake held a perplexed expression and was in no mood for guessing games. "The patrolmen said you witnessed the attack, did you see who attacked the woman or not?"

"Yup," Rollins said, "but it ain't no man. It was another woman."

Jake sat back in his chair and stared at the old man. He had a problem believing a woman could commit these murders in such a brutal way. "How do you know it was another woman?"

The old man looked at Jake and sported a toothless smile. "I'm *old*," he said. "I ain't dead." He fumbled for a cigarette. "I still remember the difference, ya know."

The statement about the murderer being a woman caused Mark to stand and approach Walter Rollins. Right behind Mark, stood John Moran. "How can you be so sure?" Mark asked. "It was dark and you were looking out a window from across the street."

"I got 20-20," Rollins replied. "She was wearing one of

Indiscriminate

them short miniskirts—red, I think—and I could see right up her skirt. She had long red hair and was wearing high heels. It was a woman, all right."

"That's why it's been so hard to catch the son-of-a-bitch," Mark said, "We've been chasing our asses around in circles because we *assumed* it was a man."

Jake thanked Walter Rollins for the information and told John to take his statement.

John escorted the old man to his desk and began typing everything into the computer.

"Son-of-a-bitch!" Jake hammered as he picked up the telephone and called Doctor Kessler. He told Kessler about the new evidence and asked his opinion of the murderer being a woman.

"Yes," the doctor answered, "as I've already explained, this type of strangulation wouldn't necessarily have to be caused by someone who has a lot of strength. A woman wouldn't have been my first choice, but it certainly is possible."

Jake's train of thought about the murderer had come to a standstill. He was back at square one, and the thought of the murderer packing up and moving on caused him more anguish than he thought he could endure. The vision of Rebecca lying in the hospital raced through his mind and he knew if he didn't find the murderer soon, he never would.

Morning came and went. Jake made several calls to the hospital, and each time he was told the same thing—there was no change. Rebecca was still unconscious.

As other detectives reported for their watch, each and every one gave Jake words of encouragement about Rebecca.

They all said the same thing: "Don't worry, Jake, she'll be okay."

Jake's anxiety reached its boiling point. "Mark, I'm going to the hospital." He walked out of the squad room.

He drove out of the police parking lot and sped toward the Riley Parking Plaza. The feeling of the warm air hitting his face was refreshing and cleared his mind. He decided to find Cameron Baird before going to the hospital and aimed the Vette in the direction of Palmer Cove, one of Baird's favorite hangouts.

Turning right onto Congress Street he drove to the end and parked facing the chain link fence. Baird was standing with some friends when Jake drove up and immediately walked over to greet him.

Standing at the driver's door of the Corvette, he said, "I got something for ya, Jake, and it's real good."

Jake could never get used to the junkie's appearance. As he was talking, Jake noticed the top of his greasy hair down to his dirty and torn sneakers.

"It's a chick," he said confidently. "The one doing all the murders is a chick."

"That's old news, Cam." Jake's tone was icy. "What else have you heard?"

Baird nervously began, "Jake, when the murderer dumped the woman in the Collins Cove Park, he was parked in front of the main entrance. The murderer must have had the body of the woman in the trunk because it was left open while the body was dragged into the park." Baird glanced nervously over his shoulder then back down at Jake. "Another woman was driving past and saw her with the trunk of her car open

Indiscriminate

and thought she had broken down. She stopped to help and got murdered, too."

Driving to the hospital, Jake wondered how a street junkie like Cameron Baird knew detailed information about what happened that morning. Deciding to find out exactly how Baird knew these things, he turned around at the Congress Street Bridge and sped back to the park. He slid to a stop as Baird looked over his shoulder at the oncoming Corvette and then jumped back.

Jake leaped over the driver's side door and walked toward Baird, his face etched in hatred. *How is it that this fucking junkie knows details about the murderer that I don't?* He wondered as he approached Baird. Jake stood directly in front of him. Softly, and with a no-nonsense tone, he said, "I want to know the name of the reporter who gave you this information. And I'm only asking once."

Baird's legs began to shake. The tone in Jake's voice and the expression on his face said it all. If he didn't tell Jake what he wanted to know, he would take the beating of his life. Without hesitation, he blurted out, "Rob Cunney... His name is Rob Cunney."

Jake's expression turned even colder. He took a step closer to Baird. "Where is he?"

"He works at the Salem Evening News." Baird's voice was laced with fear.

"Where is he right now?"

With shaking hands, Baird pointed toward the small convenience store. "He's in there. He just went in to buy cigarettes."

Jake drove to the convenience store and parked. Waiting

for the reporter to come out, he thought of Rebecca lying in the hospital and his mind raced through all the times they were together. The thought of those times coming to an end hung heavy in his heart.

A man walked out of the store and opened a package of cigarettes. Jake suspected it was Rob Cunney. As the reporter walked to his car, Jake strolled up behind him and asked him his name.

"Who wants to know?" Came an arrogant reply.

Jake held open his jacket and displayed his badge.

"What can I do for you, Detective?"

"Are you Rob Cunney?" Jake asked.

"Yes," replied Cunney, conceit lacing his tone. "I'm very busy. What can I do for you?"

"For starters," said Jake, "you can tell me how the hell you know so much about the murder at Collins Cove Park."

"I'm a news reporter, Detective." His tone was overconfident. "I can't divulge my sources. It's taken me years to develop a complex network to gather information, and that network is privileged."

Anger and resentment stirred in the pit of Jake's stomach. He was in no mood to listen to the reporter's bragging. "I can appreciate your situation, Mr. Cunney, but this is a serial murder investigation. I need to know where you get your information."

The reporter looked at Jake and shrugged. In a smug and confident tone, he simply said, "No can do, sorry."

Jake stood eye to eye with a man who could possibility help him find the murderer and his blood began to boil. "I won't ask you again," Jake warned, his blood boiling.

Indiscriminate

"Good!" Cunney retorted. "Then we have nothing else to talk about." He turned his back to Jake and leaned over to unlock the door of his car.

Jake's anger transformed into rage and he grabbed Cunney by both sides of his head, thrusting him forward. The reporter's forehead smashed through the driver's side window. Tiny cubes of glass spewed onto the front seat of the car and into the air.

Jake pulled Cunney from the window and threw him to the ground. "I told you I wouldn't *ask* you again."

The reporter rolled over onto his back. Then he sat up and leaned against another car.

Jake stood, unyielding, "Answer the fucking question."

Cunney lay against the car, his hands clutched to his head in an attempt to stop the blood from flowing onto his shirt. "I'm a professional," he stammered. "I can't divulge my sources."

Taking a step closer, Jake repeated himself in a low and menacing tone. "I won't ask you again."

Remembering what happened the first time he heard Jake say that, the reporter said, "I don't have anybody. No underground network, no sources, no anything. I have two police scanners, one in my car and one at home."

Jake looked down at a pathetic man who presented himself as a professional. "You mean you're nothing more than a fucking ambulance chaser?"

Stumbling to his feet, Cunney's voice was cracking with embarrassment as he began explaining to Jake how he gathered information. "Once I hear a report on the scanner, I rush to the scene and walked among the officers with a hidden tape recorder. I record everything that is said between the police officers. I even heard something about another woman being attacked and that she was still alive, but I didn't get the whole story."

Jake opened the door of his car and sat behind the wheel. With a cold stare, he said, "If you want to file charges, my name is Detective Jason Burnett."

He drove to the hospital and parked in the emergency parking lot. Walking to the elevator, he noticed people sitting in the waiting room and noticed their solemn expressions. Seeing the pain on their faces while waiting for a loved one that had been hurt, he quickened his pace to see Rebecca.

As the elevator doors opened Jake stepped out and saw Doctor Shaw and Nurse Cole standing at the nurse's station. Both men turned as Jake approached and Cole's face turned pasty white. Not wanting another confrontation with Jake, he told the doctor he would be in the break room and walked away.

"How is she?" was Jake's only greeting to the doctor.

Standing silent and wearing a serious expression, Shaw motioned for Jake to follow him to the end of the hallway to sit down.

Jake sensed the news he was about to hear was not good. His breathing became rapid and irregular. The thought of losing Rebecca tore into his heart.

He put his hand on the doctor's shoulder and pulled him to a stop. "Did she die?" Jake's voice cracked.

"Detective," the doctor said, "Please sit down."

"I don't want to sit down," barked Jake. "Tell me what happened."

Indiscriminate

Doctor Shaw stood face to face with Jake and spoke in a soft tone. "She went into cardiac arrest shortly after you left. The extensive injuries coupled with the severe emotional trauma she suffered caused her heart to shut down... to stop. We got her heart working again and have her on artificial breathing, but the chance that she will recover is not very good."

Jake slowly turned and walked down the hall to Rebecca's room. Sitting in a chair next to the bed, he held her hand gently. "Don't leave me," he said, "I love you."

Twelve

Jake stayed with Rebecca for most of the afternoon and talked to her as if she could hear everything he said. If there was a chance she could hear him, he wanted her to know he was there. The pain and remorse in Jake's heart slowly turned to rage. His temper had never been deemed mild, but now it was becoming hostile and his quest to find the murderer had multiplied ten-fold.

It was almost 6:00 in the afternoon when Jake left the hospital and returned to the police station. He walked into entered the squad room and saw John Moran with the telephone to his ear, scribbling notes.

Jake walked to his desk just as Moran hung up the phone. "Jake!" he said in a loud whisper.

Jake looked over at the detective and saw him excitedly waving a piece of paper over his head. He was not in the mood for guessing games and the frown on his face made

Indiscriminate

that fact obvious to Moran, who stood and hurried to show him the new information he had.

Handing Jake his notes, Moran said, "That was Detective Patel. He said there was a witness in Salem, India who swears the murderer was a woman."

Jake began reading Moran's notes but could hardly decipher the handwriting. "Your penmanship sucks. I can't read anything you wrote."

Moran snatched the paper from Jake's hands and read, "Patel said there was a witness who saw a woman running from the fourth murder. She ran to her car and sped away. The witness said she had long red hair and was wearing a red mini skirt and high heels."

"What else?" Jake barked.

Moran scanned the paper. "When I told him about our witness, he went into a rage. He said he wanted to pursue the murderer as a woman, but his captain wouldn't allow him to take that approach. His captain said that there was no way a woman could commit a murder in such a brutal way. He said he's ashamed of himself for not pursuing the case the way he should have."

"Where's Mark?" Jake asked.

"Jake, Mark left a short time ago and wants you to call him as soon as you got back to the station. Jake. He's concerned about Rebecca," Moran said. "We all are."

Jake called Mark and told him that the next seventy-two hours would determine if Rebecca would recover. Mark could hear the remorse in Jake's voice and knew this was not the time to hash over her condition. He simply said, "She's strong, Jake. She's gonna pull through."

Howard Olsen

"Jake, Bill Stoughton was in the squad room most of the afternoon, and was trying to pull information from me and Moran. He asked about the fingerprints and the witness and seemed to be looking for anything we had. I think the captain sent him on the fishing trip."

"He grilled Moran?" Jake's question was laced with concern. He still wasn't sure if Moran could keep the information quiet.

"Jake, Moran's answer to everything Stoughton asked was… That turned out to be a dead end." I was kinda proud of the way Moran handled the situation."

"What about Reins? Did he ask where I was?"

"Yes," said Mark, "he understood why you were at the hospital and seemed to have genuine concern for Rebecca. He called the florist and ordered a fruit basket to be delivered to her room."

"Mark, I'm going home to shower and then I'm going back to the hospital. "I'll see you in the morning."

Jake wanted to thank Captain Reins for the fruit basket he sent Rebecca. He walked past Moran, who was still making calls and scribbling notes, and asked, "Is Stoughton still in the captain's office?"

"No, he left about four o'clock, but he asked a million questions." Moran paused. "He asked about everything from the fingerprints to Rebecca's condition. I didn't tell him anything."

Jake thanked the detective and walked into Reins' office.

He opened the door and noticed the captain was on the

telephone and turned to leave. Reins motioned for him to come in then hung up the phone.

"It's nothing important," Jake said. "I just wanted to thank you for sending the gift to Rebecca."

"Jake, sit down," Reins motioned to a chair, then added, "please."

Jake was puzzled at the captain's tone. In all the years the two men had known each other, Reins had never called him by his first name.

Jake walked across the room and sat in the chair facing his captain. "John said that Stoughton had left," Jake said, "how's he feeling?"

Reins stared idly at the blotter on his desk as though he was trolling for something to say. He folded his hands and sat forward. "To be honest, Bill Stoughton is becoming a pain in the ass. He's here 24-7 and is always giving his opinion, or profile as he calls it, and everything he says and does is the opposite of what you are saying."

Jake was confused and didn't understand why the captain's opinion of Bill Stoughton had changed. He had defended the profiler many times and always seemed to be in his corner. "Captain, why don't you tell him to leave?"

Reins stood and walked to the window. Staring out over the parking lot he explained, "In the beginning of all this, Bill Stoughton was a valuable asset to the investigation, or so I thought. His evaluation of the murderer made sense. Then when his life was threatened, he stayed on to help. I begged him to back off out of concern for his safety, and when he was almost murdered… well, I couldn't find the words to tell him I didn't want him anymore."

Jake sat quietly while Reins vented his frustrations and couldn't understand why he was confiding in him. Had the bad blood between them passed? Jake could only hope it had. Calmly, he asked, "Do you want me to tell him?"

Reins placed both hands on the windowsill and leaned forward. "Are you going to talk to him the same way you talked to the reporter?" His tone was filled with frustration.

"Captain," Jake began, "the incident with the reporter got a little out of hand. He had information we need and I got it the only way I could." Jake sat straight in the chair, "Is he going to press charges?"

The captain turned and faced Jake. Folding his arms, he said, "The store owner saw everything that happened through the window and called the police. By the time a squad car got to the scene you were gone, and the reporter was sitting on the hood of his car bleeding into a towel."

Jake sat quietly, waiting for an outburst from Reins. It never came.

"Jake," the captain continued, "it took fourteen stitches to close the gash in his forehead. Staring at Jake with a blank stare, Reins said, I don't know what you said to him, but he's not pressing charges against you, or the department."

"Does that mean you want me to tell Stoughton to back off?"

"No! I'll handle Bill," Reins said. "I don't want him to feel as though we don't appreciate his contribution to this case. You certainly haven't cornered the market on diplomacy, Jake, and as much as I'm against your methods, I will admit they *do* get results."

Jake was amazed at the turnaround in Captain Reins'

Indiscriminate

personality. He talked as though there had never been friction between them and Jake was beginning to feel a newfound respect for the man who forced him to resign from the force.

"Captain," Jake's voice was filled with bewilderment, "I don't understand—"

Reins knew what Jake was trying to say, and he interrupted, his tone sincere. "I watched the way you took hold of this investigation and worked in many directions at once. You wouldn't take *no* for an answer about anything and kept coming up with information we couldn't find." The captain paused and the tone in his voice became even more apologetic, "When your girlfriend became one of the victims I realized how…well you know…how…"

"Are you trying to apologize, Captain?"

"Look, Jake, this isn't easy for a man like me. What I'm trying to say is…the bad blood between us just doesn't seem important any more…I'm gonna leave it at that."

"Is this an apology for what happened five years ago?" Jake asked again.

"No…well…yes."

Jake knew how difficult it was for Captain Reins to admit he was wrong and could feel the sincerity in his voice. "Let's set that aside until we find this crazy son-of-a-bitch," said Jake, "then we'll talk about it."

Reins knew that Jake saw how difficult it was for him to apologize, and deep inside he felt a sigh of relief when Jake let him off the hook.

Motioning toward the door, Reins said, "Go back to the hospital, Jake, and take all the time you need."

Jake left the captain's office with mixed feelings of doubt, suspicion and encouragement. He didn't question the complete turnaround in Reins' personality and hoped it was permanent.

He walked across the squad room and Moran motioned for him to come to his desk. "Detective Patel called while you were in with the captain and wanted you to know that there was one other thing that they found. He said it might not be important."

Jake sat on the edge of Moran's desk. Looking down at the detective, he said, "Are you going to tell me, or not?"

"Perfume," said Moran, "Patel said there was a heavy scent of perfume in the car of the last victim."

"What about the victim?" Jake asked. "Couldn't the perfume have been from her?"

"I asked him that and he said the victim wasn't wearing perfume. He also said that the perfume was overwhelming—thick and sweet to the point that it almost made his eyes water."

"There was no mention of a scent of perfume in the car at Collins Cove," said Jake. "Talk to the patrolmen and ask them if they smelled perfume in the car." He walked toward the door and, without looking back at Moran, said, "I'll be at the hospital."

When he drove out of the parking lot he noticed Bull Reins standing in front of the full-length window of his office. He couldn't help but wonder why the captain's personality had completely changed. 'I hope he doesn't go back to his old disposition,' he thought.

Jake parked in the hospital parking lot and walked

Indiscriminate

through the emergency room to the elevators, he stepped in the elevator and pushed number five. When the doors opened he walked out into the main entrance of ICU and bumped into Nurse Cole.

"She didn't have a badge," Cole said, backing up with his hands held in a defensive position. "I told her to go downstairs and register, then I would let her in."

Jake looked at Cole as he backed up and spewed something about *her* not having a badge. He didn't know what the nurse was referring to, and he took a step closer. "What the hell are you talking about?"

"Your partner," Cole pointed in the direction of the stairwell, "she's right over there."

Jake turned and looked down the hall toward the stairwell just in time to see the door closing. Turning back to Cole, he said, "My partner isn't a woman."

The look on both men's face was bewilderment. Jake looked at Nurse Cole, then back down the hall to the stairwell. All of a sudden he knew what was happening. The smell of sickening sweet perfume filled the air. He broke into a full run down the hall toward Rebecca's room. As he ran, the thought of what he might find raced through his mind. When he reached the door he turned and hollered back to Cole, "Call the police and get me some backup. Tell them to get down here right away."

Cole immediately picked up the phone and began dialing, all the while watching Jake as he rushed into Rebecca's room.

Standing just inside the door, Jake looked at Rebecca, his chest pounding with fear. He was unable to move and his hands shook like Jello in a bowl. Fearful visions raced through his mind until he heard the beeps of the machine Rebecca was connected to indicating she was still alive.

Jake turned and rushed down the hall toward the stairwell. As he ran past Nurse Cole, he hollered, "Stay with Rebecca till I get back."

He ran down the stairs two at a time, all the while the scent of sickening sweet perfume filled his nostrils. He rushed through the emergency room and out into the parking lot. He looked to his right then his left, but couldn't see anyone. He walked among the parked cars with the hope that the murderer was still there. She wasn't.

Jake went back into the hospital and stood in front of the elevator. Waiting for the doors to open, he noticed an old man sitting in a wheelchair in the hall. "Did you see a woman run past here?" he asked.

With trembling hands, the old man pointed in the direction of the hospital's main entrance. This indicated to Jake that she left the building through an exit that was on the other side of the building and there was no way he was going to find her tonight. "Shit!" he shouted.

Jake returned to Rebecca's room and looked at Nurse Cole. Pointing to the telephone, he said, "Get me an outside line."

Cole lifted the receiver and dialed nine, then handed Jake the phone.

Jake dialed the number for the squad room with the hopes Moran was still there. When Moran answered, Jake let out a sigh of relief. "I want a uniformed officer here right away," he barked. "I want someone in uniform here around the clock."

Moran acknowledged Jake's order and asked what had happened. "That son-of-a-bitch was here! He tried getting to Rebecca again! I want this motherfucker, John…I want him real bad!"

"Jake, Doctor Kessler called and said he had permission from Rachael Nickels' family to exhume her body. The body had already been exhumed and he'll be doing the autopsy in the morning. "He said he would like you to be there, Jake."

"I'll call him in the morning," said Jake. "What else did he say?"

"He said he got the results back from Ohio, and their findings were the same as his. He said there was no mistake."

Jake hung up, sat on the edge of the bed and held Rebecca's hand. Realizing Nurse Cole was still in the room, Jake got up and walked to face him. Cole's instinct was to back up into a defensive posture until he heard the soft tone in Jake's voice. "Thank you for not allowing that woman in here, you saved Rebecca's life."

"I didn't want another ass-kicking from you," Cole said, "and I almost let her in." With a confused expression, he added, "There was something about her that told me not to. I don't know what it was, just something inside telling me to send her downstairs to register."

"I want a description," Jake said. "I want to know everything you saw, what she looked like, what she wore, what she said. I even want to know *your* personal impression of this woman."

"She was definitely not my type," Cole said, "not too good looking, but she had a pretty nice body."

Jake looked at the nurse with an irritated expression. He didn't want to hear about Cole's sex life and made that fact obvious with an intense stare.

Cole knew his remark aggravated Jake and immediately changed his tone. "She was tall, almost as tall as you, and weighed about 150 pounds. She wore a ton of makeup and too much perfume."

"Did she touch anything?" asked Jake.

"She was wearing gloves," replied Cole, "but there was something else about her that stood out."

Jake looked at the nurse. "Are you going to tell me, or do I have to guess?"

"Her hair," Cole said, "it wasn't real hair."

"A wig?" Jake asked.

"Yes, but it was very unusual. I mean it was long, straight, and appeared to be expensive…"

Cole's voice trailed off and Jake blurted, "But what? What the hell are you trying to say?"

"What I'm trying to say is it looked like it was *dyed* red. I don't know of any woman who would dye an expensive wig. Do you?"

If Cole's observation were right, this information would either shed some light, or add more complexity to the confusion.

Cole walked out of the room and Jake sat with Rebecca. The events of the past two months raced through his mind and he felt more confused than ever.

Within ten minutes a uniformed police officer walked

into the room and stood at the door. Jake looked over his shoulder and saw it was the young rookie. "Don't leave this room for *any* reason," Jake said as he walked past the rookie. "I don't care what happens outside this room. You stay with her."

The officer acknowledged Jake's instructions with a nod, and sat in chair in the corner of the room facing the door. "You can count on me."

Jake walked to the nurse's station and waited for John Moran. He waited less than two minutes when the doors of the elevator opened and Moran and Mark stepped out. Their expressions were filled with concern and compassion. "Is she all right?" were Mark's first words.

"Yes," Jake answered, "thanks to Nurse Cole."

The three men talked at the end of the hall and Jake told them to go to the main entrance and talk to the receptionist. He also told them to talk to the entire staff and find out if any of them were outside within the past fifteen or twenty minutes. "Maybe someone was outside having a cigarette when the killer ran past."

Both men stepped into the elevator and Jake said, "I'll be with Doctor Kessler for most of the morning. I'll let you know what he finds."

The doors of the elevator closed and Jake walked down the stairs to see if there was anything the murderer might have dropped. There wasn't. He decided to drive home and get some rest if he could, but didn't think he'd be able to sleep. He kept thinking about Rebecca.

He pulled into his driveway and couldn't help thinking about Rebecca. His heart was filled with pain and he couldn't shake the feeling. The vision of losing Rebecca overwhelmed him and he couldn't bear the thought of being without her.

Jake stretched out on the sofa and immediately fell into a deep sleep.

The night came and went in what seemed like seconds and he awoke at 6:00 in the morning. He stood and stretched as he walked into the kitchen to make a pot of coffee. As he started the machine he thought, *I feel so guilty that I was able to sleep so soundly while Rebecca's was in the hospital fighting for her life?* He finished his cup of coffee, and then at 6:20 a.m., he walked out the door and drove to Boston to meet Doctor Kessler.

Jake pulled into the parking lot at the ME's office at the same time as Kessler. Both men walked up the stairs without saying a word. They walked through the lobby and took the elevator down to room three.

Kessler told Jake to make some coffee while he got the body of Rachael Nickels. Jake agreed, and walked to the coffeepot. He thought, *It's bad enough watching an autopsy, but to watch when the body has been exhumed is even worse.* Kessler wheeled in the gurney with Rachael Nickels covered with a plastic sheet. Depressed, he sat at Kessler's desk until the autopsy was finished.

Doctor Kessler removed his gloves and mask and washed his hands. He poured himself a cup of coffee and sat at his desk next to Jake. "This clinches it. Rachael Nickels died the same way as the others. It is my opinion that they all died by the same hand."

Jake looked at the body laying on the gurney, then back to Kessler. "There's no doubt?" Jake asked.

Indiscriminate

"None." Kessler responded as he walked over to Rachael Nickels and motioned for Jake to come and look at the rope burn around her neck.

Jake looked at the circular ring around her throat and Doctor Kessler turned her onto over onto her stomach. Jake stared at the portion on the back of her neck that had been shaved. Kessler showed Jake how the killer used the rope to drag and position his victim. "Notice how it disappears into the hair line," he said. "This is an indication that he dragged his victims face down."

The two men sat and talked for over an hour. Jake told Kessler what happened to Rebecca and how the murderer tried to enter her room by telling the nurse that she was a police officer.

Kessler sat with a confused expression and Jake asked him what was wrong. "I wouldn't have guessed it was a woman," he said. "I have trouble believing it wasn't a man."

"You said the murderer wasn't necessarily strong," Jake's tone was puzzled, "so why not a woman?"

"The savageness of the murders. Usually women don't commit such brutal crimes. They use a gun, poison or sometimes a knife. But this...this is pure evil."

Jake left Kessler sitting at his desk and drove back to the hospital. As he drove, something bothered him, but he couldn't figure out what it was. *Something's not right. It's right in front of me, but I can't put my finger on it.*

He walked through the emergency room and took the elevator to the fifth floor. Stepping out of the elevator, he was greeted by Doctor Shaw. "I've got good news," Shaw said. "She opened her eyes and has shown steady improvement.

Howard Olsen

I don't want you to get your hopes up, but this is a positive thing."

Jake's eyes popped open to the size of dinner plates and he felt them tear up. He immediately walked toward Rebecca's room, but the doctor stopped him. "She's not awake," Shaw said, "and I don't want you trying to wake her. She can't talk and I don't want you to ask her questions."

Jake felt as though a huge weight had been lifted from his shoulders. He smiled and let out a sigh of relief. This was short lived when Doctor Shaw explained that it was common for someone to go in and out of consciousness with the type of injury Rebecca had suffered. "I don't want to give you any false hopes," the doctor said. "She's in very serious condition and the prospect of her recovering is still a long way off. She's not out of the woods yet, Detective."

Jake heard what the doctor said, but couldn't conceive the thought that Rebecca would not recover. In his heart he believed she *would* recover and he wouldn't entertain any other thought.

Walking toward Rebecca's room, Jake turned and said, "You gotta believe, doc, you just gotta believe."

He told everyone in the room to go home and said he would stay the night. As they filed out, everyone looked back at Jake and smiled smiles of confidence that Rebecca would make a full recovery.

He pulled a chair close to the bed and noticed the fruit basket Captain Reins had sent. He opened the cellophane and took out an apple. When a nurse walked into the room to check the IVs, Jake asked her for something to read.

"I have just the thing," she said, and reached into the

Indiscriminate

pocket of her hospital coat. Handing Jake a book, she added, "You're going to love this."

Jake thanked the nurse and sat back in the chair to read to Rebecca. He looked at the impressive blue cover and read the name of the book aloud, *William's Island*.

Thirteen

In the morning Jake greeted a uniformed police officer at the nurse's station. "Captain Reins assigned me to Rebecca White," he said, "I'll be here until 4:00 p.m."

Jake thanked the officer and stepped into the elevator. The short descent to the first floor had him wondering why Captain Reins' demeanor had changed. He couldn't understand why his attitude toward him had inverted so drastically and decided to ask him.

It was nearly 8:00 a.m. when Jake walked into the squad room. His first responsibility was to ask his two partners if they had uncovered anything new during the night. They hadn't.

He sat at his desk facing Mark, reached into the folder, and spread the photographs of the victims across his desk.

John sat in a chair next to Jake and noticed his intense expression as he stared at the photos. "What is it Jake?" he asked.

Indiscriminate

"There's something here—right in front of me—and I can't find it. I know the answer is in these photos."

Mark stood and walked around to Jake's desk. Standing behind him he studied the pictures, also. "They all look the same. What makes you think there's something different in the photos?"

Jake clenched his teeth and slowly shook his head. "I don't know, but I can feel something is different. I just have to find it."

Lucy walked up behind Jake and gently placed her hand on his shoulder. Leaning down so that her face was touching his, she said, "I'm sorry to hear about Rebecca. I hope everything will…"

Jake covered her hand with his. "She's going to be fine, Lucy…thanks."

"Captain Reins is in his office," she said. "He wants to see you right away."

Leaving the photos spread across his desk, Jake went to the captain's office. When he walked in Reins was sitting with Mayor Sweeney and both men greeted Jake with a half-smile. He sat in a chair beside the mayor, facing Reins, and waited for them to speak.

"I talked to Doctor Shaw and he told me that Rebecca has shown slight improvement," Sweeney said. "I hope everything will be all right."

"I've heard somewhere that when a person is unconscious their subconscious can sometimes hear what's going on around them," said Jake. "I spent the night reading to her and I believe she heard me. I read her an entire book and I have *no* doubt she knew I was there." Jake paused and looked at Captain Reins. "Thank you for the fruit basket. I appreciate it."

"Maybe I'm not the cold hearted son-of-a-bitch everyone thinks I am," Reins said with a hint of humor, "but don't let that nasty rumor get out."

The lighthearted comment from the captain brought a burst of laughter from Jake and Sweeney. The ice had finally been broken. Jake felt comfortable and his mind seemed to have been set free of the animosity and contempt that had festered between them over the past five years. Jake still felt the need to talk about incident that happened between him and Reins so many years earlier, but this was not the time. In any event, he still couldn't understand the sudden and complete turnaround in Reins' disposition toward him.

Jake explained everything he was working on and told them about the information from Detective Patel. He went on to say that Patel wanted to pursue the investigation as the murderer being a woman, but his captain pushed in the direction of a man being the killer.

"What's *your* gut feeling, Jake?" the mayor asked.

"All the evidence, including the witnesses, indicates it *was* a woman." Jake said with a hint of doubt in his voice.

"That's not what the mayor asked," said Reins. "He asked what your *gut* feeling is."

Jake sat and pondered an intelligent answer. He fumbled for the right words when Sweeney said, "I'm not asking you for the name of the murderer, Jake. I'm only asking for your opinion."

"Yes," Jake finally said, "it could definitely be a woman. But there's something that bothers me and I can't put my finger on it. I believe the answer is in the photographs of the victims." Jake stared at both men with an expression of doubt. "Doctor Kessler said it could very well be a woman, but he has difficulty believing a woman would be this brutal. A garrote to commit murder is generally a weapon used by a man – not a woman."

Two knocks came from the door and then it was pushed opened. Bill Stoughton walked in and sat in a chair next to Jake, acting as if it was *his* office. Jake detected a hint of frustration in the captain's expression, but he said nothing to Stoughton.

The profiler sat with his legs crossed and arms folded in front of him. The expression on his face was that of a child who was tardy for class. "Okay," he said, "bring me up to speed."

Reins looked at Jake as if to say, "I've changed my mind and you can tell him to leave, but…use some tact and diplomacy."

Jake stepped directly in front of Stoughton. Extending his arm as if to shake his hand, Jake said, "It's nice to see you again, Bill, how are you feeling?"

Stoughton reached out and shook Jake's hand and told him he was feeling much better.

Before he realized it, Jake had pulled back gently and assisted him from his chair. Jake put his arm around Stoughton's shoulder and ushered him to the door. "There's something personal I have to talk to the captain about. You don't mind, do you, Bill?"

Fumbling for words, Stoughton said, "No problem. I'll talk to you later." As he turned and opened the door, Jake saw the scar that began in the front of his throat and ended on the back of his neck, forming a perfect circle.

The vision of Bill Stoughton struggling for his life flashed through Jake's mind, and he felt an immediate surge of compassion for the man he had always considered to be a sissy. He turned and walked back to his chair, clearly upset.

Reins knew Jake had no respect for Stoughton and seemed puzzled at his expression. "What's wrong?"

"It's no secret that I don't like Bill Stoughton," Jake said, "but I can't help feeling sorry for him. He's an asshole in every aspect of the term, but I can't get the scar around his neck out of my mind. The utter terror that man was put through must have been devastating to him

Reins didn't seem to want to discuss Bill Stoughton in front of the Mayor and immediately changed the topic. "I've assigned around-the-clock protection for Rebecca," he said. "She's a possible material witness and may be able to identify the killer." He looked at Jake with a solemn expression. "There's a good chance the murderer will try again."

Jake's blood ran cold at the thought of the murderer returning to finish what she started. All of a sudden Jake felt a strong urge to return to the hospital and stay with Rebecca until she recovered. He entertained the thought of actually living in her hospital room, but knew it was impossible. He told the captain that he would be sleeping in Rebecca's room every night and there would be no need for an officer during the evening. Reins agreed.

Jake's vision of Rebecca was interrupted when Mayor Sweeney asked, "You said that you felt the answer was in the photographs of the victims, Jake. Why do you say that? There must be a reason."

Jake explained that he didn't know why, but felt the answer was in the photos. "I'm missing something," he said, "I can't put my finger on it, but it's there. I *know* it is."

Lucy walked into the office clutching an envelope to her chest. In her eyes was a look of fear that could only mean one thing—another note from the killer.

Gently placing the envelope on the captain's desk, she looked at Jake with an alarmed expression. Without saying anything, she turned and walked out of the office.

Reins stared down at the envelope that had his name on it. It was addressed to the police station, and as before, was written in charcoal.

He lifted the envelope and held it in Jake's direction then toward the mayor, then placed it back on his desk as if he didn't want to know what it said.

"Are you going to open it, or am I?" Jake asked.

Slowly, Reins opened the bottom drawer of his desk and took out a pair of rubber gloves. He stretched the tight latex over his hands and carefully slit across the top of the envelope with a letter opener. He let the note drop out onto on the top of his desk and gently unfolded the paper.

Jake and Mayor Sweeney gathered behind the captain's desk and read the note, all the while knowing that the precaution of using the rubber gloves was for naught.

CR. YOU'RE BEGINNING TO ANGER ME.
BACK OFF AND LEAVE ME ALONE.
I TOLD YOU THIS WOULD BE OVER SOON.

Howard Olsen

"Maybe you better get Stoughton back in here," Sweeney said, "he's going to want to see this."

"No!" Jake blurted, "I don't want anyone knowing about this note. We all know there aren't going to be any fingerprints on the paper or the envelope, but I want it dusted and then I want a copy."

Jake left Reins' office and wanted to tell Mark and John about the note, but when he walked into the squad room he saw Stoughton sitting on the corner of John's desk drinking a cup of coffee. "Everything okay, Jake?" Stoughton asked.

Jake nodded in a positive gesture and sat at his desk. Turning back to Stoughton and pointing to the door, he said, "Bill, we have some sensitive matters to discuss. Do you mind?"

Stoughton obviously took offense at Jake's comment. "I'm part of this investigation, Jake—"

Jake broke into Stoughton's rebuttal in mid-sentence by saying, "Not anymore."

"We'll see about that," he said, and walked hastily into the captain's office.

In less than two minutes Stoughton came out of Reins' office and walked to the small sink that was situated beside the coffeepot. He washed and dried his cup as he always did and set it down on the counter.

The three detectives watched as Bill Stoughton slowly walked to the door of the squad room, then turned and said, "The captain said I'm still part of this case, Jake, and he's going to fill me in later."

Jake shrugged his shoulders in an unconcerned manner. "Don't bet on it."

Indiscriminate

Stoughton stormed out of the exit and down the stairs, all the while mumbling how ungrateful the department was. It was obvious he understood that his involvement in this case had come to an end, and he wasn't happy about it.

"Christ," said Mark, "even when he's pissed off he acts like a little homemaker! If it were me sitting someplace and I was told to leave, the *last* thing I would do is wash the fucking dishes."

"Enough about Bill Stoughton, let's get back to work." Jake said.

The mental strain had taken its toll and by the end of the day everyone was exhausted. Even John Moran, who spent most of his life in the squad room, wanted to go home.

"Let's call it a day," said Jake, "we'll pick it up in the morning."

Jake sat at his desk, his eyes focused on the photographs of the victims. When his two partners walked to the door, Mark stopped and turned to Jake. "Tell Rebecca I asked about her," then shut the door quietly.

Jake studied the photos and the scar on each of the victim's necks. He stared at the ugly wound that made a perfect circle, but still couldn't find what was bothering him. "It's here somewhere," he said out loud.

Jake went home, showered and then sat on the sofa staring at nothing. He noticed the VCR was still on and picked up the remote and pressed play. Rebecca had left the *Horse Whisperer* in the machine and Jake watched it with tear-filled eyes, remembering the last time he and Rebecca were together. He watched the movie for a short time before leaving for the hospital. His mind ran in several different directions when he turned onto Highland Avenue. He didn't notice the light had turned red. Without even attempting to slow down, he made the left turn and heard tires screeching from both directions as oncoming cars slid to a stop.

******

Jake walked into ICU and was immediately met by Doctor Shaw. "Any change?" Jake asked.

The doctor said there had been no improvement, but that she hadn't gotten any worse. "There have been no changes in either direction, Detective," he said, "and that isn't necessarily a bad sign. Her chance of recovery has doubled since she was brought in, and to be honest, I can't understand why. When I first examined her I didn't give her much of a chance, but now I'm not so sure."

"Well I'm sure." Jake said and walked toward Rebecca's room.

When he entered the room, he saw the young rookie sitting in a chair reading the book that Jake had left. The officer was so engrossed in the novel that he didn't notice Jake walk in.

"How do you like the book?" Jake asked, breaking the silence.

The officer jumped to his feet and set the book on the table. "I've been here since four o'clock and I just wanted something to read," he explained nervously.

"No problem," said Jake, "It's almost nine o'clock now. You can go back to your regular duties. I'll be here the rest of the night."

"I guess I'll just go home," said the rookie as he stared at the book. "This is my day off."

Indiscriminate

Jake smiled with appreciation for the help from the officer. He noticed the apparent interest he showed toward the novel. "How'd you like the book?"

"I'm only halfway through," he answered. "I couldn't set it down."

Jake walked to the table and picked up the book and tossed it to the officer, "Here, this will give you something to do tonight. You're gonna love it."

The officer thanked Jake and left walked out of the room.

Jake slid a chair close to the bed and made himself comfortable. It didn't take long before his eyes became heavy and he fell asleep with Rebecca's hand clasped in his.

At 6:00 a.m. a nurse came into the room with a cup of coffee for Jake. She gently set it down on the table and turned to leave when Jake opened his eyes. "Thank you," he said with a smile, "I *really* need this."

He held the cup with both hands and, feeling the coffee was not very hot, he gulped it down until it was gone. When he set the cup back on the table, the same nurse returned walked back into the room and told him he had a phone call at the nurse's station. Jake kissed Rebecca lightly on her forehead and left the room.

Jake answered the phone and it was Dang. He wanted to know how Rebecca was and if he and Mary could visit her. Jake explained her condition and told him she couldn't have any visitors for the next few days. "There's a police officer assigned to her during the day," Jake said, "and I spend the night in her room."

"When do you sleep?" asked Dang.

Howard Olsen

"I get a little sleep during the night, but not much." Jake's eyes were heavy as he stood waiting for the police officer who was assigned to be with Rebecca during the day. When Dang offered to spend the day with Rebecca, Jake eagerly accepted his proposal. Tired as he was, he knew that when the evening came he would be completely exhausted. Jake trusted Dang with his life and felt confident that Rebecca would be safe under the watchful eye of his friend.

"I'll be there within the hour. You or Rebecca need anything?" Dang asked.

"No, we'll be fine," Jake replied, and hung up.

Jake dialed the number for the squad room and was surprised to hear John Moran answer the phone. "Christ, John," he said, "you gotta get a life. Don't you ever go home?"

"Jake! CAIN got another hit! It came through at 5:30 this morning, and it's *definitely* our perp."

The adrenaline shot through Jake like a racecar on its last lap of the Indy 500. "Where?" he asked.

"Oregon," John said, "there were two identical murders in Salem, Oregon seven years ago."

"I'm waiting for Dang," Jake said, "I'll be there in an hour."

There was a pause on the other end of the phone and Jake thought he had lost the connection with Moran. "Are you still there?"

"Hold onto your ass, Jake," Moran said with excitement, "there's more."

"For Christ-sake, do I have to guess what's behind door number three, or are you going to tell me?"

"A fingerprint, Jake, they found a fingerprint on the rear

Indiscriminate

window of the second victim." Moran paused. "It's a perfect match with ours. There's no doubt. It's the same person."

Jake hung up and stared at the wall, thinking about the fingerprint. He knew it was only a matter of time before the murderer moved on because when a fingerprint was found, the killer vanished. He wondered why the killer still stayed in Salem after fingerprints were found at two of the crime scenes. The new information appeared to be one more part of the puzzle that didn't fit, and Jake knew that time was not on his side.

At 6:45 Dang stepped out of the elevator and saw Jake still standing at the nurse's station.

As he walked up to Jake, Nurse Cole stopped him. "Sorry, sir, you'll need to go downstairs and register."

Jake nodded at Cole to indicate it was all right to let Dang in. "Come on, Dang, follow me to Rebecca's room."

As they walked down the hall, Dang told Jake, "There's no need to have a police officer stay with Rebecca during the day, Jake. I'm on vacation and would be happy to sit with her." Dang put his hand on Jake's shoulder. "It'll only be for a couple of days, and when she wakes up it would be better if she saw a familiar face."

A wide and appreciative smile spread across Jake's face. "Thanks, buddy. You'll need to get familiar with the staff on duty and don't let anyone in that you don't recognize." He explained it was remote that she would try to get to Rebecca again, but he didn't want to take any chances.

Dang looked puzzled as he stepped into the room, "*She?*" he asked.

"It's a long story, but yes, all the evidence points to a female murderer."

Dang sat in the chair that Jake had slept in and Jake leaned down and kissed Rebecca softly. "I'll be back tonight," he whispered.

Jake turned to leave when the young patrolman walked into the room holding the book that Jake had given him. "I want to return your book before going on duty," he said. "I'll ask to be assigned to watch her if you want me to."

Jake smiled at the officer and thanked him for his consideration. "No need for you to stay," Jake pointed at Dang. "It's been covered."

The patrolman walked over to Dang and handed him the book. "Here's something for you to read. You're gonna love it."

Before leaving, the patrolman told Jake that, if he needed him, he would be there to help. Jake thanked him.

Turning his attention back to Dang Jake grumbled a low chuckle, "It's not one of those child psychology books. You ain't gonna like it."

Dang looked at the cover of the book with a blank stare. The expression on his face seemed to take on the look of a man who was outside his body, looking down, and watching. Jake had only seen this look from Dang one other time and that was during a violent fight on a street corner. Most people only saw Dang's passive side, but Jake knew Dang also had a dark side. His childhood held many secrets and Jake knew better than to talk about it.

As Dang studied the attractive blue cover, the intensity in his stare melted away. "I like fiction. I like to be entertained by a good action novel. Besides, this book was written by a local author."

Smiling, Jake walked out of Rebecca's room and down the hall. When he reached the elevator, he heard his name being called. Gazing in the direction of the stairwell he saw the patrolman holding the door open and motioning for Jake to take the stairs. "A little exercise won't hurt," he said with a grin.

Jake shook his head in an indication that he didn't need, or want the exercise. He looked over his shoulder at a nurse and said, "Youth, youth is wasted on the young."

She burst into laughter and Jake could hear her giggling as the doors closed and the elevator began its descent.

Jake drove the short distance back to the police station, all the while trying to make sense of the new evidence. It seemed that every time something new was uncovered it would add more confusion to the investigation.

Jake walked into the squad room and John Moran was arranging printouts from CAIN into a folder. As Jake approached the detective, he noticed the door to Captain Rains' office was open. He didn't understand why the captain would be there that early? In a puzzled tone, he asked, "Is the captain here?"

Jake's question startled Moran and he jumped in his chair. "Christ, you scared the shit out of me! Don't you ever make noise when you walk?"

Jake smiled and repeated the question "Is the captain here?"

John told Jake that he wasn't, but that Bill Stoughton had stopped in and wanted to wait for the captain in his office.

"Stoughton's in there?"

"No," Moran answered, as he continued organizing the printout from CAIN into a folder.

Jake was tired, confused and beginning to get annoyed at Moran. He slammed his hand down on the folder, "Talk to me, John."

Moran looked up at Jake and realized he had not made any sense with his answers. "Uh, sorry Jake, I'm trying to finish sorting the pages before Stoughton gets back. He strolled in just as the printouts were being printed. I didn't want him to see anything and told him to move away because everything that was being printed was classified."

"That must have pissed him off."

"It sure did. He told me that he was a key player in this investigation and I had no right to withhold information from him. Then he poured himself a cup of coffee and walked into the captain's office. That's when the shit hit the fan."

"How long was he in there?" Jake asked.

"About twenty seconds," Moran spouted, "I walked in behind him and told him to leave, and he got very upset. He informed me that if I wanted to continue my position as a detective—"

Jake interrupted, "That's when you tossed his ass out?"

"Yes, and he got *really* pissed off. He told me that by the time he finished talking to Captain Reins, I'd be lucky to have a job handing out parking tickets."

Jake could feel the concern if the detective's voice and knew he was worried about losing his job because of the friendship between Reins and Stoughton. "Not a chance,"

Jake said in a positive tone, "that asshole doesn't have that much juice with the captain, or anyone else."

"I hope you're right. He was so mad he smashed the coffee cup into the sink and broke it, then stormed out, mumbling that he'd be back."

"I'm surprised he didn't wash the fucking cup before he smashed it," Jake joked.

At nearly 7:30 Mark walked into the squad room and the three detectives gathered all the information they had. They went into an interrogation room to review everything, and each man spread the evidence he had across the table then sat down.

"Let's go over everything we know so far." Jake got up and walked to the chalkboard. "We know that seven years ago she killed two people in Salem, Organ, then two years later four more were murdered in Salem, India."

Jake stopped talking and looked over at Moran. "The way I see it, we met right after those people were murdered in Organ and India." In a mock tone Jake added, "Where the hell were you during that time, John."

Moran nervously twisted and turned in his chair. "Come on, Jake, let's get back to work. Plus, you met Dang around that time…didn't ya?"

Jake paid no attention to Moran's comment and began writing the place of each murder spree on the chalkboard; Mark read the latest report from CAIN.

"And five years later twelve more died in Salem, Massachusetts," Jake added as he finished writing.

He turned and faced his two partners. "The only common denominator we have is the fact that all the murders were committed in cities named Salem. For some sick reason, in the murderer's mind, there's a connection between them."

Jake sorted through the evidence in his mind. He knew the hangman's noose was not the murder weapon, but was left to reflect something that made sense in the demented mind of the killer. The rope was a part of the puzzle, but he couldn't find where it fit.

"Oh, for Christ sake," Moran bellowed, "he's back."

Jake and Mark looked through the glass partition and saw Bill Stoughton at the coffeepot. He was looking through the trash barrel as if he were a vagrant looking for cans he could cash in.

Moran stood as if he were going to go out into the squad room and confront Stoughton.

Jake said, "Sit down. I'll handle it." He left the interrogation room and quietly walked up behind Stoughton. "Hello, Bill, what the hell are you doing?"

Stoughton didn't hear Jake walk up behind him and jumped so hard it almost knocked the barrel over. "Christ, Jake, you almost scared the shit out of me."

"I've heard that a lot this morning," Jake said. "Now what the hell are you doing?"

Fumbling for an explanation Stoughton told Jake that he was ashamed of himself for the way he acted earlier, and was there to clean the mess he made in the sink and, to apologize to Detective Moran.

Jake glared at Stoughton intensely. Although he felt sorry for the self-proclaimed profiler, he wanted to solidify to Stoughton the fact that *he* was in charge of the investigation and he didn't want any outside help. "Bill, I realize your opinions were helpful in the beginning, but I don't think you should be involved any further." Not wanting to offend the man standing in front of him, he added. "You've put your life on the line in an attempt to help find this crazy son-of-a-bitch and I don't want to place you in any more danger."

To Jake's surprise and astonishment, Stoughton stepped up to within six inches of his face. "I'm not backing off, Burnett," he said in a low and confident tone.

Jake took a step backwards and noticed the twisted expression on Stoughton's face. His eyes were squinted and his teeth were clenched tightly.

"I'm not *asking* you to back off, Bill," Jake said with authority, "I'm *telling* you. You're out."

Stoughton's mannerism immediately changed back to the familiar effeminate tone that Jake knew. "Jake—"

Before Stoughton could finish his request, Jake said, "Sorry Bill, you're out."

Stoughton's slammed both hands into Jake's chest, sending him backward into a desk. The man Jake had always considered a sissy was remarkably strong and aggressive. He noticed the muscles in his arms were strong and rippled and seemed to materialize from nowhere.

"Holy shit!" Mark watched through the glass partition, "we better put a stop to this before Jake kills that asshole."

As the two detectives walked into the squad room, they saw Jake step up in front of Stoughton. "That one was a freebie," Jake said. "The next time you raise your hands to me I'll send you home wearing your asshole for a hat."

Stoughton's expression became even more twisted in anger at Jake's statement. He was enraged by the way Jake took over the case and excluded him from the investigation. The hard cold stare in Stoughton's eyes brought another note of surprise to Jake. The look in his eyes was as lifeless and cold as the eyes of the murder victims, and Jake shook his head to clear those thoughts from his mind.

"I'll talk to Captain Reins about this, Burnett," Stoughton said as he bolted to the door. "He'll straighten your ass out, once and for all!"

Fourteen

Jake motioned for Mark and John to go back into the interrogation room as he watched Bill Stoughton stomp down the stairs and out the door, slamming it behind him.

Jake strolled back into the interrogation room and stood in front of the blackboard and stared at the three cities named Salem. "Salem means something to the murderer. If w e can figure out what that is…"

"Maybe she kills in cities named Salem because there are so many of them," said Mark.

Jake turned to Moran, "John, I want you to feed all the names of the victims into the computer along with the dates that they were murdered. Then I want you to cross-reference Salem to all the names and dates. If there is any connection between them, we're going to find it."

Moran began gathering all the notes and printouts that had been spread over the table. "How far back do you want me to check?"

Jake placed both hands on the table and studied the notes the murderer had sent. There was a line in two of the notes that piqued his curiosity. They read: "HISTORY REPEATS ITSELF."

"Go back into history 300 or 400 years and start with Salem, Oregon, then Salem, India…"

"Three or 400 years!" Mark bellowed. "Do you think the killer has been reincarnated from some past life? What the hell are you thinking?"

"I don't think the killer *has* been reincarnated from a past life, but maybe she *thinks* she has."

"I'm on it," said Moran as he gathered up the paperwork and bolted to his computer.

Mark stared at Jake and saw a man who was at wit's end with the murders. He thought that Jake was grasping for straws and was about to tell him when he heard Captain Reins holler, "Burnett! In my office. Now."

Both detectives looked out the glass enclosure just in time to see Reins storm into his office. "What the hell did you do now, Jake?" Mark asked.

"He must have talked to Stoughton," said Jake. "I'll be right back."

Jake entered the captain's office and shut the door. He sat in a chair opposite Reins and noticed how irritated he was. "What's wrong, Captain?"

"What the fuck did you say to Bill? He was so upset I could barely understand what he was saying."

Knowing the friendship between the captain and Stoughton, Jake's first reaction was to apologize for everything he said to the profiler, but all of a sudden he realized the situation he was in and thought, *If Reins was in my position, he would have done the same thing. He wouldn't allow an outsider access to pertinent information in a serial murder case.*

"Captain," Jake said, "I realize that Stoughton is a friend of yours and you believe everything he says and does. He's put his life on the line to help with the investigation and was almost murdered." Jake stood and looked directly into the captain's eyes. Bill Stoughton is not a police officer or a qualified profiler with the FBI. He's not even affiliated with any other agency. He has no right to walk in here, at will, and look over the evidence we've uncovered. You would never allow anyone else to do that, right?"

Bull Reins sat silent, and Jake knew he had hit a nerve. He knew Reins worked by the book and would not be able to disagree with what he said.

Reins put his elbows on the desk and his face into his hands. He sat quietly for a moment. "You're right, Jake, but I can't help feeling as though I've betrayed Bill. He has been a good friend when the chips were down and I don't want him to think he's been used and then tossed aside."

"I'm working on another approach to the motive of the killer," Jake said, "and I would feel better if no one else knows what we're doing."

Slowly Reins stood from behind his desk and looked at Jake with an intense stare. He noticed Reins' hands were clenched. Pounding his fist on the top of his desk, the captain hollered, "You better not be insinuating that Bill Stoughton is involved in the murders, Burnett. Because if you are, you are out of here, and I don't give a fuck what the mayor wants."

"Captain," said Jake, "I didn't mean to insinuate that Stoughton was involved. I simply meant to say that the information we gather is not for civilians, that's all."

The captain knew Jake's motive to keep the information away from anyone outside the department was proper procedure and he couldn't argue with it.

"Jake, I realize police procedure does not include sharing it with non-departmental personal, but you *have* to use more diplomacy! You can't go around barking orders as though you're the fucking Gestapo! You know exactly what I'm talking about and I want it stopped. Show some fucking tact!"

Reins looked at Jake and waited for a response. "Well?"

As Jake walked to the door he turned and simply said, "You're right Captain, I will definitely work on more tact."

At nearly 11:00 that morning Jake received a phone call from the officer at the front desk. He said there was a woman downstairs who wanted to talk to him about the murders. Jake's heart pounded and he told the officer to send the woman up to the squad room.

As Jake waited for the woman to arrive, his mind wandered. He had visions that this woman would be the murderer and she was there to confess. He knew that thought was only a fantasy when she walked in. She was a middle-aged woman who walked with a severe limp. At first glance, she appeared to be Muslim. She wore a long black dress and her hair was cut short, highlighting the jet-black color. Her eyes were large, beautiful and filled with sorrow.

Jake ushered her to a chair that was situated next to his desk. "Is there anything I can do for you?"

Indiscriminate

She sat quietly for a moment. "My best friend died three months ago and her death was ruled a heart attack." In a thick Kuwaiti accent, she added, "Although she had heart problems, I believe she was murdered."

Jake began writing the report, but he didn't believe that the dead woman was one of the victims in the serial murders. The woman told Jake that her friend's name was Barbara Bowen and she had lived on Sylvan Street in Danvers. She had been in this country for nine years and worked at a restaurant on route 114. Her body was found in her apartment three days after she died.

"You said she was in this country for the past nine years." Jake said. "Where did she come from?"

"Kuwait," the woman answered, "we came to this country together."

Jake was puzzled. "Barbara Bowen's an American name, not Kuwaiti."

The woman's eyes filled with tears. "My friend wanted to be accepted in this country and had her name legally changed. She believed she would be more welcome with an American name."

Jake felt the pain this woman was going through, and although he didn't believe the woman's death was connected to the serial murders, he assured her that he would look into it as part of his investigation.

When the woman left the squad room, Jake called Doctor Kessler and told him everything the woman had said. "Can we find out who did the autopsy and look into it. I don't think this death is connected to the murders, but I'd like you to look into it. She has no family in Kuwait or in this country and the only person who could give permission to exhume the body just left the station. She said she would allow you to do another autopsy."

There was a pause on Kessler's end of the phone. "She's Kuwaiti and was buried three months ago, right?"

Jake answered that she was, but wanted to know what difference it made where she was from.

"I want you here for this one," Kessler said.

"Why?" Jake asked. "You don't need me there to observe."

"You want me to re-autopsy a Muslim woman who has been buried for three months, and according to you, has nothing to do with this case? I want you here."

"I don't understand why—"

Kessler interrupted Jake, "You'll know why when you get here. It will take a few days for the paperwork to go through. I'll let you know."

Still puzzled why Kessler wanted him at the autopsy, Jake agreed and hung up. He knew there was something the doctor wanted him to see, but didn't understand what it could possibly be.

The telephone rang and brought Jake back to the present. When he answered, he heard the familiar voice on the other end of the phone, "Jake," Dang said quietly, "Rebecca regained consciousness."

Without responding to Dang, Jake hung up and told Mark and John what happened at the hospital, then rushed out. He sped to the hospital, breaking every traffic law on the books and paid no attention to other motorists calling him names and giving him the one-finger-wave.

Indiscriminate

He stepped out of the elevator and was immediately greeted by Doctor Shaw. "She's conscious, Detective," he said, "but she can't talk yet. The damage and trauma to her esophagus and surrounding muscles restricts her ability to speak and I don't want you encouraging her to talk – understood?"

Jake's heart raced as the doctor stood in front of him, blocking his way to Rebecca's room. He tried sidestepping Shaw, but the doctor took hold of his arm and displayed amazing strength.

Jake stared into the doctor's eyes. He could see the concern that Shaw conveyed and he waited for the explanation that was about to come.

"The fact that she has regained consciousness is a miracle in itself, Detective, and she has an excellent chance of recovery…"

Jake could tell by the doctor's tone that there was something else he wanted to say. "But what?"

"What I'm trying to tell you is that she may never regain her voice, or at least the way it was. The damage is extensive and the only chance she has to recover her voice is not to try and use it now."

Jake slowly nodded in an indication he knew how serious her condition was. "Thanks, Doc."

Jake walked into Rebecca's room and listened to Dang reading to her. He was reading from the same book that Jake had read to her earlier, and although she was in and out of consciousness, she seemed to understand what he was saying.

Jake sat on the edge of the bed and Rebecca slowly opened her eyes. She looked at Jake and gave him a half-smile, then closed her eyes again. He knew she was going to completely recover and he made no attempt to hide this feeling. "Hurry up and get better, Rebecca," he said playfully, "I'm tired of watching the *Horse Whisperer* alone." He noticed a slight hint of a smile on her lips, and then kissed her gently on her forehead.

Dang walked to door and turned to Jake. "I'll be back at seven in the morning," he said. "You can finish reading that book to her."

Jake shot an appreciative smile at Dang and thanked him as he left. 'He's a good friend,' thought Jake.

Nightfall came and went, and Jake was awakened with a cup of coffee from the same nurse who had greeted him with coffee early the morning before. He sat quietly, staring at Rebecca and drinking his coffee when Dang walked in. "Where's mine?"

Jake glanced at his watch. "I didn't realize it was 7:00 o'clock, already."

It wasn't. It was only 6:30. Dang told Jake he couldn't sleep and thought he would stop by a little early and finish the book he started.

By the time Jake got back to the police station it was nearly 7:30 and Moran was already at his computer. He was trying to cross-reference every city with the name Salem, but couldn't find a common denominator. "No luck, Jake," he said, "but I'm still working on it."

Jake smiled and couldn't help but notice John's choice of words. *I'm still working on it.* "John, you're getting more like me every day."

"Is that a good thing?"

"Not if you're the captain, it isn't," Jake responded.

Moran burst into laughter then went back to punching commands into his computer. Jake watched as John Moran seemed to be oblivious of everything and everyone around him while he worked. His dedication and work habits were second to none, and Jake wondered why it took so long for him to realize it. *I guess Mark was right. Moran is an asset to the investigation.*

At 11:15 a.m. Doctor Kessler called. "Jake, I just finished with the autopsy on Molly Chrisp. My findings are identical with what I found on the other victims, from the electrical cord to the rope burn around her neck."

"There's no doubt she was murdered somewhere else?" asked Jake.

"The drag marks and abrasions on her body indicate she was dragged from one place to another," he said, "and the way the rope burn disappears up into the hairline on the back of her neck indicates this is how she was moved, or more appropriately, dragged."

The vision of Rebecca struggling for her life flashed through Jake's mind and he shook his head to clear his thoughts. He was worried about the murderer moving on to another city and in his heart he knew the next city to feel the wrath of terror would be a city named Salem, somewhere in the world.

"I'll have Barbara Bowen here on Thursday morning, Jake, and I want you here for her autopsy," Kessler said. "This one is going to be gruesome."

"If you've seen one, you've seen them all," said Jake. "I'll be there at eight."

Captain Reins walked through the squad room and

motioned for Jake to follow him into his office. Jake walked to the office while Reins held the door open.

"I don't want to get into a pissing contest with you, Jake," the captain said, "but the more I thought about what happened yesterday between you and Bill, the more I'm bothered by it."

Jake knew what Reins was getting at, but acted as though he didn't. "I'm sorry, Captain, I don't understand what you mean."

"You made every indication to Bill that for some reason you believe he can't be trusted. I know that if I ordered you to apologize to him it would be for naught, so I won't, but don't ever humiliate him like that again."

"I certainly didn't mean that he couldn't be trusted, Captain," Jake said. "I just don't think he should be involved as much as he is. He's not part of any law enforcement organization, and to give him free rein to any and all information is not part of this, or any other department's policy."

Reins knew Jake was right, but he had a difficult time excluding Stoughton from the investigation. "Jake, Bill Stoughton is my friend and offered to help when there we no leads. Even after he was almost murdered he continued to contribute. He put his own safety aside to help us and I want you to show him more respect than you've shown. Saying, *you're out, Bill...* Well, that just isn't good enough.

I'd like you to keep him in the loop, Jake," Reins said, "just enough to make him feel as though we still need him. He's a good man."

Jake agreed and left the office. He wanted to get back out

Indiscriminate

onto street and try and sift through what had happened. He had a strong feeling there was something he overlooked, but didn't know what it was, or where to start looking.

As the day wore on, the frustration increased and Mark and John became irritable. Mark asked John on a number of occasions if he found any cities named Salem that had a connection to the killer. Finally, John pushed back from his desk and barked, "That's the fourth time you asked me that. If you think you can find it any faster, be my fucking guest."

Jake immediately put an end to the bickering by telling them it was time to go home. "It's been a long day and I think we all need some rest," Jake said to end the bickering. "We'll pick it up in the morning."

Jake sat at his desk and watched the two detectives walk out the door. He knew the frustration had taken hold of everyone involved in the murders, and he didn't want it to escalate into continuous bickering.

Jake went home and showered and felt better now that he was convinced Rebecca was going to survive. His mind raced through the evidence that had been uncovered, but it always came to a standstill when he dwelled on the photographs of the victims. *The answer is in the photos. I just haven't found it yet.*

He returned to the hospital and talked briefly to Dang, who told Jake that Rebecca seemed to be more coherent, but was still in and out of consciousness. "She's getting better every day, Jake," Dang said before leaving.

At 8:00 that evening the nurse told Jake he had a phone call at the nurse's station and he slowly walked to the telephone.

"Jake," came the friendly voice of Doctor Kessler, "Barbara Bowen will here sometime tomorrow afternoon, and I want you here for this one, buddy."

Jake smiled. "How the hell did you find me?

"Doctor Shaw is a colleague and friend, Jake," Kessler said, "I know everything that goes on at the ICU, including your pain-in-the-ass overnight stays."

Jake chuckled. "Why is it so important that I attend the autopsy of Barbara Bowen? What difference does it make if I'm there?"

"She's from Kuwait, right?" Kessler asked.

"Yes, but what difference does that make? You've done autopsies on people from Muslim countries in the past. What the hell is so different about this one?"

"There's nothing different about this one," Kessler said. "I just want you to see firsthand what I have to go through every time you come up with a new theory."

"Just tell me when you want me to be there and I'll be there," Jake said.

"She'll be here late tomorrow afternoon, but I won't do the autopsy until Thursday morning," Kessler said. "It will make it a little less disgusting if she spends a night in the cold room. Not much better, but a little."

Jake had been present for autopsies of bodies that had been exhumed many times, but didn't know why Kessler was so insistent that he attended this one. Kessler had used the word, disgusting, on two different occasions and Jake didn't know why, but he would find out on Thursday morning.

On several occasions during the night Rebecca had

momentarily regained consciousness, then lapsed back into what appeared to be a deep sleep. It was almost as though she awoke just to see if Jake was still there, and this thought brought a smile to his lips. Every time she opened her eyes, Jake said, "I'm still here, honey."

Dang walked into the room at 7:00 in the morning with two large cups of coffee and a half-dozen doughnuts. He opened his backpack and pulled out a child psychology journal, then handed Jake a cup of coffee. "Go to work. I've got a lot of reading to do."

The two men sat and chatted awhile, and then Jake left for the station. Rebecca's consistent improvement and the large cup of strong coffee seemed to put Jake's mind back at 100 percent. He was anxious to get back to work and the short ride back to the station seemed to take longer than usual.

Jake drove into the parking lot, and as usual, noticed John Moran's car parked in the rear. "If anything," Jake said out loud, "he's dedicated!"

Jake ran up the stairs two at a time and walked into the squad room. Moran was sitting at his desk reading a stack of printouts that must have come in early that morning. His face beamed with excitement when he saw Jake standing at the door.

"Jake!" he bellowed, "I found a connection. It's weak, but I think we're on the right track."

Jake's adrenaline surged and he hurriedly walked hurried to where Moran was sitting. "What's the connection?"

"It bothered me why all the murders were committed in cities named, Salem," Moran said, "so I referenced the city of Salem to deaths by strangulation. Then because of the hangman's knot, I also looked for similarities of deaths by hanging." He fumbled through the pile of printouts like a child opening Christmas presents. He found the two pages he was looking for and handed them to Jake. "Notice any similarities?"

Jake studied one, then the other. He couldn't find the connection that Moran was talking about until he noticed the initials of the victims. All of a sudden he saw it. "You're right. This *is* weak, but I think you just hit a homerun."

"There's one thing that bothers me," Moran said. "There's a set of initials missing for the month of June, and if the murderer is so meticulous with detail…"

"It ain't missing," said Jake. "She will be re-autopsied tomorrow morning. Her name is Barbara Bowen."

"That's the missing piece," Moran said in a conclusive tone, "but I don't think the captain's going to buy it."

"The captain won't know anything about it." Jake's tone was laced with authority. He didn't want anyone to know what Moran found until this theory was confirmed.

When Mark walked in and saw the expression on his partners' faces. He knew they had discovered something. His heart pounded in his chest as he walked over to Moran's desk. "What is it?"

Moran handed Mark the printouts and sat down in his chair. He and Jake watched as Mark studied the paperwork, deep in thought.

All of a sudden Mark made the connection. "You gotta be shitting me."

"That's the only connection we can come up with, Mark," said Moran, "and right now it's looking pretty good."

Indiscriminate

"No way," Mark snapped. "The captain will rip you a new ass if you present this to him."

Neither Jake nor John responded to Mark's statement. They stood silent, their expressions blank. Mark knew what they had in mind.

"You're not going to tell him, are ya," Mark said. "You're going to hide this idiotic theory because you know how ridiculous it is."

Jake stared at Mark and didn't understand why he was so adamant about this theory being wrong. "Mark, I agree it's thin, but it's all we've got… give it a chance."

Mark walked to his desk and sat down with a disgusted expression on his face. Jake knew that Mark couldn't believe what the new evidence indicated, but also knew that once the names were matched, Mark would get more involved. He tossed the printouts to Mark and walked to the coffeepot, all the while knowing that Mark would reluctantly read everything that Moran had discovered.

Jake stood at the sink drinking his coffee and noticed Mark's face light up, and then the smile disappeared into a frown. He knew what his partner's next question was going to be, and he answered it before it was asked. "Barbara Bowen will be re-autopsied in the morning."

"Jesus, Jake," Mark spouted, "is this what I think it is?"

Jake stood silent as his partner continued reading, and he knew that Mark was becoming as convinced as he and Moran were about the connection.

"Every one of *our* victims' names had the same initials as the people that were hung as witches in 1692! Even the boy who was crushed under the car has the same initials as the man who was pressed to death, Giles Cory."

Mark set the printouts down on his desk with a look of disbelief. "Jake, if this is right, we're on a fucking witch hunt."

Fifteen

The three detectives sat in the interrogation room comparing the names and dates of the murders to the witch trials of 1692. John Moran had a printout from the Internet with the names of the people who were hanged as witches.

"In 1692, the only person hanged in June was Bridget Bishop," stated Moran, "and our victim is named, Barbara Bowen—same initials."

Jake picked up the printout of the names of the people who were hung as witches. "There were five people hung in July of 1692: Sarah Good, Elizabeth Howe, Susannah Martin, Rebecca Nurse and Sarah Wildes."

Moran responded with, "Sally Grogan, Ellen Hayward, Susan Martell, Rachael Nickels and Sandra Woods."

Comparing the names, Mark said, "The initials are a perfect match."

Jake continued, "There were five more people hung as

witches in August of 1692: George Burroughs, Martha Carrier, George Jacobs, John Proctor and John Willard."

Again Moran responded, "Gary Banos, Marie Chapman, Greig Jennings, John Price and James Wilson."

"That brings us up to date and into September," said Mark, "what are the names of the last two?"

Jake glanced down at the printout. In a soft voice he answered, "Martha Cory was hung and Giles Cory was pressed to death."

Moran nodded his head with conviction, and said, "Molly Chrisp and Gary Cronin."

"Every victim has the same initials as the people that were hung as witches," said Mark, "and you know what that means."

Jake's face turned to stone. "Yes, if we're right about this, there will be seven more murders before September is through." He returned to his desk, deep in thought.

When Captain Reins walked in to the squad room, he moved over to Jake's desk. "Uncover anything yet?"

He got the same answer he usually did. "Nothing yet, sir, but I'm working on it."

Reins stared at Jake, saying nothing. He knew what Jake's answer would be before he asked him the question, but felt as though it had to be asked. He continued through the squad room, past Lucy and into his office.

"John," said Jake, "go into the Internet and pull out all the information you can find on the dark side of witchcraft. I don't believe there is such a thing as a dark side, but maybe there's someone who does."

Mark and Jake followed up on every phone call that came

Indiscriminate

into the station. They both knew that the calls that came in were not going to be helpful to the case, but followed them up anyway.

Jake still had a feeling the answer was in the photos of the victims. He studied them for hours. He kept going back to the shots of the rope burns around each victim's neck and he became frustrated when he couldn't find the answer.

At 3:00 p.m. he decided to go to the hospital and spend time with Rebecca. He told his partners he was leaving and that he would be at the ME's office in the morning for the autopsy on Barbara Bowen. "I'll be here after the autopsy." He left the building and drove to the hospital.

Rebecca's condition had greatly improved and her moments of consciousness lasted much longer. She couldn't talk or stay awake very long, but Jake knew it was only a matter of time before she would be able to.

At seven the next morning, Dang walked in and set his medical journal on the table. "I should have this finished today," he said.

Jake left the hospital and drove on I-95 South en route to Boston and his meeting with Doctor Kessler. As he drove, he wondered why Kessler was so intent on having him attend this autopsy. *It's not as though I've never seen an autopsy before*, he thought. *What's so different about this one?*

Before long, Jake was sitting in room three with Kessler and they were discussing Barbara Bowen. Jake explained the theory that he had and told him about the connection between the victims and the people that were hung as witches.

"I don't think Barbara Bowen is part of the serial

murders," Jake said, "but I promised a heartbroken woman I'd look into it."

"So you wanted this autopsy even though you don't believe she is part of this case?" Kessler said as his assistant wheeled in the body of Barbara Bowen. "You don't seem to have a problem creating more work for me and I just wanted you to see, first hand, what's it's like to autopsy someone who has not been embalmed and buried for three months. You have no clue what you're in for."

Both men gathered around the body that was covered with a plastic sheet. Jake still didn't understand what Kessler meant until he pulled off the cover that hid the grotesque remains of the Muslim woman.

Immediately Jake backed up and gasped for air. He turned around and walked to the door in an attempt to breathe the air from out in the hall.

"Jake," Kessler said, "I need you to help me turn her over."

Jake walked to the cabinet and retrieved a pair of heavy-duty gloves from the cabinet drawer. He walked back to the table and helped the doctor turn the body over onto the stomach.

The body was covered with a slimy film and Jake's hands slid off of the woman's arm and almost went right through the skin and into the inside of her body. The stench was unbearable. He leaned over into the bucket on the floor and vomited.

Jake walked back to the door and stood with his hands at his side. He had never seen anything like this in his life, and didn't think he couldn't continue helping Doctor Kessler. "I can't do it, Doc," was all he said.

Indiscriminate

Kessler told Jake he was only going to make one incision on the back of the neck and he needed Jake to help turn her over.

"You brought me down here to watch you make only one incision, Doc?"

"It will only take one incision to either prove or disprove if she was murdered by the serial killer," Kessler said. "Now give me a hand."

Reluctantly, Jake turned and walked back to the table to assist the doctor. Both men pushed and turned the body as fluid gushed from every orifice. The skin was mushy and fell off the bone as they finally turned Barbara Bowen onto her stomach. Jake vomited two more times into the bucket.

Doctor Kessler looked at Jake and decided that he had had enough. "Go outside and get some air, this will only take me a minute."

There was no need for Jake to hear Kessler's offer twice and he bolted for the door, tossing his gloves onto the floor.

Sitting on a bench in the hallway, Jake could still feel the decaying body of Barbara Bowen on his hands. The stench of rotting flesh filled his entire being and he thought of nothing else but taking a shower.

Within minutes, Doctor Kessler joined Jake in the hallway. "You're finished already?" Jake asked.

"No need to do a complete autopsy," replied Kessler. "I only needed to find out if the rope burn was consistent with the other victims. It was."

Jake stared at Kessler, perplexed. "Are you telling me that whoever did the autopsy the first time missed it?"

"Yes…and no," replied Kessler. "When we do an autopsy,

we always consider the medical history of the deceased. In this case, Barbara Bowen had a history of heart problems and was found three days after she died. The condition of the body was bloated and discolored and at that time there was no reason to suspect that she was strangled, and certainly no reason to cut into the back of the neck looking for a coagulation of blood. The Holyoke office followed procedure to the letter."

Jake stood and walked to the far wall of the hallway. His mind raced. He was angry. "Then why the fuck did you insist on me being here?"

"You never have a problem insisting that I do a re-autopsy on someone, even though you believe it will have no impact on the investigation. You make these requests as though they're nothing. I just wanted you to know what I have to go through every time you pull something like this," Kessler explained.

Walking back to the bench, Jake sat back down next to Kessler. "You did this to teach me a fucking lesson?" Jake's voice was cold.

"One good experience is worth a thousand lectures," Kessler replied. "And yes, I did it to teach you a lesson."

The doctor stared at Jake, anticipating an outburst. To his surprise, Jake turned with a half-smile and remarked, "It sure as hell worked."

Doctor Kessler returned to the autopsy room. Jake asked, "How the hell did you know it would be this gruesome?"

"You told me she was Kuwaiti, and Muslims don't usually embalm their dead," Kessler said. "And being buried for three months…"

Indiscriminate

"Okay, Doc, I've learned my lesson." Jake walked away.

When Jake returned to the squad room, he noticed Mark studying the photos in the interrogation room while Moran was sorting more printouts from the Internet. The expression on Moran's face piqued Jake's interest and he walked to where the detective was sitting.

"Hold on, Jake," Moran said excitedly, "you gotta read this." He handed Jake the printouts.

Jake read the data that Moran had found on the Internet. Everything began to make sense. "Did Mark see this?"

"Not yet," replied Moran, "but as soon as I have everything in order I'll explain it to the both of you."

Jake walked into the interrogation room with Mark and waited for Moran. He knew Moran wanted to have all the pages in order and also wanted to explain everything himself.

Within minutes John Moran entered the room and sat across the table from Jake and Mark. Clearing his throat, he began, "I found a woman named Norma Stiles in Oregon who was committed to an asylum twelve years ago. She was a self-proclaimed witch who practiced the darker side of witchcraft."

Jake interrupted, "Witchcraft is a peaceful religion. I didn't know there was a dark side, other than the phony shit we see in the movies."

"Well," continued Moran, "according to the information I downloaded from the Internet, the good and bad magic is neither black nor white. The energy is the same on both sides, except…" Moran paused.

"Except what?" asked Mark.

Moran continued, "This woman worked with Kali, the goddess of destruction, and she was able to cause a lot of pain and heartache to people around her. She had a thirteen-year-old child at the time she was committed and the child was forced to go from one foster home to another. Every time the kid was placed in a home, the foster parents had him removed. The signs of abuse were evident in the bruises on his back and cigarette burns on his body, including his fingers."

This statement brought a heightened reaction from Jake. "A cigarette burn would leave a small round circular scar on the skin, just like the fingerprints we found."

"The child was only thirteen years old when the mother was committed, and that would have made him eighteen years old when the murders started in Salem, Oregon."

Jake looked at Moran with a perplexed expression. "You referred to the child as *he*."

Moran fumbled through the paperwork. "The child's name is Whitney Stiles, and I just used the name as a *him*. It could be either."

"We closed the gap on that question," said Mark. "We know it ain't a he. It's a *she*."

As the three detectives discussed the new theory, Captain Reins and Bill Stoughton walked into the squad room. Stoughton immediately headed for the coffeepot while Reins walked toward went into his office. The captain stopped in front of the glass partition of the interrogation room and stared at Jake. The stare let him know it was time to talk to Stoughton and bring him back into the loop.

Jake nodded to Reins and gave him a thumbs-up sign,

then turned to his partners and told them not to divulge any information to anyone. Jake walked out of the interrogation room and intercepted Stoughton as he was walking toward the captain's office. "Bill, I think you misunderstood what I was trying to say yesterday."

"In what way?" Stoughton asked.

"I certainly didn't mean to insinuate that I didn't trust you. I was only trying to say that there were things I was working on that were only halfway confirmed. I'll bring you up to speed as soon as I separate the fact from the bullshit."

Stoughton looked through the glass partition directly at Mark and John as if he wanted to be invited to the meeting. Jake could see the frustration on his face and knew he didn't like being excluded from what was taking place. "Fair enough." Stoughton's tone was laced with animosity as he entered the captain's office.

The hours passed quickly with the new theory on everyone's mind and it was five o'clock before Jake realized it. He called it a day and went home and showered before going to the hospital.

Driving back to the hospital, his mind wasn't as scattered as before. He knew he was closing in on the murderer and that thought brought on a feeling of satisfaction. His only concern now was to find her before she moved on.

Jake walked into Rebecca's room and saw Dang standing next to the bed talking to her. Her eyes were open and she was completely conscious. A wide smile burst across his face and he walked toward the bed.

When she saw Jake, Rebecca's eyes lit up and it was obvious she was happy to see him. He sat on the edge of the bed and held her hand. "Don't try to say anything. You're gonna be fine."

"I was telling Rebecca how much of a pain in the ass you've been to the nurses," said Dang. "I told her you've been sleeping here every night and that she had better get well soon because the staff can't put up with you much longer."

Jake looked down at Rebecca and said, "Don't listen to him, honey. They all love me."

A scant smile spread across her face and Jake could see a hint of tear in her eyes as she squeezed his hand. He could do nothing more than imagine what she was going through and vowed to himself that no one else would suffer at the hands of this murderer, ever again.

The night passed quickly and Rebecca remained conscious for longer periods of time. Although she couldn't speak, her eyes were so vibrant that Jake could understand what she was trying to say.

When Dang came into the room at 7:00, Jake left and drove to the station. As he drove he thought about the connection between the victims and the people that were hung in 1692. "Their initials," he said aloud, "the next victim will have the same initials as one of the people hung for witchcraft."

Walking into the squad room, Jake hurried to Moran, "I want you to find every person with the same initials as the people who were hung in September, 1692. Check in Salem, Peabody, Danvers…"

John handed Jake a piece of paper and said, "I've already taken the liberty of doing that, there are seventeen names that fit the bill."

Indiscriminate

Jake listened as Moran read the names of the people who were hung as witches. "Mary Easty, Alice Parker, Mary Parker, Ann Pudeator, Margaret Scott, Wilmot Redd and Samuel Wardwell."

Jake saw that there was a perfect match for each and every name on the list. "It's difficult to believe that anyone could be so ignorant as to hang someone for being a witch." He hung his head and added, "Man, these people had a lot of spare time on their hands to be able to sit around and come up with something as idiotic as this."

Jake walked back in the interrogation room and spread out the photographs of the victims. "What the hell am I missing?" he asked aloud. "I know it's here."

Moran walked into the interrogation room and asked Jake what he wanted to do about the list of potential victims.

"Split the list between you and Mark, then contact each name on the list," said Jake, "I want you to offer them a free, all-expenses-paid stay in the Hawthorn Hotel. Don't tell them any more than you have to to get them there."

"Jake, I don't think the captain will foot the bill for this one," Moran said. "He's gonna hit the roof when he finds out."

"If he barks at picking up the tab, I'll pay for it myself. Now get to work."

John Moran was aware that Jake had won a two million-dollar lottery ticket and simply shrugged his shoulders and turned to leave the room.

"Get me everything you can on Whitney Stiles and his mother," Jake said as he studied the photographs. "I want to know where the hell they are now."

Howard Olsen

Moments later Jake walked out of the interrogation room and told Moran that he also wanted the names of the foster parents that had custody of Whitney Stiles.

"I have the agency in Oregon on the line now," said Moran, "and they have all the information we need on Norma and Whitney Stiles. They'll fax it to us within the hour."

"Christ, John, you're turning into a regular, Radar O'Riley!"

True to their word, the agency in Oregon faxed six pages of information on the Stiles family, along with five names and telephone numbers of the foster parents that made an attempt at caring for Whitney. Moran immediately called the foster parents while Jake studied the report on Norma Stiles.

Satisfied that the murderer he was looking for was Whitney Stiles, Jake called the institution where Norma Stiles had been committed.

He talked to a half-dozen people before finally getting the chief of staff on the line. The doctor was reluctant to divulge any information over the telephone until Jake told him about the murders in Salem, Massachusetts.

"The person you're asking about was completely out of control, detective, and was beyond help. She had visions of being a black witch and spent every waking moment causing terror to everyone around her."

Jake listened to the doctor as he told him how Norma had abused Whitney from the moment the child was born. "She used to make the Whitney kneel on the floor while she chanted and burned the child with cigarettes and candles. She would pour hot wax on the his back and stomach until she rendered him unconscious, then would pour water over his head to wake him up and start over. This was the poor child's life, from the moment of birth until Norma was committed. It's no wonder none of the foster homes could control that child."

"Doc, you refer to the child as a, *him*... Don't you mean, *she*? Plus, you talked about Norma Stiles in the past tense, is she still living?"

"No," replied the doctor, "Norma Stiles hung herself five years ago. She was found in the morning by an orderly. By the time I got to her room she had been cut down and was lying on her bed. Her matted, fire engine red wig was lying on the floor beside her. Detective, I've already told you more than I should have. I have a responsibility to keep all medical information confidential. I've already gone too far."

"Okay, just one more thing. You said she wore and expensive wig dyed red?"

The doctor cleared his throat. "The only reason I'm telling you this is because Norma Stiles is now deceased. Yes, the wig was dyed red and, was very expensive."

"Do you feel Whitney is capable of multiple murder?"

"There is no doubt that as an adult, Whitney was more than capable of multiple murder."

The doctor's tone became aggravated when he said, "No more questions, detective...not without a warrant."

"I understand, Doc. Thank you very much for the information, you've been a big help."

Mark told Jake that out of the seventeen people who matched the initials of the people who were hung, four died and four were in homes for the elderly. "That leaves nine people who could possibly be the next victims," Mark said, "and every one of them jumped at the chance to spend a few days at the Hawthorn Hotel, free of charge."

Jake gave Mark his credit card and told him to make all the arrangements and that he wanted the nine people in the hotel that night. "Whatever it takes, Mark," said Jake, "I want them all tucked away safely by tonight."

Moran was still deeply engrossed in downloading information about the witch trials of 1692 and had compiled a stack of printouts that was over one-inch thick. He hadn't read any of the files yet because he was ready to call it a day. "This file will continue to download until all the pages have been printed out, Jake," he said. "I'll decipher the information in the morning."

Jake nodded in approval and watched Mark and John leave the squad room. He thought of how tired they must be after the long hours of paperwork that was involved in the case, and how well they held up under all the scrutiny they have been put through. *Hell*, he thought, *we all need a rest*.

As he did every night since Rebecca was attacked, Jake went home, showered and then drove to the hospital. When he walked into the ICU, Doctor Shaw told him that Rebecca would be moved to a private room in the main hospital in the morning. "I have no reason to doubt that she will make a complete recovery, Detective," said Shaw, "and I'm beginning to believe that a lot of the progress is due to you and your friend. She's a lucky woman, in more ways than one."

That evening Jake noticed the progress Rebecca had made as he read to her from another book. She seemed to be as much into the book as Jake was, and she smiled and frowned at the different emotions the book projected.

Rebecca's rapid recovery, coupled with knowing the identity of the murderer, allowed Jake the luxury of beginning to feel some peace of mind. He felt as though he was finally in control of what was happening around him, and his only concern now was to find Whitney Stiles before she moved to another city and unleashed her wrath.

The night passed and both Jake and Rebecca had a restful night's sleep. As usual, Dang was there at 7 o'clock with coffee and more journals to read. After talking briefly with Dang, Jake kissed Rebecca and went home to shower before going to work.

Jake walked into the squad room at eight o'clock and immediately called Mark and John into the interrogation room. He wanted to format a strategy for each detective to devote his time to and didn't have the luxury of time in his favor.

Moran sat at the table with a stack of printouts measuring six inches high. "I haven't had the chance to sort through this yet, Jake," he said. "It's gonna take some time."

"Time is the only thing we *don't* have," said Jake. "Let's split up the printouts and skim through the bullshit and pull out what we can use."

Each detective took a stack of printouts and began reading. Most of what they read, although interesting, had no connection to their case.

When Captain Reins arrived at the station, he asked Jake about Rebecca.

"She's doing much better, Captain. She has been moved

out of the ICU and into a room in the main hospital…Thanks for asking."

"That's great, Jake, I'll go up and visit her during lunch. Maybe we *all* should go to see her at lunchtime. It might make her feel better if she knows everyone is concerned."

Jake agreed and thanked the captain for his concern. "Thanks Captain, it will mean a lot to her."

The three detectives spent the morning reading some of the information surrounding the witch trials of 1692. When Bill Stoughton walked into the squad room, the first thing he did was to pour himself a cup of coffee and look through the glass partition as though he was expecting to hear an invitation to join the meeting.

Stoughton walked toward the interrogation room and Jake told Moran to gather all the printouts and put them into a folder. Within seconds, Stoughton walked into the room just in time to see Moran closing a folder. He walked past Bill and walked out of the room.

"More classified stuff, Jake?" Stoughton's tone was cold. He made no attempt to conceal his animosity about not being included in the meetings. His eyes were filled with hatred toward Jake because of Jake's control over the case, and resentment hung thick in the air.

Jake simply said, "We're all going to the hospital to visit Rebecca. Would you like to come with us?"

Stoughton stood silent for a moment as though he was trying to think of an excuse why he couldn't go to with them. "I don't know, Jake," he said, "I have a lot of things I have to do today. Besides, I have business to discuss with the Captain."

When Jake told him that Captain Reins was going

with them to the hospital, Stoughton managed a half-smile. "Okay," he said, "if I have the time I'll go to the hospital with the Captain."

It was nearly noon when Jake left for the hospital. He knew Rebecca would be happy with the show of support from everyone at the police station and he was anxious to see her expression.

Jake turned left into the hospital entrance and almost drove down into the hollow where the emergency room and the ICU were located. He drove up to the main hospital parking lot and parked the Vette. He felt much better about where Rebecca was staying now. Since she was out of the ICU that meant her recovery was imminent.

The receptionist told Jake that Rebecca was in a section of the hospital called Davenport 8 and to follow the stripes on the wall to the elevator. "She's on the eighth floor," she said with a smile. "You can't miss it."

Jake thanked her and walked the length of the hall following the painted stripe to the elevator and pushed the button marked 8.

When the doors opened, he noticed that there was much more activity in the main hospital than there was at ICU. He reasoned that was because there were more people in the main portion of the hospital that were allowed visitors.

He walked to at the nurse's station he was told that Rebecca was in room number 209. He scurried down the hall in that direction. He was anxious to see Rebecca and made no attempt to conceal his cheerfulness with flair in his stride.

He walked into room number 209 and saw Rebecca was

watching the television. Her eyes were open and she looked strong and well, almost as though the brutal attack never took place.

When Rebecca saw Jake walking toward her, a surge of comfort raced through her entire body. Her eyes were the size of dinner plates and Jake never saw her looking so beautiful. He leaned down and kissed her gently on her lips and she responded passionately. This was the first time since the attack that Jake felt completely at ease with her condition.

"Some of the guys from the station are on their way here to see you," Jake said, "but I'll make sure they don't stay very long."

Rebecca's smile and her bright eyes told Jake that she was happy to have someone visit her and that she was even happier to have him there.

Jake and Dang talked briefly before everyone from the station arrived. He told Dang about Norma and Whitney Stiles and how she tormented and tortured Whitney when she was very young. He also told Dang about Norma's delusions of black magic and how she practiced her dark energy on the one person that was most available to her, her own daughter.

It wasn't long before everyone from the station walked in. The first to enter the room was Captain Reins, followed by Mark, John and Lucy. The captain walked to Rebecca and handed her a dozen roses, "I'm glad you're feeling better, Rebecca. I thought the roses might brighten your day," pointing to Jake, he added, "considering who you have to put up with."

Indiscriminate

Rebecca smiled at the man she had heard about, but never met. She imagined him to be somewhat of a monster because of everything that Jake had told her about him, but after meeting him, she felt differently.

Lucy was next to greet Rebecca. "I'll put these in some water for you." She picked up the flowers and placed them into a plastic container. Looking at the captain, she said in a mock tone, "Men, men don't do anything right."

Everyone laughed at Lucy's statement, including Rebecca. It was obvious that she was feeling much better.

"Where's Stoughton?" Jake asked Mark.

Mark shrugged in an indication that he didn't know, but told Jake to ask the captain. Jake did, and Reins told him that Bill would try and stop by later because he had pressing business at noon.

Captain Reins walked to Dang and thanked him for spending his days with Rebecca. "You staying here during the day made it possible for me to keep that officer out on the street."

Dang said nothing, but smiled and nodded.

Jake was sitting on the edge of the bed when everyone was about to leave. John Moran turned to Jake and told him that he was going to re-run the request for people who have had their passports stamped from India. "Now that we know that it's a woman we're looking for, I'm going to narrow down the search to just women."

Rebecca's hand flinched. While Moran told Jake how he was going to refine his search to women only, Jake sensed Rebecca's piercing stare. His head turned slowly toward her as though everything was in slow motion. When his eyes met hers, he saw her terror.

He cupped her small fragile hand in his and continued looking into her fright-filled eyes. She was trying to tell him something, but he already knew what it was.

Jake stood and leaned over Rebecca so that his face was within inches from hers. "It was a man, wasn't it?"

Rebecca closed her eyes and nodded, yes.

Sixteen

Jake and Dang stayed with Rebecca for two hours after everyone left. They knew she was reliving the attack and wanted to be with her until she felt safe again. Before Jake went back to the station he called Mark and told him what Rebecca said. He told him to have Moran continue the search for a man when he delved into the childhood of Whitney Stiles.

"The kid was a boy?" Mark snapped. "That makes a lot more sense, Jake."

Rebecca finally fell asleep and Jake left for the station while Dang remained sitting in the same chair he'd been in all morning. Jake knew everything was coming to a head, and also knew that Rebecca would continue to be safe under the watchful eye of his friend.

Jake walked into the squad room and noticed that Moran was standing next to the coffeepot, sipping coffee. He knew the detective had been working very hard at digging through the Internet for the information they needed, but was upset when he saw him doing nothing.

He walked to Moran and asked him if he already found what they were looking for. His voice carried a tone of annoyance and Moran knew the sarcastic tone in Jake's voice was because he needed the information immediately. Seeing Moran doing nothing annoyed Jake, and Moran knew it. Without saying a word and still sipping his coffee, Moran motioned toward the captain's office with his head.

Jake looked in the direction of Reins' office and noticed that the door was halfway open. He could hear someone talking but couldn't make out who it was or what they were saying.

"He's been here for that past two hours," Moran said. "He was here when we got back from the hospital."

"Stoughton?" Jake asked.

"Yes, and he's been a pain in the ass," Moran replied. "He's been asking more questions than a hooker at a banquet! Every time I started doing something he was all over me wanting to know what the hell I was doing, so I finally stopped doing everything until you got back."

Jake looked through the half-open door and into the captain's office. Bill Stoughton paced back and forth while talking to Reins and his hands moved in every direction. It was obvious he was upset and was venting his displeasure on the captain.

Jake told Moran to continue searching the Internet for the information surrounding Whitney Stiles, "If Stoughton noses around again, *I'll* put a stop to it!"

Jake called the home of Detective Patel in Salem India,

and with the ten-hour time difference he hoped the detective wouldn't be too upset with the late night call.

The telephone rang four short rings and Patel answered in a sleepy voice. Jake apologized for calling so late and explained how important the call was. Patel said, "It's okay," and was receptive to Jake's request for information and listened to everything he had to say.

When Jake told him the murderer was a man named Whitney Stiles, he sensed anxiety in Patel's voice, "Are you sure?" he asked.

Jake assured him there was no mistake and asked him to check passports on anyone who left his country shortly after the murders.

Jake heard Patel rustling around on the other end of the phone and knew he was getting dressed while he talked.

"Detective Patel," said Jake, "you don't have to run the check tonight. It can wait until the morning."

"You and I both know it's only a matter of time before the murderer vanishes," he replied. "I'll get back to you within two hours."

Jake was pleased at Patel's zest to look back into the information that had been gathered in India. He thanked the detective for his eagerness to help and hung up.

Jake sat at his desk and listened to Mark talking to one of the foster parents who used to care for Whitney Stiles. He only heard one side of the conversation and was anxious to know everything that was said. Mark continued scribbling notes on piece of paper while the other person talked. Finally he hung up the phone.

Jake stared across his desk at Mark, "Well?"

Howard Olsen

"Whitney Stiles was placed in six different foster homes," said Mark. "The first two families have moved away and can't be found. The third family, Mr. and Mrs. Bernard Thatcher, had Whitney for six months until Mr. Thatcher was found lying at the bottom of the stairs with a broken neck. The death was ruled an accident, but the authorities believe Whitney pushed the man down the stairs."

"And the last three?" asked Jake.

"The fourth family refused to talk about what happened while Whitney was under their care because they said they don't want to be involved, while the fifth and sixth families who foster-parented the boy couldn't stop talking.

"Whitney was placed in his fifth foster home when he was fifteen and stayed with them for one year. The neighbor's pets began turning up dead and it was suspected that Whitney did all the killing, but no one knew for sure."

Jake listened in awe at the life of Whitney Stiles. He envisioned a child whose life had been condemned from the moment he was conceived. He wondered why Whitney hadn't been committed to a place where he could have been helped. Instead, the boy was shuffled from home to home with the hopes that he would somehow straighten out his own life. That was a mistake. The system failed more than just Whitney Stiles, it also failed everyone he's murdered. And everyone he would murder in the future if Jake didn't catch him first.

"He was placed in his sixth foster home at the age of sixteen," Mark continued, "but that only lasted three months. He was removed from the home when the father caught him trying to strangle one of the other children with an electrical cord."

Indiscriminate

"And he still wasn't committed?" Jake's tone was laced with anger and frustration.

"Yes, he was committed," said Mark, "but not for long. In fact, he was locked up less than a week when he escaped. According to the doctor at the hospital, he simply walked off into the night and was never seen again."

Two hours had passed and true to his word, Detective Patel called and said he had information, but didn't think it would be helpful. He went on to say that they had conducted a massive door-to-door search in the same area where the last victim was found and discovered what *he* believed was the home of the murderer. "It was rented to a young woman named Whitney Stiles," he said. "She was tall, about 5' 10, with long red hair. She wasn't very sociable and no one got to know her very well."

"That's our guy." Jake barked.

"Your *guy?*" responded Patel, "Whitney Stiles is a woman."

"Whitney Stiles is cunning. Whitney Stiles is evil. Whitney Stiles is a wolf in sheep's clothing. Whitney Stiles is a man," Jake replied in a low voice.

"A man dressed as a woman?" Patel asked, "How could this be? How could a man deceive everyone into believing he was a *she?* Someone must have noticed."

Jake told the detective everything that had been uncovered about Whitney Stiles, and Patel was mesmerized at Jake's description of how the murders were committed. "It looks like I owe my captain an apology," said Patel. "He said it was a man and I thought otherwise. I was wrong."

Jake asked Patel if he had any evidence that would

solidify his theory of the murders being connected to witchcraft. The detective told him that they found a partially burned note. In his thick Indian accent, he read the portion that was readable: "You have been judged and found to be possessed by the devil. You are a witch. You know you are a witch. You are a consort of the devil…" Patel stopped reading and told Jake that the rest of the paper was unreadable except for two lines on the bottom. It read: "Your limbs have been bound, rendering you unable to cast your evil to anyone. You will be hanged as a witch and I will sign the order of execution."

"That's it?" Jake asked.

"Yes," Patel answered, "there was more, but any of the names that may have been written have been burned away."

After hanging up with Detective Patel, Jake looked up and saw Bill Stoughton walking out of the captain's office. As usual, the first thing he did was wash his coffee cup and place it back into the rack. He turned and faced Jake, and from across the room he said, "Captain Reins has put me back into the loop, Burnett. When I return I'm going to be included in your meetings." He said, "you *will* fill me in…"

Jake said nothing and smiled at the profiler as he walked out of the squad room. He knew the captain had no intention of filling him in on everything they had uncovered. He walked into Reins' office to ask him what information he wanted him to reveal to Stoughton.

When Jake shut the door to the captain's office, Reins was standing in front of the window staring out into the parking lot. He knew it was Jake who came into his office, but he didn't turn around.

Indiscriminate

There was something bothering Reins and Jake knew it. "Captain, what's wrong?"

"Bill was in here for two hours reminding me why I drove you out of the department five years ago," Reins said. "He went on about the night my brother, Ben, and I busted through the door at the motel and found you in bed with a woman, with Ben's wife."

"Captain, I tried to explain what happened that night but you wouldn't listen. I didn't know she was married, and certainly didn't know she was married to your brother. I met her for the first time that night."

Reins turned and faced Jake with his hand in the air as if to stop him. "Ben was devastated when he found out about his wife. You weren't the only one, Jake. She flaunted the men she was with right in front of my brother without any regard for what she was doing to him."

"You knew this five years ago?" Jake asked.

Reins sat at his desk, looking embarrassed. "I knew it, but couldn't admit to myself that it was true. Ben loved her with all his heart and I couldn't bear watching him go through the torment. I blamed everyone for my brother's breakdown, but mostly I blamed you. I'm sorry for the nasty way you've been treated over the past five years."

Jake sat in silence while his captain vented what caused Jake to leave the police force five years earlier. He never knew there was another side to Reins' personality, a soft side that went against the arrogant persona the captain worked so hard to project. He could see how hard it was for Reins to admit what had really happened that night, and felt sorry for the way it affected him and his brother. "Captain, if I had known it was you and your brother who came through the door that night…"

"It wasn't your fault," Reins admitted. "We both got our asses kicked and it was our own fault."

"Everything that happened five years ago is past history," said Jake. "Let's leave it where it belongs, in the past."

Captain Reins cleared his throat. With a half-smile he said, "Okay Jake, tell me about the new theory."

After five long years of hatred between the two men, the slate was finally wiped clean.

Jake felt a huge weight removed from his shoulders and his mind was at ease. Looking at his captain he could see that the heavy weight of aversion had been removed from his shoulders, also.

Jake explained his theory of the murderer imitating the witch trials of 1692 and he noticed the blank expression on Reins' face. He knew this motive was difficult to believe, but when he showed the captain the initials of the murdered victims and compared them to the initials of the people who were convicted of witchcraft.

"Jesus Christ," Reins snapped, "This can't be! No way Jake, you don't really expect me to believe this shit… Do ya? I mean… Come on, Jake!"

Reins continued to study the initials of each victim, then scanned over the initials of all the people who were executed in 1692. "Holy fuck, Jake… A perfect match! This is not a coincidence, this is pure fact! It looks like you did it, Jake, you found the connection!"

" Captain, Moran downloaded a one-foot high stack

Indiscriminate

of printouts surrounding witchcraft and the witch trials of 1692, but it's going to take quite some time to read it all.

"You feel the answer is in there?" Reins asked.

"Yes," said Jake, "there's a ton of information on the Internet and what we're looking for is a theory on a possible motive, prophecies, predictions, quotes from someone from 1692, and a possible connection with their initials that will give us a clue as to where to look.

Before he left the office Jake asked the captain about Bill Stoughton. "I saw him pacing back and forth. What's his problem?"

Reins looked at Jake with frustration in his eyes. He slowly walked back to the window. "To be completely honest, he's beginning to drive me crazy. He's here all the time, and when he isn't here, he's calling me on the phone. Christ, he even stops by my house and asks questions about the case! Isn't there something you can tell him to keep him in the loop?"

Jake told Reins there wasn't any information he could divulge at this time, but he would try and come up with something to pacify Stoughton.

Jake went back to his desk and waited for his partners to finish reading the information from the Internet. Looking at Mark and John he could see their fatigue surrounded by fascination over what they read in the reports. "It's getting late," he said, "let's pick it up in the morning."

The two detectives left for home and Jake was preparing to leave when Bill Stoughton walked in. He walked up to Jake and told him that he was there to hear the update on the new evidence. "I'm not leaving until you bring me up to speed," he said, "and neither are you!"

Jake looked directly into Stoughton's face. The cold tone in the profiler's voice coupled with the hatred in his eyes told Jake it was time to leave.

Without saying a word, Jake turned and walked toward the door. All of a sudden Stoughton grabbed Jake by his shoulder and spun him around. He stepped within inches from Jake's face. "I'm not going to tell you again, Burnett."

Jake placed his hand on Stoughton's chest and was about to push him away when Stoughton wrapped his arm around Jake's arm, locking Jake's elbow in a painful position. He thrust his right hand into Jake's throat sending him back and landing on the top of a desk, all the while applying pressure to Jake's elbow and pressing on his throat.

Lying flat on his back on the top of a desk, Jake looked up and saw a man filled with hatred. He wanted to be included in solving the murders and resented the fact that Jake had taken over.

Jake tried to get up from the desk but Stoughton applied more pressure to his elbow and to his throat, causing him to gasp for breath. He couldn't breathe and Stoughton was beginning to squeeze even harder. "I'm tired of you looking down on me," said the profiler, "and now I'm going to teach you a lesson."

The grip around Jake's throat became even tighter as he struggled. He was ready to pass out. Looking up into the eyes of Stoughton, Jake saw nothing—no emotion, no compassion and no sign of a loosening grip. Without hesitation, Jake grabbed the telephone with his left hand and slammed it into the side of Stoughton's head, sending him crashing to the floor.

Indiscriminate

Jake stood up from the desk and inhaled as hard as he could, trying to fill his lungs with air. He had difficulty breathing and wanted to catch his breath before Stoughton got to his feet.

By the time both men were standing face to face, Captain Reins had heard the commotion and came rushing into the squad room. The first thing he saw was Jake throwing a punch at Stoughton. The profiler sidestepped Jake's attack and hit him square on his forehead with a straight right hand.

Jake's head snapped back and Stoughton stepped in to throw another blow. That was a mistake. Jake ducked under the punch and grabbed onto the back of Stoughton's shirt and pulled in a downward motion. Stoughton leaned forward and the shirt was pulled over his head. Jake hit the profiler four times before he fell to the floor.

"Enough!" commanded Reins.

Jake stepped back and Stoughton struggled to his feet with his shirt still wrapped around his head. He pulled until the shirt came free and fell to the floor.

Jake looked at the captain then turned back to Bill Stoughton, but the profiler had already picked up his shirt and run out of the squad room.

"When I told you to include him in your procedures," Reins said, "I didn't mean for you to beat the shit out of him."

The captain hurried after Stoughton apparently hoping he could salvage the relationship between them. Jake knew that he would be put through a grueling ass-chewing from Reins, but he couldn't care less. He was not in the habit of being pushed around by anyone, and he wasn't about to start now.

He put the folder with the photographs of the victims back into his desk and locked it, then left the squad room. He walked across the parking lot toward his Corvette and could see neither Captain Reins nor Bill Stoughton. He figured they were discussing how they could get rid of him. He decided not to go home and shower before going to the hospital, and instead he drove to see Rebecca. On the way, he rubbed his forehead and felt a large lump. *He's got a pretty good punch for a fucking sissy.*

When Jake walked into Rebecca's room and saw her eyes lit up with joy. That put an end to the vision of the altercation he had with Bill Stoughton. He felt at ease and the problems that plagued him earlier had vanished.

Before leaving, Dang told him that he had to go back to work in the morning and wouldn't be able to stay with Rebecca during the day. Jake thanked his friend and told him he would have a police officer there in the morning.

It was nearly 7:30 when a nurse walked in and handed Jake an envelope. "This was left at the nurse's station," she said. "It has this room number and your name written on it."

Jake looked down at the envelope and saw the handwriting was written in charcoal. A surge of uneasiness raced through his body at the thought of Whitney Stiles still stalking Rebecca. He walked out of the room and read the letter.

Standing at the door of Rebecca's room, he slowly opened the envelope. The note read:

I AM BUT ONE OF THE FOUR MEN
WHO CONDEMNS YOU TO DEATH.

Indiscriminate

Jake folded the note and placed it back into the envelope. He walked back into the room. When he returned and looked into Rebecca's eyes, he knew she felt something was wrong. He smiled in an effort to soften her fear and told her not to worry.

Jake noticed an empty room across the hall from Rebecca's that was used by the hospital staff during their breaks. He decided to call Mark and John and have them bring all the evidence to the hospital. They would use the empty room to review everything, even if it took them all night. That way, they would be able to see Rebecca as they worked.

Jake picked up the telephone situated next to Rebecca's bed and called Mark. He told him about the note and asked him to call John, then go to the station and use his spare key to get the folder that was in his desk. "Bring the folder and all the printouts that you and John have been working on," he said. "We're gonna be here all night."

An hour passed and Rebecca had fallen asleep when the two detectives entered the room carrying everything Jake had requested. Jake pointed in the direction of the break room and whispered that he would join them in a moment.

Mark and John spread out all the evidence on the large table that was usually used for the staff's coffee breaks. Jake kissed Rebecca lightly and joined his partners for a night of research. The first thing he did was make a pot of coffee, "We're gonna need this."

It was almost midnight and three men sat quietly reviewing their portion of the evidence when Mark looked up and saw the expression on Jake's face. He was staring at the photographs of the victims with an expression of disbelief.

Jake gathered all the photos into one large collage and hovered over them like mother hen. Staring down at the photos, he exclaimed, "This can't be!"

Mark got up from his chair and stood beside Jake. In a bewildered tone he asked, "What is it? What do you see?"

Jake pointed to the rope burn around the front portion of the throat of each victim, then pointed to the photos of the same rope burn on the back of their necks.

Mark was perplexed. "Jake, what the hell do you see? I don't see any difference. They're all the same."

Jake slowly turned and faced his partner. "Exactly. Every one of the rope burns is identical."

"We already know this. What's your point?"

"Do you remember the rope burn on Bill Stoughton?" Jake asked. "The burn on Stoughton's neck made a *perfect* circle. The rope burns on the victims' necks disappear up into the hairline, but not on Stoughton. There is no way that *he* was a victim."

"Are you saying Bill Stoughton is the murderer?" Mark walked around the table and sat back down in his chair. Looking as though he couldn't believe what his partner was insinuating, he said, "That's weak, Jake. Captain Reins will never go along with it."

"I know," Jake said, "especially after I kicked Stoughton's ass in the squad room. The captain will think I'm just trying to implicate Stoughton because of the fight."

"Maybe not," Moran blurted out. "There were four magistrates involved in most of the interrogations involving the people who were accused of being witches."

Jake glanced down at the note that was delivered that

evening to the hospital. "The note said that he, the murderer, was but *one* of four men who have condemned me to death."

"The four men who questioned most of the accused in 1692 were John Hathorne, Jonathan Corwin, Samuel Sewall," Moran said, "and the last magistrate was named William Stoughton."

"Holy shit!" Mark barked. "This is too much to be a coincidence."

"I agree," Jake said, "but we need more than just the two names being the same. We need *hard* evidence. We need something that the captain can hold in his hand and look at, something that will knock him out of his fucking chair."

An eerie silence fell over the room. The three detectives stared at everything, and nothing. They looked at each other as though they expected an answer to appear from thin air.

"That son-of-a-bitch is too smart to leave anything we could use," said Mark. "Christ, he even washes his fucking coffee cup when he's in the middle of an argument."

The statement from Mark brought Jake's mind to attention. "He *always* washes his coffee cup, no matter what's going on in the squad room. And he *always* puts the cup back where it belongs."

"Yeah, so what?" Mark said. "We all know how anal he is when it comes to washing his cup."

"That's right," Jake said, "except when his temper took over. Remember when I walked up behind him when he was digging through the trash barrel? What do you think he was looking for?"

"Son-of-a-bitch!" Mark said. "He was looking for the cup he smashed when he was pissed off."

A large smile spread across Jake's face. "He knew the cup was covered with his fingerprints," Jake said, "and wanted to wash it."

Jake turned to John, but before he could give the order to go back to the station and find the cup, Moran said, "Okay, okay, I'm on it." Moran hurried out of the room and scurried down the hall en route to his car. He knew the gravity of time was not in his favor, and didn't want to waste it.

Jake watched as John Moran burst through the stairwell door and down the stairs. Turning to face Mark, Jake said, "He didn't even wait for the elevator."

A nurse came into the break room and looked at Jake. "I just received a telephone call from a man named Captain Reins," she said. "He asked if you were here and I told him that you were. He wants you to wait for him and said he's on his way."

Jake thanked the nurse and turned to Mark. "He's not going to like what I have to say."

"He's not going to *believe* what you have to say," Mark snapped. "Bill Stoughton is his friend and you phased him out of the case within a week after you took over." Mark poured another cup of coffee. "Then you opened up a can of whoop-ass on him right in the fucking squad room. Now you're going to tell him that his friend, probably his *only* friend, is a serial murderer."

Jake looked across the hall into Rebecca's room and said nothing. He knew that everything Mark said was true and the only thing that would solidify his suspicions would be if Stoughton's fingerprints matched the killer's.

It wasn't long before Captain Reins stormed into the

break room wearing an expression of sheer anger and resentment. There was no misinterpreting his intentions. "You're finished as a police officer, Burnett." Reins turned and faced Mark. "If I can connect you to any of this insanity, you can join your *partner*."

"You put me in charge of this case, Captain," Jake said. "Detective Roads only followed my orders. If there is any blame here it's mine and mine alone."

Mark sat and listened to the two men bicker over what had happened. He listened to Reins' threats to fire Jake for the fight he had with Stoughton and felt a surge of rage race through his body. When Reins added that everyone involved would either be terminated or demoted, Mark exploded, "Who the fuck do you think you are?" He slammed his fist onto the table. "You had nothing until Jake took over. You come in here and threaten to fire everyone and you have no fucking clue what's going on."

Mark's outburst stunned both Reins and Jake. The violent eruption was out of character for Mark and the change in mannerism was what made the outburst so impressive. Jake sat down and Reins immediately followed suit.

"We have strong evidence that Bill Stoughton is the murderer," Mark said in much calmer tone, "and when John Moran gets back we will know for sure."

Jake winced at Mark's statement. He didn't want to tell the captain of his suspicions until he was absolutely sure. He knew there was an outburst about to come from Reins and the captain didn't disappoint him.

"I'm not going to wait until tomorrow," Reins bellowed. "I want both your badges and weapons. Now!"

Mark reached down and unhooked his badge from his belt and set it on the table. The look in his eyes was nothing short of devastation at being fired. When he reached for his weapon, Jake held his hand in the air in an indication for him to stop. Turning to Reins, Jake said, "Captain, before you commit yourself to something that's going to come back and bite you in the ass, I think you should wait for Moran."

"I'll wait twenty minutes," Reins said, "then both your careers with law enforcement will come to an end."

The minutes ticked by and Jake looked in on Rebecca frequently. In his heart he knew Bill Stoughton was the man he was looking for, but only hoped he could prove it. The captain was well aware of how much Jake disliked the profiler and Jake knew that Reins' interpretation of the evidence would be different than his – unless he could match the fingerprints.

At 2:00 a.m. Reins announced again that he wanted the badge and weapons from Jake and Mark. "I'm wasting my time sitting here," he said. "You have no evidence that Bill is involved in the murders and I'm not going to be involved in your attempt to smear his name."

Mark looked at Jake and shrugged. He removed his badge from his belt and tossed it on the table, followed by his gun. "You're making a mistake, Captain."

As Jake unhooked the badge from his belt, he heard one of the nurses talking to someone in the hall. "This is a hospital. You can't come in here like this." There was a pause, and in an aggravated tone, she added, "Do the words 'germs' or 'sanitary conditions' mean anything to you?"

Jake placed his badge back onto his belt and motioned

Indiscriminate

for Mark to do the same. He walked out into the hall and saw a nurse scolding John Moran. Walking up to greet the detective he saw why. Moran was covered in garbage and dirt and his hair was matted with squalor. He looked like a transient looking for a place to sleep. He took hold of Moran's arm and told the nurse it was all right to let him through, "He's with me," Jake said as he ushered Moran down the hall, leaving the nurse dumbfounded and angry.

When Jake and Moran entered the break room, Captain Reins went into a fit of rage. "You're as fucked-up as these two are," he barked at Moran while pointing at Jake and Mark. "This better be good."

Moran swallowed hard and carefully removed the broken cup from a plastic evidence bag. He opened the fingerprint case and motioned for Mark to dust the cup.

"You haven't even checked the prints yet," Reins bellowed. "You condemn a man on speculation just because you don't like him and I'm not going to be a party to it." He strode to the door.

"Sit your fucking ass down," Jake commanded. "You're not going anywhere until you see what we have."

Jake's shocking statement to the captain stunned everyone, including Reins. He turned and sat down at the table, obviously startled at Jake's commanding tone.

Moran motioned for Jake to follow him out into the hallway and it was obvious to Jake that he wasn't going to like what Moran had to say.

"Housekeeping emptied the trash before I got there. I had to climb into the dumpster to find the cup." He looked down at his clothing. "The cup is in the same condition as my clothes,

Jake. I don't think Mark will find any readable fingerprints. Even if he does, the evidence has been contaminated and will never hold up in court."

Jake nodded in appreciation of what his partner had to do to get the cup, and hoped the cup would reciprocate by giving up a readable print. When he walked back into the room he knew his hopes were for naught. The expression on Mark's face said it all.

At that moment the nurse who handed Jake the note walked in to get a cup of coffee and Jake desperately played his last card. "Did you talk to the person who gave you the note?" he asked.

"Briefly," the nurse replied as she poured the coffee. "The only thing she said was to give the note to Detective Burnett. Then she left."

The nurse turned and walked out of the break room and Jake knew there was nothing else he had that would convince Reins that Stoughton was the murderer. He knew the information he had was weak to say the least, and he felt guilty about being responsible for Mark losing his job.

Reins motioned for Mark to turn over his badge and weapon. Once again, Mark placed his badge on the table and reached for his gun. Jake was about to follow Mark's lead when the nurse came back into the room.

"There was one thing I thought a little odd about the woman who delivered the note," she said to Jake. "She held the note by the edges, as though she didn't want to touch it, as though the envelope was *dirty*."

"She wasn't wearing gloves?" Jake asked.

"No," said the nurse, "she just leaned against the counter and handed me the note."

"Show me exactly where she stood," Jake said quietly, glancing at Mark.

Mark knew what Jake's next move was going to be. He picked up the fingerprint case and walked to the nurse's station.

After the nurse showed Mark where the woman stood, he began dusting the black powder with a brush. The tension was thick as Jake and Moran watched Mark work feverishly in his search for the evidence. The harder Mark worked, the more evident it became that he wasn't going to find anything.

"This has gone on long enough," Reins said.

Before the captain could finish what he was about to say, Jake asked the nurse if the woman used the elevator when she left.

"No," replied the nurse, "she pushed the door to the stairwell open with her shoulder and walked down the stairs."

Jake looked in the direction of the stairwell, then looked at Mark. "I guess the situation is fourth and ten."

"Detective," the nurse said, "she didn't use the elevator when she left, but she used it when she came."

Without hesitation, Jake pushed the button for the elevator and stepped back, knowing this was going to be his last chance. It was his last chance to prove his suspicion of Stoughton being the murderer and help Mark save his job.

When the doors opened, Mark scurried inside and began dusting the button marked 8. The light was poor in the elevator and Mark asked Jake to get the small flashlight from the fingerprint case. Jake handed Mark the flashlight, and Mark held it firm between his teeth while he worked.

Everyone stood silent while Mark dusted the button, and tension hung heavy in the air. The eerie silence was finally broken when Mark said, "We not only got the first down, Jake, we scored a fucking touchdown."

Reins watched as Mark lifted the fingerprint off of the button onto a piece of tape. They walked back into the break room and transferred the print from the tape to a fingerprint card. Mark took the card of the fingerprint that was taken from one of the murder scenes and placed it beside the print that was taken from button number 8.

He stepped back and handed Captain Reins the magnifying glass. "See for yourself, Captain. It's a perfect match."

Reins studied the fingerprints carefully. "Yes, they are a perfect match. Now what the hell does this have to do with Bill Stoughton?"

The three detectives looked at each other and realized the captain was right. All it proved was that the murderer was at the hospital and nothing more.

"Let me try one more thing," Mark said. "I looked for prints on the outside of the coffee cup, but didn't check inside. I remember when Stoughton smashed the cup he held it from the outside and the little bit of coffee that was left in the cup spilled on his shirt. His thumb went inside the cup when he threw it."

Reins looked at Mark with an expression of contempt,

Indiscriminate

and Mark knew that he was only moments away from losing his job with the Salem Police Department.

He turned the cup over gently and looked inside. It was dry and clean as he applied the black fingerprint powder.

Reins stood next to Mark, all the while holding the magnifying glass until Mark tore it from his hand. Jake and Moran took a step closer just as Mark mumbled, "We just got a two-point conversion."

Reins snatched the glass from Mark and looked into the inside of the coffee cup. There it was, Bill Stoughton's fingerprint. "No," said Reins, "this can't be. How the hell could he deceive everyone for so long? It has to be a mistake."

Jake looked at Reins and realized that his captain knew it wasn't a mistake. Reins now knew that his friend was the man who murdered twelve people in less than three months, and probably was responsible for many others.

Reins reached into his inside pocket and pulled out his cell phone. He called the station and ordered an All Points Bulletin on William Stoughton. He told the officer on duty to send two squad cars to Stoughton's home and arrest him on suspicion of multiple murders. "Call me on my cell phone when you pick him up," Reins ordered. "I'll be waiting at the hospital with my *three* detectives."

The captain turned and pointed to the badge that was still resting on the table. "Are you in the habit of leaving your badge lying around, *Detective* Roads?"

Within an hour the captain's cell phone rang and everyone's attention was focused on Reins as he answered. It was evident in his tone that he was not pleased with what he was told. "Are you sure?" he barked.

Captain Reins hung up the phone and looked at Jake. "I just realized that Bill has a police radio in his car and must have heard the APB when it went out."

The room fell silent while everyone waited for Reins to continue. "A witness said he saw Bill Stoughton leaving his apartment caring a suitcase."

Mark looked at Jake. "Just like the doctor said, he simply walked off into the night and disappeared."

Seventeen

Before Captain Reins left the hospital, Jake asked him to assign an officer to Rebecca in the morning. "I doubt Whitney Stiles will come back to the hospital, but I don't want to take any chances."

"I was an asshole five years ago when I pursued something I knew was wrong," Reins said solemnly, "and if it weren't for you I would have been an asshole again tonight. You saved my ass again… Thanks."

He stepped close to Jake and placed his hand on Jake's shoulder. "I'll make sure someone is here at 7:00 a.m. You can depend on it."

Jake nodded in appreciation and the captain added, "I have a confession to make. It wasn't by chance that I had your gold shield in my desk. I have a gold shield for all my detectives in the event that a situation arises and I feel as though a promotion is warranted—of course it would have to be something big."

Jake knew the captain was trying to tell him something, but as usual he had difficulty expressing it. "You're beating around the bush again, Captain."

"I've been thinking about having someone run the squad room," Reins said. "I've been thinking about taking on a Chief of Detectives."

"You want to promote me to Chief of Detectives?" Jake asked.

"Jake, some of the detectives don't like you, but they *all* respect you. Although there are times that I don't like your methods, you have ways of getting results when no one else can."

The captain's offer took Jake by surprise and he leaned back against the wall. He looked into Rebecca's room, then into the break room at Mark and John. His mind raced in different directions.

Being a member of the Salem police department was all he ever wanted to do. He could not remember a time in his life when he wanted to be anything else but a police officer. The only deterrent to the promotion was that Jake was a street cop and the thought of spending his time behind a desk made him shiver.

"Captain," Jake began, "I appreciate the offer, but I belong on the street, not behind a desk. I wouldn't last a week."

"You're always looking at the downside of everything. Maybe that's because you *are* a street cop. My Chief of Detectives would make the decision who is out on the street and who rides a desk. In fact, my Chief of Detectives could even have *two* partners."

Jake felt a rush of mixed emotions ranging from pride

Indiscriminate

and conceit, to inhibition and apprehension. He stood eye-to-eye with Captain Reins and knew the captain was waiting for an answer. In a soft and clear tone, Jake said, "Any Chief of Detectives worth his salt wouldn't have a partner that hasn't earned his gold shield."

The captain's eyes lit up when he heard Jake's remark. He knew what Jake was saying that he'd take the job if he promoted his two partners. "Jake," Reins said, "there is no money in the budget for three promotions. There's no way I could get it approved."

"I don't need the extra money, Captain. I know you can pull it off for Mark and John."

"Christ, Jake! Do you always get what you want? I bet you were a spoiled brat when you were a kid." Reins turned his back to Jake and paced back and forth. Turning back to Jake, he added, "I guess this is why you get things done, because you're so fucking persistent."

"Then it's a deal?" Jake asked.

Reins stood silent for a moment then held out his hand. The two men shook hands and Reins said, "It's a done deal, Jake." He pulled Jake closer. "But you do the honors in the morning. You're the one who will have to deal with all the flack from the other detectives, so you will be the one to give them their new shields. I will announce *your* promotion to the rest of the squad in the morning and then the ball is in your court."

Jake smiled. "We won't let you down, Captain."

"You're damned right you won't let me down. Those gold shields can be taken back as easily as they were given out." Giving Jake a wink, Reins turned and walked away.

Jake watched his captain walk down the hall toward the elevator. His stride was different. The confident way he once carried himself gave way seemed to slow with a tinge of unforgiving guilt. Jake knew the guilt was from being deceived by someone he thought of as a fellow professional, an ally and a friend. Jake knew the captain entertained the thought that if he weren't taken in by the captivating personality of Bill Stoughton, maybe some lives would have been spared.

Jake went into the break room to help Mark and John gather all the information into folders. He watched as his two partners worked and he listened to them talk about how the case turned out. Pride rushed through Jake over the grueling effort his partners displayed during the investigation. Jake didn't coddle Mark, or John, and at times he was somewhat demanding.

What the hell, Jake thought, *why make them wait until they're in the squad room to find out they've earned their gold shield.* "The captain just promoted me to Chief of Detectives," Jake announced. "He said I could continue to have two partners if I wanted them."

Both detectives bolted to Jake and shook his hand in congratulations.

"You're gonna be a desk jockey?" Mark asked in a playful tone.

Jake told them what the captain said and explained he would need their support when Reins informed the rest of the squad they would be answering to him.

"Wow," said Mark, "Chief of Detectives, Jason Burnett. That has a nice ring to it. Makes you sound so important. So powerful…So smart."

Indiscriminate

"You're right," said Jake, "the job does carry a lot of visibility to the public and to the media." Jake walked to the door. In a sarcastic tone he added, "I told the captain that any Chief of Detectives worth his salt would never have squad room detectives as partners. That would be degrading to his position. Of course, if his partners had earned their gold shield…"

Mark's face exploded with pride. Slowly he sat down and stared at Jake with an electrified expression. "Are you saying that you got me my gold shield?" His voice cracked.

"That's what I'm saying," Jake said.

"One minute you almost get me fired, the next minute you get me something that I've only fantasized about—my gold shield."

Moran rushed to Mark and placed his arm around his shoulder. In an excited voice he congratulated Mark over and over until Jake said, "John, I have *two* partners."

Jake saw Moran's legs begin to shake as he backed away from Mark. He leaned against the counter and tried to speak. His mouth moved, but no words came out.

"How long will it take before I'll have my gold shield in my hand, Jake?" Mark asked. "I mean, how long will it take before my shield comes in?" Stumbling for words, Mark continued, "What I mean is, how long does it take to make it?"

"You will have your shield before 8:00 this morning," Jake said. "Reins has gold shields for everyone in the squad room tucked away in his desk. He will never give them to any of his detectives, but has them just in case."

"How the hell did you pull this off, Jake?" Mark asked. "What did you have to promise the captain?"

"He called me a spoiled brat. Said he felt sorry for my parents because I never take no for an answer." Jake turned to leave the break room. "Leave the folders here and I'll bring them to the station in the morning. You better go home and get a couple hours sleep. We're gonna have a long day tomorrow."

On that note the two detectives thanked Jake again and scurried down the hall to the elevator. As they walked, Jake noticed the cocky way they carried themselves. Their strides were laced with a cocky arrogance and pride. Jake knew neither man would sleep a wink.

Jake had no problem falling asleep when he sat in the chair next to Rebecca's bed. It was as though he just sat down when he opened his eyes slightly, twisted in the chair, and noticed a patrolman standing in the doorway. "I'm here to relieve you, Detective Burnett."

Jake rubbed his forehead for a moment to try and clear his thoughts. He looked at Rebecca as she slept, then thanked the officer and left the hospital to go home and shower before going to work. The events that happened that night raced through his mind and he felt an unbelievable sense of fulfillment. *Everything came together*, he thought, *Rebecca is going to be fine…proving who the killer is…Mark and John earning their gold shield…and my promotion…*

Jake turned into his driveway and shut off the engine. He sat in his Vette for a moment. The only thing left to do now was to find Whitney Stiles and put the son-of-a-bitch away.

Jake walked through the front door into the living

Indiscriminate

room, tossed his keys on the table, went to the refrigerator, and took out a carton of orange juice. As he drank from the carton, the familiar scent of sickening sweet perfume filled the air. Before he could react, something crashed down on his head and sent him to the floor, rendering him unconscious.

When Jake woke up, he found himself sitting in a kitchen chair with his hands bound behind his back with duct tape. He shook his head to clear his thoughts and felt blood streaming down the side of his face. Looking up, he saw a blurry figure sitting across the table. As his eyes focused, he saw the long red hair of Whitney Stiles.

Jake cleared his throat. He knew the only way he was going to live to see another day was to talk Whitney Stiles into giving up. He also knew that the chance of him surrendering was slim.

"Your time has come," Stiles said. "You have interrupted what has to be done—what *must* be done."

"What must be done? There is no reason you could possibly come up with to justify all the murders, Whitney. You need help."

"I knew you wouldn't understand," Stiles barked. "No one ever does. They're everywhere and someone has to put an end to their destruction and torment. Jake listened to Whitney Stiles explain why he had taken the lives of so many people. They have been sent by the devil to cause pain and torment, and they all must be condemned to death."

"You believe that all those people were witches because their names had the same initials as the people who were hung in, *1692?*" Jake asked. "Even if they were witches, why the hell would you want to kill them? Witchcraft is a peaceful religion."

Stiles stepped directly in front of Jake. "You're one of *them*. You're one of the millions of sheep that walks through life without seeing the evil all around them. You're small-minded and don't take the time to seek out the devil's disciples and destroy them." Whitney's voice was filled with contempt. "You are content with your pathetic little life and give no thought to those of us who have been through hell."

Jake looked into the eyes of the unstable man standing in front of him. He knew there was nothing he could say that would be rationalized in the afflicted mind of Whitney Stiles.

"It's been said that neither positive nor negative energy will produce perfect balance," Stiles said, "but the person who said that was never introduced to the goddesses, Hecate and Kali."

Jake saw Whitney's hands tremble as he sat down and knew he had to keep him talking about the dark side of energy. If he could convince Stiles that he understood what he was doing, and agreed with it, he might be able to get him to undo the tape from his hands. "Tell me about the dark energy," Jake said. "I want to know. Maybe there's something I can do to help if I knew more about the goddesses."

"They are very powerful," Stiles said. "Hecate and Kali are capable of inflicting tremendous pain and torment when their powers are used by someone who is unaware of their capability. Everything that's done through their powers comes back—times three."

Indiscriminate

"How do you know this?" Jake asked. "How do you *really* know?"

Stiles burst into a rage and slammed his fist on the table. "I know because I've lived with destruction. I've lived in the dark side of energy all my life. I've felt the wrath of Kali!"

For the second time in his life Jake felt completely helpless. The first time was when Rebecca lay on her deathbed. He watched as Whitney Stiles emptied out a small satchel onto the counter and saw what was about to be his fate. A rope tied into a hangman's knot, a roll of duct tape and a two-foot piece of electrical cord with a dowel tied to each end.

Stiles carefully picked up the garrote and stood behind Jake as he sat bound in the chair. Staring at the weapon as though it had some kind of magical power of good, he said, "You are a witch. You know you are a witch. I will sign your death warrant and send you back to the devil."

He wrapped the cord around Jake's neck and slowly pulled until the slack was gone and the skin around Jake's neck began to crimp. "The devil has willed you to stop me from finding his children," Stiles said as he began to tighten the cord, "I condemn you to death in the name of the lord."

As the cord slowly became tighter, Jake knew Stiles was deliberately prolonging the event, and in his mind, was enjoying the momentous occasion.

Jake struggled, but his efforts were to no avail. Excruciating pain gripped Jake's throat as he twisted and struggled to get free, desperately trying to breathe. The harder he sucked for air, the more air he seemed to lose.

He pushed with his feet in a desperate attempt to stand, but Stiles wrestled him to the floor. This was the position that the other victims had met their death and Jake knew it. Stiles had his knee in the middle of his back and pulled even harder on the garrote.

"Fight me, witch," Stiles said with a hint of pleasure. "My power is much stronger than yours."

Jake felt his life slipping away as he was rendered unconscious.

Voices and movement caused Jake's eyes to open and he saw two figures standing in his kitchen. "Officer down!" came the voice of Mark Roads as he stood with the telephone in his hand.

Jake's eyes began to clear on what was happening around him and Mark and John came into focus. A slight smile spread across Jake's face. In a raspy voice he said, "What the fuck took you guys so long to get here?" He slipped back into unconsciousness.

The next time Jake opened his eyes, he found himself lying in a hospital bed next to Rebecca. "Hi sweetheart," he joked, "we *have* to stop meeting this way."

A burst of laughter erupted from inside the room and Jake turned to see where it came from. "He's gonna be just fine," came the friendly voice of Mark Roads.

Before anyone spoke, John Moran told Jake that he would have the front window replaced and that he and Mark would pay for it.

Jake didn't know what he was talking about until Captain Reins explained, "Your two partners couldn't wait until they got to the station to get their gold shields," he said. "They decided to drive to your house with the hopes that you already had them. They walked up onto the front stairs and knocked on the door and when you didn't answer they looked through the window. That's when they *both* opened fire—right though the window."

Jake looked at Mark and John and asked, "Is he dead?"

"As a Christmas goose," Mark said soberly.

"The review board will hold a hearing to determine if discharging their weapons was warranted," Reins said as he glanced at Dang.

Dang didn't know the captain well enough to recognize that he was only joking, and shook his head in disbelief.

Again with a playful tone and a smile, Reins asked Dang if he had a comment to add about the hearing.

Dang looked at Jake with an expression of frustration. "Je refuse à entre dans un combat d'esprits avec un homme de unarmed." He winked at Jake and left the room.

Captain Reins watched Dang walk out of the room. He turned to Jake, "What the hell did he just say?"

In a raspy voice, Jake answered, "He said he refused go into a battle of wits against an unarmed man."

THE END

CPSIA information can be obtained at www.ICGtesting.com
Printed in the USA
BVOW010921170113

310830BV00001B/1/P